What Remains

Maxine Roël

What Remains

Vanguard Press

A CIP catalogue record for this title is
available from the British Library.

ISBN 978 1 80016 740 7

*Vanguard Press is an imprint of
Pegasus Elliot Mackenzie Publishers Ltd.*
www.pegasuspublishers.com

First Published in 2023

**Vanguard Press
Sheraton House Castle Park
Cambridge England**

Printed & Bound in Great Britain

To my mother.

Acknowledgements

To Pegasus for making my dream a reality.

Dawn Rebecky, Nitza Wilon, and Rebecca Baum – my original writing group – where the seeds of this novel were sewn. We met, we laughed, we drank tea, we created. Carolyn Mackler, I will be forever grateful to you. You read the first draft of the first decade and encouraged me to keep writing. Just the boost I needed. Heather Jackson, your constant willingness to talk shop and share your expertise and insight. Jeff Ourvan, who helped me mold, shape, ponder and re-write many-many times. And to my partners at The Write Workshop in NYC: Greg Basham, Jeremy Goldstein, Ann Harson, Dawn Rebecky, Tatsha Robertson, Anne Rourke, and Aliah Dorene Wright, what a fun (and sometimes excruciating) way to spend Saturday mornings.

I have received an abundance of encouragement from my family and friends without which this process would not have been as fulfilling. I am especially grateful to Jennifer Factor, Harry Factor, Marcia Menter, Lara Morrison, Paulina Perera, Christa Scott-Reed, Dennis Roel, and Josee Roel, who generously agreed to read this novel at its various stages of maturation.

Suzette Avila-Berkey, you know how to make a shy girl take a great photo.

To my mother, who has read What Remains more times than I have.

To my children for their exuberance to get Sophie Gold out from under my bed and into the hands of others.

To Peter, who knows that without a creative endeavor we are not fully alive.

CHAPTER ONE

At exactly three-thirty, the yellow school bus stopped in front of 23 Birch Street, depositing the girl. She ran up the slate steps two at a time and pushed open the front-porch door, which waited unlocked for her arrival. She slipped off her moccasins and raced toward the stairs. Knowing she had just thirty minutes to pretend she was an only child, she wasted no time.

She shouted hi to her mom, and dashed upstairs and into the bedroom she shared with her younger sister. Her toy chest held twenty Barbie dolls clad in groovy halter tops, tight-fitting skirts and short-shorts. They would make up the girl's audience. They were placed with precision, one at a time, against the wall in a sitting position on her bed.

The girl lifted her yellow sun dress from the bottom hem and over her head, throwing it down onto the beige carpet. Her closet was filled with many dresses, but she wanted to wear the one her mom had just bought. It was pink with purple polka dots and had a satin ribbon, that tied into a bow on her back. It was for her eighth birthday party, which was eight days away. To

11

accompany the dress, she wore a pair of black patent-leather Mary Janes. She grabbed her hairbrush from her desk.

"*Introducing…*" she said, in a booming voice, "*Sophie Gold.*"

Her slim finger pushed play on a tape recorder and Sophie lip synched to all her favorite tunes. Her hips and head swayed side to side so much that her wavy brown hair followed. And when she smiled, her lips could no longer conceal her overbite.

As the tape moved from *The Bee Gees' Stayin' Alive* to *Night Fever,* Sophie added a twirl here and there, and the hem of her party dress was carried up to waist height exposing her trim olive-skinned legs.

A gentle knock on the door stopped Sophie mid spin.

"Hi love. What are you doing?"

"Just singing to a very large audience, Mama," she said, as she turned to her dolls.

"I see. I didn't mean to interrupt you during a show, but I baked cookies. Wanna be my first taster?" Only thirty-six years old and a mother of four, streaks of gray had begun to permeate her light-brown hair.

"Mama?"

"Yes, Sophie."

"Can we eat them in my room together?"

"No sweetie, not upstairs."

By this time, her mom, Sarah, was in the bedroom, leaning against the walls she had painted marigold for her daughter. She had picked the color because they were her favorite flowers, which she had strewn all over the back garden.

Sophie turned off the music. "Please, Mom? We can be all alone up here before everyone else gets home."

"Okay, just this once, but take off your party dress so it's not ruined for next weekend."

Before she left for the kitchen, Sophie's mom scooped up her daughter. Sophie wrapped her legs around her mom's waist, leaned her head on her shoulder and squeezed as hard as she could.

"Superhero grip! You're getting so big, I may not be able to do this much longer." Her mom put her down, kissed both cheeks and then the tip of her nose. "Be right back."

Sophie's desk clock read three-forty-five. Fifteen minutes gone and fifteen left – no time to spare. She changed back into her school clothes and hung up her party dress.

Picking up one Barbie at the end of the bed, she said, "I got Mama all to myself," and gave it a kiss on both cheeks and tip of the nose.

Her mom walked in with a tray of milk and cookies for two. "Here we go."

"Mama, want to play Barbies with me?"

"I don't have time, sweetie. Did you forget that Dad and I are going to the opera tonight?"

Sophie never forgot when her parents were going out. "Please don't go, Mama. It's not the same when you're gone," Sophie said, her mouth filled with salty, sweet crumbs.

"I know you girls don't always get along, but you can work it out."

They sat on the floor leaning against Sophie's bed. "Remember how I told you that when I was a kid, I begged my mom and dad for a brother or sister? It was really hard growing up with no one to play with. You all have each other," Sarah said, as she wiped a crumb off Sophie's cheek.

Sophie bit her fingernails, "I remember."

Sophie's mom placed her hand onto the one she was biting and held it. "That's why Dad and I wanted such a big family."

Sophie had to admit it seemed kind of lonely to be an only child. Maybe her mom had a point.

Downstairs, the front door slammed. Everyone was home now except for Sam Gold, Sophie's dad. He would stay in the city and meet her mom straight from work.

Footsteps clattered up the stairs.

"I'm going to say hello. Enjoy the snack." Sarah smiled and closed the door behind her. Sophie's shoulders slumped.

Picking up her favorite doll, she cut her blonde hair in thirds and began a braid.

"Cindy, Mom doesn't understand."

It didn't take long before she heard whispering and laughter fill the hallway, and then a door slam. She didn't feel hungry any more, or in the mood to play, and dropped Cindy on the carpet. Sophie's face turned sullen, until her mom reappeared.

"I almost forgot," Sarah said, as she re-entered and sat beside Sophie. "I wanted to give you an early birthday gift." She handed her daughter a wrapped box with a pink ribbon fastened around it.

Sophie slid off the ribbon without tearing it, so she could keep it for her collection, undid the tape on each end, and opened the box. Inside was a delicate gold chain-link necklace with a small heart at the end. It was engraved with an S.

"Mama, I love it. Will you put it on for me?" Sophie lifted her hair off her neck and smiled.

"Of course." Sarah fastened the clasp. She kissed Sophie again, on each cheek and then the tip of her nose. "See you downstairs later, big girl."

Sophie left her room in a mess. The gold necklace gave her superpower confidence. She was ready to face her sisters.

Hannah, fourteen, Amy, twelve, and five-year-old Jane were in the upstairs bathroom doing their nails. Hannah was polishing her toes bright red and Amy was giving Jane her favorite, deep purple for fingers and rainbow for toes.

"Will you do mine, Hannah?" Sophie asked softly.

"Huh?" Hannah replied, without looking up from her slumped over position. At 5'8" she towered above the secrets shared between girls of her age. She was taller than most of the boys she was beginning to find cute. From bottom to top, her body screamed pubescent boy: flat feet, lanky, muscular legs, narrow hips, flat chest and rounded broad shoulders. Her body looked like a long rectangular storage box. It was perfect for tracks meets, where she often came in first in the sprinting competitions.

"Hannah, will you polish mine rainbow like Jane's?" Sophie tried asking a little louder. She didn't dare walk past the doorway.

"I don't want to," Hannah replied. She pressed her knee into her chest and blew on her big toe. "Damn, I smudged it." She glanced over at Sophie. "Another time, I'm busy." She grabbed the remover off the counter.

"You're always too busy," Sophie said, leaving the bathroom. She went downstairs to the kitchen and read a book at the table. She clung to her necklace with both hands. She thought about how special her mom made her feel, even though her sisters had a knack for giving her the invisible vibe or worse, the vibe that she was an utter nuisance.

At five o'clock the bell rang, Hannah and Amy dashed toward the door, a perfect opportunity for them to compete.

"I'm gonna beat you," Amy shouted.

Sophie thought Amy looked like she belonged to a different family, with her pale skin and perfectly pink cheeks. She didn't look anything like the rest of them, or any other Jewish families Sophie knew in Queens. And Amy's boobs were gigantic. Even Sophie knew a D-cup was too big for twelve.

There was a physical argument along the stairs, as always, and down the hall to the glass door, where Amy jabbed her elbow into Hannah to slow down her runner's legs.

"You're way too slow, Amy!" Hannah shrieked.

Hannah retaliated with a tug of Amy's long brown braid that swayed across her belt line as she ran. Sophie took her position on the staircase landing, pressed against the wall, her toes drenched in the green fuzzy carpet. From this vantage point she watched the impending race that was replayed week after week. As always, Jane snuck up from behind the kitchen door, two rooms away from the finish line, and beat them both.

"Janie, how do you always do that?" Hannah asked playfully, as she and Amy raced back up the way they came down. They screamed their hellos to their grandparents as they departed.

"Hi," Jane said, in her raspy voice. She stood at the door and looked up, her mangled orange curls draping her face. Her green eyes drifted up to their grandfather's mouth. His thin lips slightly parted, and then she gazed at his large, calloused hands, "Do you have my present?"

"May we come in, please?" Sophie's grandfather said, with a small bow of his head. He handed Jane another new outfit for her Barbie collection.

"Thank you, Grandpa," Jane said. She waited for him to pass and then looked up at their grandmother. "Hi, Grammy," she said as she skipped away, passing Sophie on the stairs.

"Can I see it, Jane?"

"*No!*" Jane put the outfit behind her back. "You have your own."

"That's not fair. I always share with you."

Jane shrugged, "I don't care."

It burned. She hadn't received a gift from her grandfather all year, since he announced it was Jane's turn.

"There's only one beautiful Gold girl I haven't seen yet." Sophie heard her grandma's voice and scooted into the living room to take her usual place. Her grandma always knew where Sophie hid. She crawled on her belly, placed her cheeks in her hands, propped on her elbows, and looked at Sophie under the piano. "Hello, my sweet, and how are you this evening?"

Sophie didn't say a word. She waited with anticipation.

"May I put some make-up on your face for dinner?" her grandma asked.

With this Sophie lay down, still under the piano, and closed her eyes.

Her grandmother opened her imaginary compact and began with the foundation. She made one light stroke with her middle and forefinger, smooth across Sophie's entire face, until her jaw loosened. Then she applied eye shadow and whispered, "I brought brown today to match your deep chocolate eyes, Sophie." She used just her pinkie to slide across Sophie's lids. "Keep that smile for the lipstick. I brought my special ruby red. It's a bit bright, but I think you can handle it now that you're just about eight."

The corners of Sophie's mouth stayed lifted until the moment she felt her grandmother's hand part from her face and knew their ritual was ending. "Thank you, Grandma." Sophie crawled back out from under the piano and sat down to play her scales.

From her seat she could peer into the dining room at the only painting that hung against the stark white walls. It was centered above the credenza. The large canvas boasted bright red with freckles of orange and deep smudges of paint that gave way in the middle to a thick blue line. The blue reminded Sophie of swimming in the ocean on a hot summer day. Other than that, she didn't really understand what it was about, but remembered her parents saying that it was *abstract,* and that meant you could make up your own story.

Sophie was so enthralled with the colors that she didn't hear her mom come up behind her. "I'm going to meet Dad now, don't forget what I told you. You're so lucky to have three sisters. Try and have some fun with them," her mom said, while she brushed Sophie's hair behind her ears. Sophie noticed the sparkle of the circular diamonds she wore. And then her mom dashed off.

Sophie began to cry. She went to the window and stared out. The warm spring night was filled with neighborhood kids: on bikes, throwing footballs, and jumping rope.

She heard Jane call, "Dinner is ready! Come to the table."

Sophie remained in position, with her forehead firmly pressed to the glass. She knew it wouldn't make her mother reappear, but it gave her the illusion of being closer to her. Once she went to sit with the rest of her family, she would be propelled into a reality that made her feel like a dog with its fur on end.

Hannah and Amy sat on one side of the table; Sophie and Jane were on the other, and their grandparents at the heads. Within minutes Hannah whispered something to Amy and Amy laughed. Sophie wished she knew what was so funny. Her sisters leaned so close to each other that Hannah's chair tilted.

Moments into the meal, their grandfather began his usual barrage, "Amy, what happened at school this week? How did you do on your biology test?" He barely paused for a beat or waited for her reply. "Did you hand in your essay on *Catcher in the Rye*?"

"Yes."

Sophie put her chin down, feeling anxious. Her eyes followed her grandfather's still fixed on Amy. She felt like a swarm of bees were buzzing in her chest and belly.

"Can you elaborate?" he snapped.

Oh God, he's being so mean. At least it's at Amy. Sophie thought.

Amy's giggling ceased. She took hold of her braid and fidgeted with the sections of hair.

"Do not play with your hair at the table!" their grandfather said. "So…," he continued, "tell me."

Amy stopped unbraiding, but held onto her ponytail like a rope ladder. She looked like she was ready to climb her way up to the ceiling, through a trap door, to safe landing in her bedroom above.

"Everything is fine, Grandpa. Don't worry about it," Amy mumbled. Normally she would have been more daring, but tonight avoided eye contact. Her pink cheeks grew a shade darker. Her neck got blotchy.

Before their grandfather was able to respond, their grandma chimed in, "So, girls," in a sing-song voice, "shall we do some homework together tonight?"

"It's Friday night, Grandma. Can't we just watch TV? I don't even have homework," Jane whined, like she always did when she really wanted something. Sophie knew that if they didn't figure things out soon Jane would scream.

Sophie watched her grandma inch toward the edge of her seat, her spine lifting from the back cushion. Her orange lips pressed together slightly as she looked over at her husband.

"Grandfather," Jane said glaring with her green eyes locked firmly on his. "It's Friday night, it's *not* fair."

He stood up and planted his fists on the table. "Don't you speak to me that way, missy!" Saliva pooled at the corners of his mouth. Sophie thought it was gross. She watched Jane, who continued looking directly at him. She crumpled the paper-napkin resting on her lap into a tight wad. How could he go from being so kind at the door to getting angry over nothing?

Without missing a beat, their grandmother said, "Okay, we will settle on a compromise. First you finish your dinner, the lasagna is getting cold, then homework, and one show before bed."

"Grandma, we *cannot* watch the same show as Jane and Sophie. They watch baby stuff," Hannah objected. "Sorry, Janie," she added.

"Can we watch *Happy Days*, Grammy?" asked Jane.

"I love that show," Sophie joined in. "Fonzie is so cool, and Marion is just like you, Grandma."

"*No way!*" Amy said. "How about *Three's Company*?" She and Hannah high-fived each other.

"*Happy Days* is lovely for all ages. It's a family show, not that silliness that goes on with a grown man

22

living with two grown women frolicking around," her grandma said.

"What's frolicking?"

"It's fun, Sophie. But we aren't allowed to have too much fun. Don't you know that by now?" Amy piped in.

"Oh, hush now. None of that," their grandma said. "Start eating, girls, please."

"I've heard enough jibber-jabber for one night," their grandfather said. He wiped the corners of his mouth with his napkin and placed it on the table in a clump. It seemed to Sophie he was always looking for a way out. "I'll take my dinner in the living room, Eva," he said, and retreated to the couch. He picked up the newspaper and began to read. His skinny legs crossed and his top foot bounced as if he was keeping time.

Their grandmother quickly gathered up his plate and brought it to the coffee table, setting it in front of him. "Here you go, dear," she said with a smile, though her husband didn't look up.

"What's wrong with her? Can't he do anything for himself?" Hannah whispered to Amy. "At least he's gone. Let's eat fast and get to our room," she added, with a forkful by her mouth.

"Hannah, did Mom say when she'll be home?"

"I don't know, Sophie, but it's definitely going to be laaaate." Hannah smiled as she spoke.

"Hannah, that's so mean. You know how Sophie gets when Mom is gone," Amy replied, but Sophie saw the collaborative smirk on her face.

Sophie thought growing up without her sisters, an only child like her mom, seemed a better alternative. She took a few more hurried bites of dinner, wanting desperately to retreat to her own room. She gulped her milk and placed the empty glass carefully on the table. "Grandma, may I be excused?"

"You may all be excused."

Sophie and her sisters headed upstairs. Jane was in the lead, her small hands gripping the banister. She swiveled as she hit the landing, prompting the rest of the girls to stop short. Jane turned to her grandfather in the living room and shouted, "Grandpa, someone named Leslie called for you this afternoon." When he didn't answer she shouted again, even louder. "Grandpa! Leslie called you."

"It must have been for your father," he answered, without looking up from his paper. Although his voice remained steady, his legs suddenly stopped bouncing.

"Nope," Jane said. "She said your name, Robert Gold. Daddy is Sam Gold."

Their grandmother peered around from the kitchen, a dishtowel in her hands. "Girls, go up and do your work now." No one moved. "Go on," she added, a quiver in her voice. "Let me know when you're done and we'll turn on the TV."

Before Sophie continued upstairs, she saw her grandmother frown as she brought the towel to her chest.

An hour later, the girls had finished their homework. They gathered in the den upstairs, and their grandmother turned on *Happy Days*. The music began and the girls plopped down in their respective places. Jane sat smack in front of the set, Hannah and Amy squished their bodies to fit in the corner chaise of the large gray sectional, and Sophie found her way to the far end where she tucked her legs to her chest and leaned on her knees to watch.

Sunday, Monday, Happy Days...

Usually the girls hummed along, even Hannah and Amy. This Friday night Jane hummed alone. Sophie was distracted by her grandmother, who was constantly getting up. She walked to the staircase and then rounded back to sit again beside Sophie. She did this several times. Hannah and Amy pushed each other's bodies like rambunctious boys.

"Move over," Hannah grumbled.

"You move. Your legs are squishing me."

"NO."

"Grandma, will you make me a braid?" Sophie whispered in her grandmother's ear.

"Sure, sweet. Come sit in front of me on the floor."

But as soon as Sophie sat, her grandmother bounced up from her seat again, "I think I left something on the stove. I'll be right back."

She didn't come right back. The show carried on, the laugh tracked played and all four girls sat mesmerized by the fight they tried to hear between their grandparents. Their voices were muffled except for the occasional words they couldn't contain.

"Hush, you're being a ridiculous female." Then more whispers.

"I will not stand for this inquisition!" Their grandfather's voice again.

This time he sounded ferocious. Sophie imagined him standing very close to their grandmother and leaning over her as he shouted.

They heard their grandmother crying. Then more whispers. And then the front door creaked open.

"*You*," he said with disdain. "Are a disrespectful woman!"

The door slammed shut behind him. There was a long silence before the girls heard dishes being put away in the cupboards and the vacuum as it sucked up the last bits of crumbs from the floor.

Sophie struggled to fall asleep after her grandparent's argument. Even though her grandma had refreshed her make-up and kissed them at bedtime, she didn't linger as usual. She gave Jane and Sophie a meek good night and shut the lights and door.

Jane fell asleep easily, but Sophie twisted around in her covers, listening to the hum of Hannah and Amy, who were allowed to stay up until eleven p.m. Sophie was still awake when she heard her grandpa come back into the house, and smelled tobacco from his pipe, wafting up from the living room.

While listening to crickets sing outside her open window, Sophie succumbed to the heat, and was lulled to sleep. Her lids closed just in time. If she had been awake another minute, she would have seen the sudden flash of blue and red lights blaring, as a police car stopped in front of her house.

CHAPTER TWO

When Sophie woke up Saturday morning, she noticed an unusual smell coming from the kitchen. The weekend ritual of pancakes, waffles, and syrup was replaced by the aroma of eggs, toast, and frying bacon. That was a breakfast reserved for special occasions, which piqued Sophie's interest. Her party wasn't for another week. Rolling over in bed she saw that it was only seven-thirty. The rule was to stay in her room until eight, zero, zero. She was allowed to read, whisper with Jane, or play with dolls quietly. Jane was not in her bed. Sophie was torn between following the rules and exploring.

"What should I do?" she whispered into Teddy's ear, the only stuffed animal she kept on her bed. It was given to her as a baby, a classic brown teddy bear with a red ribbon bow around the neck. It never left the confines of the mattress.

"I'll go down and check it out. Maybe it's an early surprise for my birthday."

Tired from tossing and turning the night before, she released an enormous yawn. Sophie slid out of bed and pulled the covers over Teddy, "I'll be right back after breakfast." She gave his matted furry nose a kiss.

She passed the bathroom and heard Hannah wheezing like she was having an asthma attack. The door was open a crack already, so she swung it the rest of the way full force. It hit the pink tile wall with a bang. After twenty years, the tiles contained multiple blemishes: chips, mildew, and splits that made divisions like highways on a map.

"Go..." Hannah yelled between breaths, "to Grandma, Sophie." And she started coughing. Hannah hung over the toilet bowl rim, her back all hunched, inhaler in hand. Amy leaned on Hannah, burrowed into her own nightgown, her hands clenched around her toes.

"Are you okay? Where's Mom?" Sophie asked.

"Just go," Amy screamed with her head still down.

Sophie saw a panic in Hannah's expression that she had only experienced once before, the previous year. Jane had fallen down the stairs head first. A trip to the ER confirmed a concussion. Hannah and Amy had been playing with her, seeing who could slide down faster on their bellies, with arms reaching out in front. They didn't calculate how Jane's tiny body might propel forward, not yet having the coordination to pace herself on the way down. Having witnessed and participated in the fall, they were riddled with fear and guilt. In her room at the time, Sophie came out when she heard Jane's shrieking.

Sophie remembered how Hannah couldn't catch her breath that day either, so she ran down to the kitchen as fast as she could. She halted when she saw Jane eating breakfast at the table. Jane sat on their grandma's lap, while she hummed and licked cherry jam off her toast.

"Hannah's having an asthma attack!" Sophie began, but stopped when she looked at her grandma, who was usually so composed. She wore the same outfit as the previous night, only now her emerald green Izod shirt appeared crumpled like she had slept in it. "Grandma, what's going on?" Sophie continued with a furrowed brow, "Amy's crying. Where's Grandpa? Where are Mom and Dad?" Sophie stood across the table. She bit her finger nails.

"I've already tended to Hannah, she's going to be fine," her grandma said calmly.

"We need Mom!" Sophie shouted.

"Grandpa had some business to sort out. Please sit and eat, Sophie. Then I want to talk with you and Jane."

Sophie watched her grandma try to smile as she spoke, but it ended up looking like she had just taken a bite of spoiled yogurt. And the plate of food on the table looked odd: the eggs were perfect, but the bacon was raw, and the toast charcoaled. Sophie slid out the wooden chair and sat on the seat.

"I'm not feeling very hungry."

"Okay then." Her grandma paused. "Jane, Sophie, I need to tell you…" she lowered her head to her chest and frowned, displaying the many wrinkles she usually covered with make-up.

"Your Mom and Dad…" Her eyes were surrounded by mascara smudges.

"Why are you crying, Grammy?" Jane asked, as she placed her hands on either side of their grandma's face, tilting her head to one side.

"Your mom and dad… were in a bad car accident," her grandma's breath turned choppy. "Your Dad is in the hospital."

Sophie watched one reckless tear fall after the next. Her grandma batted them each away, like flies becoming a nuisance.

Sophie imagined her dad lying in the hospital bed, snug inside the covers. He never wore pajamas, only his Hanes boxers. Even though her older sisters were embarrassed when he did this, her dad would say things like, *I don't see the difference between this and a bathing suit.* Then he'd run after Hannah or Amy teasing, *Want a hug?* With his arms outstretched, chasing them.

Lost in the thought of her father's muscular body running up the stairs, and wondering if they gave him pajamas in the hospital, Sophie almost forgot that her grandma hadn't said anything about her mom yet. "My Mom?"

"Your mom," her grandma pursed her lips and finished, "didn't make it."

Sophie looked at her grandma and asked the question that would age her that very second. "Make what?"

"She died," her grandma finally admitted.

As words tumbled from her grandma's bare lips, Sophie heard them again, like the flash cards she used to study her times table.

Dad Hospital, Mom Died.

After her grandma had finished speaking, she held Jane like a mother with a newborn, kissed her face as many times as she could, no longer fighting the falling tears. The quietest, "I'm so sorry girls, I'm so very sorry," exited from her lips.

Sophie felt like she was falling backwards. Into a pool. No, into the painting in the living room. Right into the sea of blue, in the center of the canvas. She wanted to rip off her pajamas. Sophie closed her eyes.

Dad Hospital

A free fall, the moment right before hitting the pool water. Doubt creeping in. Who would catch her?

Mom Died

Smack! Backside in first, and then bubbles surrounded her on all sides, like the orange and red smudges of paint. Sophie scrambled like she couldn't breathe. Her arms and legs went wild. *I have to get to the surface,* she thought.

I need… breath!

"Sophie, Sophie, are you okay?"

Sophie heard her grandma's voice and opened her eyes. It was still just her, Jane, and Grandma. All still in the kitchen.

Jane pushed herself out of their grandma's arms. Her small hand grabbed the edge of the plate and threw it across the room. The food splattered.

"I want my Mommy and Daddy," she screamed as the plate shattered. The fried egg over-easy slid down the cabinet. It oozed yoke. Jane ran out of the kitchen and up the stairs to find Hannah and Amy.

Sophie sat still, fixated on a piece of floral wallpaper that had torn from the wall. She wanted to rip it off and unravel the whole thing.

***

Sophie's already slender body looked emaciated after the very long week that followed.

"You should try and eat something, honey," Mrs. Long, her neighbor, said. Her chubby brown fingers pushed a plate of cold cuts and coleslaw in front of Sophie, who sat at the dining room table. The Longs had been living next door when Sophie's parents bought their house. Each spring her mom and Mrs. Long planted annuals in the garden together, tanning their fair skin to a beautiful golden hue. Sophie loved to watch their collective fingers maneuvering the dirt, worms squirming about un-phased by the uprooting around them.

Sophie sat silently, holding her necklace, and stared at the blue paint on the canvas before her. Having no experience with death she didn't know how to register what was happening to her. She and her mom had just eaten cookies together in her room the week before. She could still feel how her mom had fastened the necklace around her neck, the faint smell of Ivory soap on her hands, the brush of her white linen sleeves resting on Sophie's shoulders.

"That must be the necklace your mom bought you. She told me all about it," Mrs. Long said.

Sophie pushed the plate to the very end of the glass table, as if daring it to drop and crash into thousands of ceramic shards on the floor. Instead, it just teetered there, like Sophie, not knowing what to do next.

For seven days she, her sisters and grandparents held themselves captive in the house, impotent and reliant on the care and generosity of friends and neighbors. Hannah and Amy would not leave their room, except for trips to the bathroom, which were sparse. They lay in one bed together all day and night with their bodies braided like the trunk of an old tree. They only ate when the hunger pains were so unbearable, they could no longer ignore their bellies. A few nibbles of bread or fruit from a tray brought to them sufficed.

Jane clung to their grandpa like a baby monkey, incessantly asking, "When are Mommy and Daddy coming back?" Her green eyes were wild with confusion. Grandpa held on to Jane and stroked her mane of orange hair, but was unable to answer her question. He walked around the house, room to room, as if searching for them himself. He took small respites on the couch and went straight back to pacing. Exhausted and bewildered, Jane periodically fell asleep while being carried, her head drifting onto his bony shoulder.

"Honey, I'm so sorry about your mom. She was such a dear friend and neighbor," Mrs. Long began. She pulled up a chair and placed it against Sophie's. Mrs. Long had only one daughter, Chloe, also eight, and she and Sophie were the best of friends. "I went with your grandma yesterday to visit your dad. It seems he's making a great recovery. I'm sure it won't be too long before he's home with you girls." Mrs. Long reached her thick hand over to stroke Sophie's hair. Sophie didn't move a muscle. Mrs. Longs hand felt so warm, like a wool hat on a chilly January day. The thought of her dad coming home soon eased her disappointment that he wouldn't be at the funeral the next day. They had waited all week, despite the Jewish tradition of immediate burial, in hopes that he would recover in time.

"Chloe can come by later, after her ballet class. Would you like that?" Mrs. Long asked.

Sophie's brown eyes searched the painting.

"Well, okay then. I'll be back with her later." She gave Sophie a loving kiss on the top of her head and removed the plate from the table as she left.

Sophie sat in the same position all day. Her grandma either milled around doing chores or scurried down to the basement, locked the door behind her and wailed like a wounded animal.

Sophie thought about the eighth birthday party she was supposed to be having at that very moment. She and her mom had mapped it out together in advance; they were going to begin with relay races in the yard, three-legged race, egg pass, then to pin the tail on the donkey, and the final game was going to be duck-duck goose. They were going to order pizza from Mario's, their favorite local place, but the cake was going to be homemade. The plan was to bake together, Friday after school, Sophie's favorite white sheet cake with lemon frosting and pink icing that said.

Happy 8ᵗʰ Birthday
Sophie

Sophie got up and ran into the backyard. She sat among the marigolds.

As promised, Chloe came by. She sat beside Sophie. Chloe was a slight girl with long blonde pigtails, and gigantic blue eyes that looked like they belonged to a Siamese cat. Chloe weaved her fingers into Sophie's and said, "My mom says your mom is watching you from Heaven." She spoke softly. If they hadn't been sitting right beside each other, Sophie would have missed every word.

When Sophie didn't respond, Chloe added, "Here," and placed a tray of cupcakes with lemon icing and pink flower decorations on top. "We baked them as soon as I got home."

Sophie didn't move, but peeked at the cupcakes and then back to the grass.

"Meet me in our passageway after the funeral tomorrow, okay? My mom won't let me come. She says it's not for kids." Chloe's eyebrows furrowed, realizing what she had just said. "Well, except for you, of course."

Sophie nodded yes.

Chloe hugged Sophie's stiff body, stood and waved good-bye, even though her friend didn't look up.

At the very back of both their yards sat a dirt path that linked their two homes. They called it their "tree house." When the weather cooperated, they covered the dirt with a towel and lounged together, until they were called inside by their moms. Chloe smuggled two lollipops, and Sophie, two of Hannah's training bras. Hidden behind enormous maple trees, they giggled as they climbed into the bras, like they were stepping into hula hoops. They pulled them up to their chests before removing their shirts. Once the shirts hit the ground, they pulled on the straps, looked at each other in the baggy material and shared hysterical fits of laughter until their bellies ached.

At least now Sophie had something to look forward to the next day.

***

The slate was moist that Sunday morning, when all four girls walked down the front steps of their home, en route to their mother's funeral. Fat slugs had pasted themselves on the center of every few steps. The girls would normally squeal in disgust while avoiding each one, but today remained silent. Sophie was the last of them to come out of the house, with a steady stream of tears rolling down her cheeks and dripping over the edge of her nose. She followed in the path of the others until the very last step, where she lifted her black leather half inch pump and brought down the toe on the belly of the last slug. She looked at it as the flesh spread onto the gray slate. She walked to the black limo in front of the house.

"Good morning, Miss," said the driver. He was a small white man with a large nose and tiny brown eyes. He had one hand on the door waiting for her to enter and the other behind his back. His black suit and cap were crisp and fresh.

Sophie gingerly stepped in and sat beside her grandma, who looked perfect. Her makeup made her look like a movie star. She wore a black silk blouse and trousers. She had pulled back her shoulder length gray hair in a tight bun, displaying her pearl earrings.

The windshield wipers swooshed a few times: back and forth, back and forth, back and forth, until the fallen pollen was pushed to the edges.

Sophie's grandpa was the last to leave the house. She watched him drop his keys twice before locking the door, and as he approached the car, he mumbled and shook his head multiple times. The driver still held the door open, which allowed Sophie, her sisters, and their grandma to see him look inside the back and decidedly turn away. "You can close the door, I'm going upfront," he said briskly.

The way to the temple was silent except for a nose being blown or a leg crossing over leg. They wound along Grand Central Parkway at a steady fifty miles an hour and the girl's bodies swayed with the motion of the car. No one steadied themselves by holding the sides or each other. Sophie had never been in such a fancy car before: with snacks, water that could be poured in pretty glasses and windows that moved with the touch of a button. The windows of their Volvo needed muscle to roll up and down.

When they finally made their way into the driveway of the temple and around the back to park, Hannah took Amy's hand, Amy reached for Jane, and Jane placed her deep purple nail-polished fingers over Sophie's to lace between. Sophie retreated, putting her hands together in her lap, between her top inner thighs. A small moan escaped her mouth, then turned into sobs.

"Stop crying, Sophie. Please stop crying," Amy pleaded. She had pulled her hair back into an especially tight French braid and wore her best navy-blue dress with a thin white pin stripe.

"Can we get out of the car now? I have those needle things," Jane said, turning to Hannah.

"Almost, Janie."

Jane had been impossible to dress. Each outfit their grandma had tried to put on her was ripped off and thrown back into the closet. "I hate that!" Jane said, over and over. Finally, Hannah stepped in and took Jane's favorite pair of dark blue jeans and Snoopy T-shirt from her dresser and handed them to Jane. "I can do it myself," Jane scolded her grandma, as she placed each article on her small frame.

Amy smoothed Jane's curls away from her face.

Sophie pulled in tighter toward the door on her left. If she stayed in the car, she could pretend her mom was still alive. She could practically hear her mom whispering in her ear, "*It's going to be okay, Sophie. I love you so...go with your sisters.*"

The driver had already come around, opened the door and stood outside. He waited for someone to get out.

"You need to get out of the car now, Robert," Sophie's grandma said, as she leaned over the open glass partition and placed her hand on his shoulder.

"I should have married Leslie," he mumbled a little too loudly. "None of this — none of this would have happened."

Grandma removed her hand and hissed in his ear, "Don't you dare do this today, Robert."

"I want to see Mom. Can we see Mom now, Hannah?" Jane cried.

"No Jane. We won't see Mom, we're Jewish."

"What do we do?" Jane asked.

Sophie counted the white lint on the limo floor, hoping it would stop her crying. From her periphery, she spied her grandpa slinking out of the car, and out of sight.

"We listen to people talk and then go the cemetery. They bury Mom there," Hannah said, gathering momentum in her motherly role to Jane.

"I have to pee, Hannah. Can we go now?" Jane whined.

"I don't want to go," Sophie said.

"It's time now, girls," their grandma replied.

"What are they going to do with my mom?" Sophie probed her grandmother's eyes.

"Come, we'll talk on the way in," her grandma gestured to Hannah to leave the car.

"Amy, take Jane. We need to go now," Hannah insisted.

Amy did as Hannah told. She pulled Jane onto her lap and scooted out after Hannah. Jane clung on, her orange hair laid out on Amy's back like fusilli pasta.

41

Sophie nudged closer to the door and pressed the control for the window. She watched it glide up and down.

"It's just us now, love. We have to go," her grandma said.

"What's going to happen to us?"

Her grandma sat closer and took Sophie's hand. "Grandpa and I will stay with you until your dad is home from the hospital."

Sophie left the window down and put her face on the edge of the glass. It was just a mist coming down, but it made her blink. She wished that her father had recovered enough to be with her. She wished that her grandparents weren't so protective. They kept telling her and her sisters that their dad didn't look himself yet, with all his bumps and bruises, and that he drifted in and out of sleep all day from the medicine he took.

"Everything is going to be okay, Sophie, you'll see. Once your dad is home, things will get back to normal. And Grandpa and I will be around to make things easier."

Normal. Sophie didn't know what that meant any more. She knew other kids whose families looked more like hers now. Mark, who lived down the block, was adopted by his mom, but had no dad. He always killed bugs and threatened to kill the birds in his backyard trees with homemade swords. Amy's friend, Barbara, had both parents, but her mom always travelled for work and was never home. She pulled out all her eyelashes and some of her pin-straight black hair. Lucy, in her class, her dad died when she was only three, and, well, she was just weird.

CHAPTER THREE

As soon as the limo dropped them at the curb, back home, Sophie ran. She ran around the side of the house, through the thorns of the rose bushes. Her bare arms and ankles sustained paper thin scratches along the way. She ran straight to the tree house, hoping that Chloe hadn't forgotten to come. Sophie was out of breath. She put her hands on her bent knees, while her belly rapidly moved out and in, slowly returning to equilibrium. There was Chloe, holding two lollipops.

"My mom just got home from the temple a while ago. I knew you'd be here soon."

More than anything in the whole wide world, Sophie did not want to talk about the funeral. She didn't want to share with Chloe that all the adults cried, even ones she had never seen before. She could barely move a step before someone, even strangers, asked her if she was okay, or worse told her she was going to be okay. She was never going to be okay.

"This is a stupid dress," Sophie tugged on the elastic waist.

"Here," Chloe handed Sophie a cherry lollipop, "it has the tootsie in the middle."

Sophie thought Chloe was great, not only did she know that that was her favorite kind of lollipop, but she knew not to ask, *how was it*? "Thanks," Sophie said, unwrapping it. She sat down as close to Chloe as she could, on an orange and yellow striped beach towel that had already been warmed by the sun.

"They put my mom in the ground." Sophie held the lollipop in one hand and flicked an ant off the towel with her other. "Do you think there will be bugs on her?"

"No. They make those boxes really tight." Chloe sucked on her lollipop so hard her cheeks caved in. She pulled it out just in time for the POP. Sophie laughed for the first time in days. "I know," Chloe said. "You'll come with me to ballet."

"What?"

"It's really fun. My mom says it's good to have a distraction when you're sad."

Sophie thought this over. "I don't have anything to wear. I can't ask my... I can't ask my dad either. He hasn't woken up yet."

It was impossible for Sophie to understand why her grandparents wouldn't let her go to the hospital to see him. When she asked, they gave her the same lame answer, over and over, that he slept so much he wouldn't even know she was there. But that didn't matter to Sophie, she just wanted to crawl into bed beside him and snuggle. Maybe just because she was there, he would open his eyes. Maybe he just needed to be told a story, like she did when she couldn't sleep. Maybe it worked both ways.

"You can borrow my stuff. Say you'll come, please?" Chloe leaned her head on Sophie's shoulder. Her blonde hair fanned out along Sophie's chest.

Sophie twirled the ends of Chloe's hair, "I guess I have to ask my grandma. I don't know."

"I'll take care of everything," Chloe turned toward Sophie, so their knees touched and they faced each other. "Pinkie promise you'll come?" She put her right pinkie out for Sophie.

Sophie gave her a pinkie.

***

Monday morning, all the Gold girls prepared for school. Sophie's grandparents wouldn't allow them to miss another day, for the sake of their routine.

"Hurry up, Amy! We barely have time to see Dad before Grandma and Grandpa get there." Sophie stood on the opposite side of the door holding her breath, like she practiced in the pool, so Hannah and Amy wouldn't hear her.

"What if they catch us? What if we're not allowed to see him once we get to the hospital?" Amy sounded worried.

"Who cares? He's our father. Don't you want to see him? Don't you think he needs to know what happened to Mom?" Sophie could hear the crack in Hannah's voice with the last words. She imagined Hannah's hands on her hips.

Bags rustled on the other side of the door. "But Grandma and Grandpa say he's not even awake yet, how is he even gonna know what we say?"

"Just get your bag, Amy. We have to boogie."

Sophie scurried back to her room, like a squirrel running up a tree trunk with a newly acquired nut. She stayed huddled in the corner by her desk until it was time to go.

When she got into her grandparents' car, she imagined a reunion between her sisters and dad. Her hands curled into fists. She needed to see her dad too.

"Put your seat belts on, girls," Sophie's grandma said as she turned toward them in the backseat.

"*No*," Jane answered.

"Jane, put it on please," Sophie pleaded, as she buckled her own. She had never worn it before and it gave her a belly an ache the moment she heard it lock into place.

"You're not the boss of me," Jane crossed her arms at her chest. "I'm not going to school anyway. I'm going to see Daddy."

"Jane, please. It will be fun at school today. You'll see your friends there," Grandma said.

"*No!*"

"She doesn't need a seat belt, Eva," Sophie's grandpa piped in, as he started the car. His beard had grown wilder, with spotty bald patches. Sophie thought it looked like their lawn after the family had been away on vacation.

"Do I need to remind you, Robert…"

"He's my son! You don't need to remind me of anything!" Sophie noticed a look of disgust on his face. He got out of the car, went around to Jane's side and opened the door. He buckled her in. Jane kept her arms crossed. She pouted, but didn't fuss.

"When can we see Daddy?" Sophie snuck the question in, as her grandfather made his way back to the driver's seat.

"I don't know yet, Sophie," grandma said.

The rest of the five-minute ride was silent. Jane kept sulking, even when her grandma walked her up the path to her kindergarten class, which was just a house in the neighborhood a mile away from theirs, an old brick colonial with great columns and porch swings out front. It converted into a school the year Hannah was ready to attend, and all the Gold girls had gone. The head teacher, Mrs. Birch, knew the family all those years, so when Sophie's grandma reached the door and passed Jane over the threshold, she was greeted with a big hug. Sophie shifted lower in her seat, not wanting to be seen by her old teacher. She bit her nails.

"Don't do that, it's a disgusting habit," her grandpa peered at her through the rearview mirror.

Sophie placed her hands in her lap and closed her eyes. She imagined her mom in the driver's seat. When she looked through the mirror, her mom always winked at her. *"Hi Mom,"* she thought, *"I wish you were here. Grandma and Grandpa keep fighting, Hannah and Amy won't talk to me, Jane's getting in trouble, and worst of all Daddy won't wake up."* The thought made her nose burn, the feeling that always preceded her tears. Sophie did not want to cry. Instead, she thought of her pact with Chloe, made in the tree house, and prayed that Mrs. Long had spoken with her grandma.

***

Sophie pushed her mushy white noodles around her plate, unable to consume her grandma's tuna casserole, loaded with cream and mushrooms. It made Sophie's stomach turn. Never mind the fact that she had no appetite at all since the night of the accident. It didn't seem to matter, no one paid attention.

Her grandmother had delivered the food to the table, one slow serving at a time, and then stood at the sink, looking out the kitchen window above it. She placed on yellow rubber gloves, ready for dishes that weren't there. The sun had just begun to set. It was a completely still evening, no rain, no wind, no clattering tree branches against the panes. "Sophie, Mrs. Long called today."

Spoons scraped across the plain white bowls, the weekday glasses were put down mindlessly, a bang here, a splash of water there, and her grandfather's newspaper pages crinkled with every turn.

"What for, Eva?" her grandpa asked. He and Jane were huddled behind the *New York Times*. The only sign that she was even back there, behind the black and white print, were her little purple fingernails, exposed and grasping the edges. Her polish was now chipped and peeling.

"Chloe would like Sophie to join her ballet class on Saturday morning, Robert," her back still faced the table.

"Can I, Grandma, please?" Sophie practically begged.

Hannah and Amy both read Nancy Drew mysteries, with their elbows against the table. Sophie knew that Amy had Judy Blume's book *Forever* tucked within her Nancy Drew. Her mom had forbidden Hannah from reading *Forever* just months before. Neither Hannah nor Amy looked up as they scooped their noodles into their spoons and shoved them in their mouths.

"I said yes."

"I want to go too, Grandma, can I go too?" Jane asked, pushing the newspaper down.

"No dear, this is just for Sophie."

"Just for Sophie. Of course, it is," Hannah piped in from behind her book.

"Just like the piano lessons. Sophie was the only one allowed to have those too. What makes her so special?" Amy asked.

"That's not fair," Jane shouted.

Sophie could hardly contain her smile. "Thanks, Grandma." She walked over to the sink and gave her a hug, then went back to sit down.

"You're a suck up, Sophie. You did that with Mom too – always!" Amy spit out.

"None of that, girls," her grandma responded, without much conviction.

Sophie saw Hannah gaze over the top of her book, perusing the table and the fact that no one was eating. She nudged Amy with her elbow. Amy took the signal and stood to go upstairs, books tucked under her arm. Hannah handed her mystery to Amy so she could lift Jane out of their grandfather's lap.

"Time for bed, Jane." Sophie's heart quickened when Hannah pulled Jane in. Her head turned to the side without thought to accommodate Jane's, just like her mom would have. Jane clamped on and the three were gone.

Sophie followed her sisters up, even though they were all mad at her. She didn't know what else to do. She certainly didn't want to be alone in the kitchen with her grandparents.

Just as her foot hit the bottom step, Sophie heard the sound of her grandpa's newspaper and imagined him folding it down to peer at her grandma. "Why does Sophie need to do this ballet thing, Eva?"

"She needs something right now, Robert. Don't we all need something?"

"We're going to meet Sam's doctor Saturday, remember?"

"She'll go with Mr. Long. Hannah and Amy can stay with Jane."

"How long are we going to keep this up, Eva? This is supposed to be the time we…"

She cut him off, "As long as it takes."

And then they stopped. Like the bell that rang at school before the pledge of allegiance, utter quiet.

Sophie ran up the stairs two at a time, thrilled that her grandma had agreed to class, especially before discussing it with her grandfather, who might have ruined it. When she got to her bedroom Hannah and Amy were helping Jane into her pajamas.

"Step in Jane," Hannah said. Jane's feet looked so small and delicate. She stepped into each pant leg and then Amy pulled them to her waist.

"Can you believe what a brat Sophie is, always getting special treatment, even now?" Amy said to Hannah.

Hannah kissed Jane's nose as she slid her shirt over Jane's head. "She's as spoiled as she's always been. Did you think that would change?"

"At least we got to see dad before her."

Sophie's face flushed; it was such a lie, she was never given special treatment, and what about Jane? Hannah and Amy doted over her, she'd been doing her pajamas by herself since the age of two, when she insisted "Jamas, self!" in her foreign toddler tongue, her pudgy hands pounding her chest.

"You saw Dad today?" Sophie stepped into the room.

Amy looked over at Hannah, while she grabbed for her braid, at her back.

"You know we're not allowed at the hospital yet, Princess Sophie," Hannah said, avoiding eye contact. She looked at Jane, patted her tush, and said, "Come, let's brush teeth." They headed to the bathroom, hand in hand.

"Where would you get a silly idea like that from, Sophie?" Amy asked, putting her hands on her hips. "Shouldn't you get ready for bed too?" she added, turning to leave the bedroom. She twirled her braid between her fingers, giving herself away. Sophie knew she only did this when she was nervous or lying.

"I just heard you."

"You're imagining things."

"You're mean, Amy. You're so mean," Sophie shouted. She felt like a race car revving up.

Amy didn't turn as she left, but released her braid with gusto, so it whipped onto her back like a horse's mane swatting a fly. "And you're so spoiled!"

Engine cut, Sophie slipped on her nightgown, like she would each night until Saturday, waiting for ballet class.

***

Saturday morning Chloe's dad idled in the driveway between their homes. He waited while the girls used every last minute possible to select the perfect leotard for Sophie's first class.

There was spaghetti strap, cap sleeve, long sleeve, low back V-neck, and more. Finally, Sophie closed her eyes and yanked one from the pile on Chloe's bedroom floor. They ran out of the house together and climbed into the car.

"How's your dad doing?" Mr. Long asked Sophie, after they were a few blocks along.

Sophie looked up at him from the back seat. She knew, from Chloe, that he was the same age as her father, but his bald head and pudgy belly aged him. "He's not awake yet."

"I bet he'll be home sooner than you think," Mr. Long turned his head toward her for a moment and smiled.

"Thanks."

"Soph, remember what I said — Mrs. Reilly isn't the warm and fuzzy type, but you'll still have a lot of fun," Chloe said.

"What if everyone stares at me? I don't know anything about ballet. I think this was a bad idea," Sophie's eyes welled.

"You're gonna be great."

When they arrived at the dance school, a building not far from home, Chloe pulled Sophie down the steep concrete ramp to the basement. When they opened the large steel door and entered the lobby, the smell hit them – a mixture of sweat, ballet shoes, and damp wooden floors.

"First position," a woman called as she walked in smoking a cigarette.

Every girl in the room placed their left hands onto the barre, Sophie followed, not knowing what to expect. Her belly tightened. She was so grateful Chloe was in front of her.

"That's Mrs. Reilly," Chloe said, her head cocked. Mrs. Reilly's dyed black hair stretched in a bun. She wore a black leotard with long sleeves, black tights and a black ballet skirt tied at her waist, unable to hold back the roll of fat that hung around her middle. The only hint of color was the pink of her shoes, and they looked as old as she did.

She told everyone to take first position, as she placed her own feet into a turned -out stance. They were to mirror her every move as the pianist played.

"Plié," she said in her raspy voice. They followed her as she bent her knees just half way. She carried her right arm in a circular position down, then across her body from belly button to chest and back out to the side. As her arm landed by her side, her legs straightened.

Mrs. Reilly didn't seem to notice Sophie and that allowed her to relax and absorb the many instructions given. Each sequence was repeated over and over, eventually bending down all the way until their butts hit their feet and back up again they uncoiled like springs. Then again, with legs in various other positions, Mrs. Reilly called second and fourth and fifth. Sophie's legs tried to twist and turn to fit each shape. Her eyes stayed plastered onto Mrs. Reilly, who didn't smile or praise anyone. The pianist's fingers danced across the keys, as the dancers accompanied him by moving across the floor.

Sophie completely forgot about her family as she moved from one exercise into the next, legs bending and kicking to different heights and in different directions. Their arms were supposed to do something else with every move of their legs. There were so many body parts to coordinate and Sophie enjoyed every moment of it, even the constant sound of Mrs. Reilly shouting, "Round your arms, legs up… up higher, kick girls, kick, stretch those lazy toes to the floor."

***

The following Saturday, Sophie sat on the marley floor and slipped on her ballet shoes. When she looked up at her reflection, she almost didn't recognize herself. Her tight bun made the dark circles under her eyes more pronounced. It was hard to sleep. Sophie was eager for her dad to come home. It had been two weeks since her mom's funeral and still she was given excuse after excuse for not being allowed to the hospital, *he just woke up, he's too weak, he needs his rest.* She inhaled the aroma of the room and recalled her dad's sweaty smell after garden work or gutter cleanings each fall, when he climbed a great ladder to get rid of dirt, leaves, and debris. Last year he pulled out a pink sock that he insisted belonged to Jane.

Her mom had been in the garden, pulling weeds and raking the leaves.

"Jane!" he shouted from above, waving the pink sock in the air.

"Sam, she's only four, leave her be," her mom had replied, looking up at him, covering her eyes from the blaring morning sun.

All the girls were hanging out in the garden, reading in lounge chairs on the grass before doing their afternoon chores.

"Sarah, no time to learn but the present. She must have thrown it from her window," he waved the sock like a flag up toward Sophie and Jane's bedroom, just a couple of feet above the section of the gutter he worked on.

Sophie closed her eyes and saw him descending the ladder that day. His T-shirt was marked with sweaty yellow patches. He never wore more than that when he worked outside. Even when the temperature fell, he seemed immune to the cold.

Her mom walked over to him, all bundled up in a beige cable-knit sweater, and just as he was about to step off the ladder, hugged his body and whispered in his ear. Sophie couldn't hear what she had said that day, but back up he went smiling.

"Soph, open your eyes. Mrs. Reilly just walked in," Chloe whispered.

Sophie took a breath, the smoke smell confirming Chloe's words. She stood, straightened her pink chiffon skirt and took first position, left hand to the barre. The next sixty minutes transported Sophie. She focused on the piano playing classical music, she had to focus on what her body was supposed to do or she would be lost; *stretch my toes, legs higher, round my arms, stretch my legs... "* Sophie repeated the list over and over. She was in a la seconde, her right leg lifted up to waist height, when Mrs. Reilly walked over, took her leg in hand and lifted it all the way up to Sophie's ear. Sophie felt a slight pull along the back of her leg, but didn't make a peep.

"That will do," Mrs. Reilly said, then walked away.

When she took her last grand jete of the day, her mom's face flashed in front of her and Sophie felt like she had to start the day all over again, waking to reality.

"Come on Wednesdays three-thirty to five," Mrs. Reilly said, as she lit a half used cigarette, "Tell your mother," she exhaled a long line of smoke toward Sophie.

"Thank you, Mrs. Reilly. I'll ask." Sophie blinked as the smoke evaporated in front of her.

Mrs. Reilly walked out of the studio before Sophie finished speaking.

Sophie held her necklace in her hands.

***

The next morning Sophie couldn't stop smiling at the thought of another class each week. Her body ached with life and her feet were sore and red from class. The carpet stung her toes. She strolled down to the kitchen.

"Here, you mix the eggs while I grab the challah," their grandma said, and walked to the fridge. "Take your time, Janie, or the eggs will spill all over the counter." Her grandma moved around the kitchen in circles. "Now where is that bread?" she asked, sounding scattered.

Sophie's grandma bent over to look in the fridge and the sheer material of her nightgown exposed her underwear. Sophie's cheeks turned red. She turned her head and spied the challah on the counter.

Sophie grabbed it and held it out as she walked over to her grandmother. "Hi, Grandma," she said, gingerly.

"Huh?" she stood up, startled by Sophie's appearance. She looked down at her toes, "What is this?"

"They're just blisters, Grandma," Sophie tried to hold back her smirk, but she was so proud of her damaged toes.

"Is that going to happen all the time now?" her grandmother asked as she took the bread from Sophie.

"Just until I have calluses, don't worry. All the girls have them."

"I don't care about all the girls."

Sophie hated it when her mom used to say that. She didn't expect that from her grandma too. Of course, it mattered that other girls had them, you had to have them!

"GRANDMA, I'm done," Jane stood there with the whisk in her hand, dangling it over the linoleum floor. Little droplets of egg sprinkled down.

"Oh, Janie," she shook her head in exasperation. "What a mess."

Sophie grabbed a paper towel from the table and helped clean up the egg while Jane watched from her stool. Her hair wildly fell all over her face and shoulders.

"I'm hungry. Can you make the French toast already?" Jane rocked back and forth on the stool.

Grandma looked up at Jane, as if she was about to say something, and then directed her focus back to Sophie, who jumped in before she could speak. "Mrs. Reilly told me to come on Wednesday too. Please, Grandma, can I?"

"Will your feet always look like this?" she walked over to the stove and turned on the burner. "You could take an extra piano lesson or… something else."

"I don't want something else," Sophie snapped and stomped upstairs and back to her room to wait until breakfast was ready. She opened her closet door so she could look in the full-length mirror glued to the inside. Sophie took fifth position and rounded her arms in front of her chest. She closed her eyes for a moment, took a deep breath, and began to repeat the exercises from class. As her left arm lifted above her head Sophie imagined being picked up and carried across the room by her dad. Her face lifted toward her hand and she smiled. She would never stop dancing.

CHAPTER FOUR

Still bleary-eyed, Sophie rolled out of bed and meandered to her desk chair where she had set out her ballet outfit. She pulled her tights up to her waist and recalled an exchange from the previous day. While heading for her beginner class she passed an older girl of about twelve, huddled over her toes. It was impossible not to stare.

The girl turned and looked up. "It's gonna fall off you know," she said, tilting her head to the side as she spoke, while staring at her black toenail. Her wavy hair surrounded her face and hung to her waist. She held her bobby pins in one hand and the ribbons of her pointe shoes in another. Her center part was stark white in contrast to her jet-black strands.

"It is?" Sophie smirked.

She had watched this girl for weeks and all of a sudden they were actually talking. Whenever Sophie arrived early to ballet, she studied the advanced class before hers. Most of the girls were on pointe, which raised them inches off the floor, like sprouting buds. Sophie marveled at how well they could jump, turn, and balance on such a tiny surface. What she found most intriguing was how quickly they could imitate what

Mrs. Reilly demonstrated. The girls would make all the movements with hand gestures and small steps. When it was their turn to dance, they had the whole thing memorized.

"I don't know why you're smiling. It hurts like hell," the girl said, as she untied her pink ballet skirt and walked away.

Now, a day later, it seemed silly. If it hurt that much, why would she and the other girls keep doing it?

Sophie released the elastic band around her waist and picked up her leotard.

"Where's Dad, Grandma? He's not at the hospital."

Sophie heard the question, but couldn't identify the voice. She rubbed her eyes and quickly pulled up her leotard as she walked toward Hannah and Amy's room.

"They moved him, dears."

"Where?" *That was definitely Hannah*. Sophie moved to the entrance of their bedroom door.

"To a more suitable place – for his condition."

"That's why he wasn't at the hospital when we went back," Amy blurted out.

"Amy!" Hannah shrieked.

"Ooops."

"What does that mean, Grandma?" Hannah quickly brushed over Amy's admission.

"Did you girls go to the hospital?"

Sophie edged as close to the door as she could and sat down. She didn't want to miss anything.

"Only once before, Grandma," Amy said. "In the beginning…"

"What's wrong with you?" Hannah cut her off.

"What? You said it yourself, he's our dad. We have a right to see him."

"Grandma, what type of place? For concussions?" Hannah asked. She had a knack for swerving conversations back to point. Sophie had heard her use this tactic before with their parents. She would stay on topic, even though she knew she had done something against their rules. It was quite impressive to Sophie, how it often threw her parents off the rails, and it seemed it might be working now too.

"Not exactly, Hannah. We'll discuss this more later. I need to drop Sophie at ballet this morning."

"It's Sunday. She doesn't go on Sunday." Jane protested. *Jane's in there too?*

"She added a class at the recommendation of her teacher."

"Again?" Amy asked.

"Where's my father? It's been weeks," Hannah's voice escalated.

"I know you're concerned, but some circumstances are not ideal for children. Just know he's in a good place for his situation." Sophie thought her grandma sounded like she was trying to convince herself.

"What situation would that be, Grandma?" Hannah pressed. It made Sophie nervous, but also grateful. She too wanted to uncover the mystery of her dad's homecoming.

"Where's my Daddy?" Jane's raspy voice had a quiver in it.

"Hannah, I don't want to upset your sister. Later!" her grandma said sternly.

"*Where – is he*?" Hannah asked, like a tea kettle at full boil.

Sophie waited to hear the answer, but instead was side swiped when Hannah directed her venom toward her, "What the fuck, Sophie?" Hannah towered over her. She wore her red flannel pajamas and a loose ponytail with wisps of hair scattered all over her face and neck. "Just come in like the rest of us. You're getting creepier by the day, always skulking around."

Sophie sat on the carpet in a lump, dumbstruck.

"Of course not. Just sit there, like always, totally inept," Hannah pushed back the most immediate hairs blocking her eyes.

Sophie had no idea what inept meant, but she was sure that Hannah had just insulted her.

"Are you capable of doing anything anymore, other than ballet?"

Sophie wanted to weep or run into her room, but knew that would only feed her frenzy.

"That's enough!" Sophie's grandma came out of Hannah and Amy's room. "You're behaving abysmally. I'm so ashamed of you. You are the oldest sister in this house. Start acting like it."

"Really, Grandma? You've been walking around like a zombie. Now, you're gonna tell me what to do and how to act?"

"STOP," Jane shouted as she burst into the hallway, her hands covering her ears.

Hannah stopped, but only after she walked over to her grandma. She stood as close as she could, her head rising above her grandma's hair. "I – hate – you," she seethed. Hannah slammed the door to her room, shoving Amy in as she went.

"Come, Sophie. Jane, you too," her grandma pulled Sophie up by the elbow with a strong grip. "Jane, get dressed. You'll come with me to drop Sophie off at ballet."

"Why can't I stay with Grandpa?" Jane fully recovered, bounced into their room and onto her bed.

"Grandpa is away. He left this morning." Sophie thought her grandma sounded a bit too cheery.

"Is he visiting his friend again?" Jane asked, as she got undressed and sat in her underwear.

"Yes, Jane. He'll be back in a couple of days. Now, find something cool to wear, shorts, tank top," her voice trailed off, as she walked toward the door, "it's brutal out there today."

***

"I'm ready." Sophie took a seat at the kitchen table and put a pile of bobby pins and a hairbrush down.

Her grandma stood by the phone with a steaming cup of black coffee in her hands. Upon seeing Sophie, she replaced the mug for brush and started to make her a ponytail.

"I can do that."

Her grandma kept brushing. "You know, I always wanted to be a ballerina. Too tall, too buxom," her hands cupped under her breasts. Sophie blushed.

"What happened, Grandma?"

"Well, I decided to be a wife and mother instead. Best choice ever," she twirled and twisted Sophie's hair into a bun.

"No, to Dad?"

"Oh." She placed a few pins equally around until Sophie's hair gathered stiffly in place. "Perfect!" She paused and straightened her shirt. "Well, your dad, he's very sad."

"About Mom?"

"Yes," she said, stroking her granddaughter's hair. "Sometimes, when you're really sad, you – you just can't do things the way you normally do and you need some help. You kind of shut down like, like…"

"An old battery?" Sophie filled in the gap.

"Exactly," her grandma sounded relieved.

"Will he be okay?"

"Yes, Sophie. He'll be just fine."

***

Yes, Sophie. He'll be fine. Tendu.

Sophie stretched her leg out in front of her, along the floor, foot pointed.

Yes, Sophie. He'll be fine.   Ronde jambe.

Her tendu moved from front, to side, to back.

Yes, Sophie. He'll be fine.   Passe.

Sophie lifted her left foot up to the side of her knee.

Sophie stopped mid-develope. It struck her like one of those moments when a ball slams you in the nose. You didn't even know it was coming your way and all of a sudden you're on fire. *He's not fine,* Sophie finally realized. She had carried her grandmother's words for weeks, acting like things would soon go back to normal: she went swimming in the local pool, played mini golf with friends, and even ate ice cream and enjoyed it. And with her grandpa often away on a trip, she and her grandma had begun to renew their strong bond. But Sophie felt unsure she would ever see her father again.

She ran out of ballet class, to the office, a musty room the size of a walk-in closet. The carpet was torn and ripped along the edges of the wall. It had coffee stains and burn holes from too many ashes dropped. Mrs. Reilly's husband ran things from a desk that was really a card table with a fold-up chair. He smoked almost as much as she did, so the smell in the room was intense. Sophie ran in with urgency.

The lighting was so dismal she had to squint to adjust. "Mr. Reilly, I have to call home," Sophie said. If

Chloe had been in class on Sundays, she would have been right at Sophie's heels, but she was only allowed to take one class a week.

Mr. Reilly slid the phone toward Sophie, who immediately dialed. Her delicate fingers raced to circle through all the numbers she needed to hit.

"Is he really coming home?" Sophie asked franticly.

Ten minutes later, her grandmother walked into the office, took Sophie's hand, and pulled her out of the school. They went up the ramp and straight into the car, which waited double parked, engine on, hazards flashing.

Once the car door closed and they were tucked inside the backseat, Sophie cried. It began slowly, a shake, a tear, and then a sob that made her body crumble like decayed plaster. Sophie collapsed the full force of her sixty pounds, into her grandmother's lap.

Her grandmother seemed to know not to speak, but to just stroke Sophie's hair, gently from part to tip, over and over, for the duration of the next half hour. When Sophie's body quieted down, her grandma went around to the front seat and drove. Sophie drifted in and out of sleep, exhausted. Her grandma smoothly glided them in the car. The route was unfamiliar. She could always tell when they were close to home by the swerves in the road, first a left off the parkway, quick right, then the zig zag of Downey Drive, stop light, another right and they were home. Recognizing none of the usual signs, she allowed herself to be lulled by the hum of the wind whipping the doors of the car and the wheels rolling over the pavement.

When she saw her father for the first time, she didn't run to him as she anticipated, she didn't jump in his arms and cry, "Daddy, I missed you so much!" Instead, she stood in front of him and stared. He sat by the window in a room the size of the one she shared with Jane. She had been surprised when they pulled up in front of a house that looked similar to her own, like a miniature fairy-tale castle, with a tower on the second floor and stained-glass windows on the first. They were greeted by a nurse who smiled at her grandma. They walked up a spiral staircase to the threshold of a bedroom.

"Sophie," her name came out of his mouth in a whisper, like he was parched. His face was gray and had no expression. His body slack in his jeans and black turtleneck sweater. Sophie had never seen him wear a turtleneck before, especially not on a ninety-degree day. The newspaper sat on his lap, his hands folded on top, the way Sophie saw him do when they had company over.

An urge came over her to punch her father, right in the gut, as hard and fast as she could. He had been sitting in that chair, in a house close to theirs, when he could have been with her, all this time. "Hi," she said and walked over to him.

He picked up her fingers, like strayed threads and moved them around his hand, "Sophie," he said a bit louder this time.

His hands were cold. "Are you coming home now?"

He held her hand tighter and then released it.

"Why did you bring her, Mom? I begged you not to tell the girls. None of them. Not till I was ready." Sophie had never heard her father plead before.

Sophie's grandma smiled. "Enough, Sam. I've abided by your wishes, but the girls are suffering. I can't make excuses any longer. They need you."

She began packing. The one mahogany bureau in the room held four drawers, each pulled open by Sophie's grandma and the contents spilled onto her father's bed. The method, both sloppy and deliberate, delighted Sophie. It had a purpose. Her eyes, a little brighter, travelled along his single mattress where she spotted an old black and white photo of her mom, taped to the mahogany headboard. Her hair was long and straight, Sophie couldn't imagine her mom taking the time to blow it dry – she always washed and went.

"That's Mom," Sophie declared.

"Yes, it sure is. That's around the time she and your dad met." Her grandma opened the closet and grabbed the suitcase inside. She tossed it on the bed, swinging it up with more force than necessary and proceeded to throw all his clothing inside. Sophie found it fun to watch the chaos being strewn about, sleeves tangled up with pant legs and underwear, all tumbling like the autumn leaves, into one big pile. Once the zipper made its way to the end of its journey, her grandma declared, "Mission accomplished." She walked to the door and added, "I'm going to tell the doctor we're leaving. I'll be right back. Collect your photos, Sam."

And they were alone. He obeyed his mother. Slowly he lifted himself from the arm chair, moving like a stiff old man. Once upright, his shoulders slumped forward, as he reached for each frame on the window sill. One photo for each daughter, in age order from left to right. He picked up Hannah's first, a shot taken at the starting line of her last race. Her arms and legs were bulging with definition, her hips so tiny in her blue short shorts and racer-back tank. The front read *'QUEENS TRACK'* in white print.

The picture of Amy – quintessential teenager – dressed up for a school dance, with a little too much eye liner surrounding her lids and loud red lip gloss to match her pant suit. Sophie knew that once Amy got to her friend Dina's house, she would add to the make-up and probably pull down the already low scoop-neck top to reveal her bounty of cleavage.

Sophie's picture was taken on recital night. Mrs. Reilly had chosen excerpts from *The Nutcracker Suite*. Sophie danced as a snowflake. She was in arabesque, her front arm reaching forward, head slightly turned toward her shoulder. *My leg should have been higher*, she thought looking at it as her father picked it up and piled it on Amy's. *I could have pointed my foot more. Chloe told me it was perfect, was she just being nice?*

Jane's was a head shot from the day she lost her first tooth, bottom left. It had been loose for weeks, dangling in a way that Sophie thought was so cool, all twisted and hanging forward. One bite into the corner of her Rubix Cube and it dropped to the ground.

Before getting in the car, Sophie watched her father fumble. "Be ready, be steady," he kept mumbling. He clung to the picture frames of the girls, pressed to his chest with his left arm, as he maneuvered the black and white of her mom. He managed to fold it against his thigh and tuck it in his back pocket, after several failed attempts.

He paused at the car door and mumbled. "Can't get in, can't get in," his breath getting loud and swift. *What's wrong with him?* Sophie wondered.

"Sam, go sit in the back with Sophie and close your eyes. Deep breaths," her grandma coached. She opened the door for him and guided him in by the arm.

Once they were all seated and buckled in, Sophie took her dad's hand and squeezed. She looked up and met her grandma's eyes through the rearview mirror. Her grandma winked and mouthed, "Thank you!"

The engine rumbled.

CHAPTER FIVE

Sophie, her grandma, and dad entered an empty house. Lunch dishes littered the dining table with crusts of uneaten bread, and a knife stood upright in an open peanut butter jar like a stick thrust in the mud. The chairs were left pushed back from the table.

"I wonder where the girls went," her grandma mumbled as she glided the chairs, one by one, into position. "Sam, why don't you relax in the living room. I'll make you some lunch. And I have some beautiful pears. Sophie, you must be starving too."

"I'm fine," Sophie and her dad replied in unison.

"Sit down, you two. Lunch will be ready in a jiffy." She left for the kitchen, humming.

From her position on the sofa, she watched her dad circle, like a dog looking for its tail. He touched the mantle first. "Dusty." One arm reached into a caramel covered lamp shaped like a tulip and turned the switch. "It's supposed to be off during the day." He lowered his head to his chest as he dragged his body over to the couch and landed beside Sophie. His shoulders collapsed.

Sophie dug her fingernails into her palms as she listened to the clamoring of dishes in the kitchen and the fridge door swinging open and shut repeatedly. She lived with her grandmother long enough to recognize the signs. She was nervous too.

The space between Sophie's body and her dad's was narrow, like two cars merging too close together on the parkway. She looked down at his lap and saw him clutching the picture frames. Her father had become a stranger.

"Grandpa took all those photos," Sophie tried to break the ice, or at least thaw it, but her father's gaze stayed attached to his brown moccasins, with fur on the inside and a tassel on the front. They looked like old man slippers, the kind her dad would never have bought for himself. "I'm glad you're home, Dad." *Was she?*

The corners of his mouth moved, but not upward to make a smile, more a flat line across. "Your mom makes me the best lunches." Sophie could barely hear him, even though her pink tights almost touched his blue jeans. "Turkey, with mustard, never mayo," he stopped to clear his throat, "she knows I hate mayo."

"Knew. Mom died, Dad." It was the first time she had uttered those words. They came out a bit harsher than she intended.

Tray in hand and apron tied around her waist, her grandma strolled into the room. "You're chatting. Terrific!" Her father blinked rapidly a few times. "This was not what I expected when I started my day," she added.

Sophie stood to help her grandma, relieved to have something to do. As her hands touched the sides of the tray, she looked up quizzically and whispered, "Does he know that Mom died?"

"Of course, he does, sweetie," she said. "Take your plate and sit down next to your dad."

"But we never eat here."

"It's a very special occasion." Her pale pink lips formed a Marion Howard smile.

As far as Sophie could tell, there were no markings of special around. Her dad looked like a loaf of stale white bread, beginning to get moldy.

"Here honey, take your plate," her grandma insisted, but Sophie's dad didn't react. "When you're ready, dear." As she placed the tray on the coffee table, the front door flew open.

Sophie heard the stamping of her sister's shoes. A rare sense of relief overcame her.

"That's the last time I take you along, Amy. It's like you're the five-year-old, not Jane."

Relief turned to satisfaction at hearing Hannah's fury.

"You were supposed to take care of Jane, so I could have pizza with Mark. You messed the whole thing up."

Sophie listened to the next wave of stamping and the slide and creak of the front coat closet. Then the turn of the glass knob on the French doors leading into the living room. She watched as her sisters registered their father on the couch beside her. Sophie would have gloated at being the first at something for once, but not being alone with this shell of her father consoled her.

Hannah, Amy, and Jane all looked sweaty and worn out by the heat. Their cheeks were cherry red and each had their hair pulled back in a ponytail, even Jane. And though her sisters looked nothing alike, the expression they wore when seeing their dad for the first time was unmistakably related.

Jane, with her usual flare, broke the ice, "Is that you, Daddy? You look so… weird."

Sophie had a moment where she imagined them all embracing in a family hug. Her grandma would evaporate and turn into her mom.

Then they ran, nearly pushing each other over. Hannah jumped a chair and got to him first. "Daddy, oh my God, I'm so glad you're home," she hugged him tightly around the neck. He remained stiff.

Jane scooted in between, shoving Hannah away. She climbed into his lap and began kissing his hollow cheeks over and over. Jane's legs shoved Sophie aside as they wiggled to wrap around their dad's lap.

Hannah dropped to her knees in front of his and placed her hands on his legs. "We missed you so much, Dad, we're so glad you're home."

"Give me some space," Amy piped in, as she knocked Hannah over. "We tried to see you at the hospital."

"Don't push me, that's so nasty," Hannah fell on her butt, wedged by the coffee table and rammed Amy with her elbow.

"Daddy, want to see my new Barbie?" Jane gave him a squeeze and one more kiss. "I'll be right back." She ran upstairs.

Sophie was crammed into the corner of the couch. She watched her dad press his eyes shut over and over again.

"Give him some space, Amy," Hannah said, having sat down on his left side. She wiped some sweat off her forehead.

"No, you give him space," Amy said loudly, "you're always so pushy."

Their dad started to rock back and forth, with his arms crossed at his chest. The photos that he had held so tightly on his lap slipped to the floor in disarray. He didn't react.

"What's the matter, Dad?" Hannah asked. "Do you need something?"

"You know what's the matter, Hannah – YOU!" Amy screamed.

Sophie put her hands over her ears. "Stop – please stop you guys," she said, but too softly for anyone to hear. She couldn't bear it, her dad wasn't answering and her sisters were shouting.

"Girls, that's enough. Your Dad just needs a little rest," Grandma said.

He didn't flinch. Sophie's heart pounded rapidly.

"You know why Mom and Dad needed all those dates, Hannah?" Amy pointed her finger at her sister. "You're always so pushy. You need to be first at everything and you ALWAYS have to be right."

"ME? Are you kidding? Mom wanted to escape from all your neeeeds… Mom, I need new make-up, Mom I need a new outfit, Mom…" Hannah said in a bratty voice.

"I'm so sick of you always telling me what to do," Amy screamed. She crossed her arms at her chest and stared at Hannah.

"You're on your own. Don't follow me anywhere – any more," Hannah shouted back, her face beet red.

Sophie felt like lava surrounded her, "*STOP!*" She bellowed as loud as possible.

The room went still. Her dad moved, but only to readjust his back cushion, and then his head bobbed back toward his chest.

"Girls, no one, none of you, are to blame for what happened to your mom." Her grandma walked toward their dad as she spoke, picked up his hands and held them, "Accidents happen. That's all."

"You should tell Grandpa to get home already," Hannah said. "Don't you think he would like to see his only son?"

Grandma's hand shot out and slapped Hannah across the face.

***

The following weeks were dreadful. Her dad sat in the same position on the couch like a dark cloud. He barely ate, or slept, and never spoke to anyone. What was worse in Sophie's mind was that they all began to function as if he wasn't even there.

Her grandfather continued to travel for days at a time and when he did come back there were arguments between her grandparents. They were the kind of fights that began muffled and always ended with the same phrases − "And when will it be our time, Eva? Tell me that!" The louder he got, the less responsive her grandmother became. Sophie would lie in her bed and wonder what "our time" meant, it seemed so vital to them, but nothing changed.

One night Sophie woke up at one-fifty-seven a.m. and couldn't get back to sleep. She tossed and turned like she had the night of her parent's accident. After about an hour, she went downstairs.

She could hear her mom in her head, "*A warm cup of milk always helps*." This was her mom's remedy for Sophie's occasional nightmares. It would have to be cold milk, but she was willing to give it a try. Sophie adjusted her eyes to the dark and walked down slowly, holding onto the banister.

Her dad snored on the couch, still in his clothes, like he'd taken a cat nap. A small lamp on the side table was on its dimmest setting. At first Sophie turned away from him and toward the kitchen, but something drew her back.. He seemed approachable in the soft lighting. His face looked more familiar and unchanged, like the couch cushions had absorbed all his pain.

Sophie grabbed a plaid red blanket from the closet in the living room and curled up beside him. She felt rigid at first, but after only a few awkward seconds she succumbed to her dad's familiar scent. She nestled in and covered both of them.

"Hold on Sarah. Hold on, they're coming for us... I hear an ambulance."

It was still dark when Sophie woke to her dad's voice. "It's okay, Dad. You're home. It's Sophie." She mimicked the words her mom and dad would say to her, when her dreams felt like reality in the black night.

He wasn't okay. She knew that now. Everything at home seemed uncertain like constant tremors of a quake. The only thing she could count on was ballet and the reliability that one exercise led to the next and so on. When she danced the real world dropped away. As she swept her body around the studio, immersed in movement and music, she felt safe. Sophie promised herself in that moment that she was going to be the greatest dancer in the world.

CHAPTER SIX

1988

Sophie Gold's hand stretched out of the warm covers and slammed the alarm off. She looked over at the red fluorescent light on her clock for confirmation: five-thirty a.m. Like ripping off a band aid, she threw the covers down to the edge of the bed. Every morning she woke up at the same time, and every morning it sucked. Her long, lanky, olive-skinned legs dropped over the side and her bare feet wiggled as they hit the hard wood floor. She let out one big yawn and stretched her skinny arms toward the ceiling as she stood up to her full five foot eight inches.

She tip-toed out of the living/bedroom, as not to disturb her best friend from childhood and roommate, Chloe, and closed the French doors that led to the kitchen. Her tired fingers opened the fridge for a bit of light and then she turned on the coffee pot that had been prepared the night before. While she waited, she sat down on the linoleum floor. "Fuck, it's cold," she whispered to herself while twirling her long wavy hair into a ponytail at the top of her head. Her hair had grown so long that it still made its way down half her back, even when it was pulled up. She used her foot to close the fridge and lay down. The floor was hard against her bony spine. As the coffee pot gurgled, she put her hands behind her neck, bent her knees, and began a circuit of crunches; ten fast, ten slow, repeat... until the coffee stopped brewing and two hundred crunches had been accomplished. She pulled on her belly skin with one hand and grabbed a mug with the other. She poured in the black French roast and took a few sips.

Sophie got back down on the floor and counted fifty push-ups and then sprang up for one hundred jumping jacks. Another sip of coffee − after which she reached for her pack of Marlboro Lights. Her elbows hit the counter and she lit up. The cigarettes were a newly acquired habit. When she learned they were an appetite suppressant, she instantly bought a pack of Marlboro Reds. They were so heavy that she choked non-stop for a few minutes, so she switched. Sophie took her time inhaling, allowing the smoke to cascade through her, leaving a slight feeling of light-headedness. She closed her eyes, still groggy, and frowned. It was only six a.m. and already Sophie felt depressed. She was eighteen years old, still a virgin, and didn't have a job with a ballet company yet, despite several auditions in the past few weeks.

She flicked her cigarette butt in Chloe's dirty dinner bowl, only to catch sight of three roaches hanging around the remnants of pasta sauce and spinach leaves. Sophie walked away in no mood to attempt her usual bug squashing. She went into the bathroom, turned on the hot water and peeled off her cut off T-shirt and pink undies. Before stepping into the shower stall, she inspected her body, pulling any loose skin she could find. "Gross," she whispered, with every bit that would fit in her fingers.

She walked into the steamy hot water and slid down the side of the slick tile till she hit the tub floor. Elbows on knees, head in hands, she cried. It was the silent type that feels lost at the throat, preventing any sound from escaping. She shook and rocked herself until the feeling subsided. She placed her head back, imagining herself as Martha Graham, adorning a long-sleeve Lycra bodice extending into a floor-length dress, her hair severely pulled back, lips pursed in a perfect red heart shape. She could see herself exiting stage left, hobbling around backstage toward her dressing room, body aching from finishing a twenty-minute solo, only to be stopped by some faceless admirer who would firmly push her against the wall. He would press his body against hers as his hands held her jawline and his lips made contact.

The bathroom door swung open. "Wow, how long have you been in here? It's like a sauna," Chloe said.

"Morning," Sophie mumbled back.

"Yes, it's gonna be great. Graham One today, remember? No cold feet, you have to come with me," Chloe said with enthusiasm while sitting down to pee.

How the hell was she always so perky? Chloe flushed, causing a rush of scalding hot water onto

Sophie. "CHLOE!" Sophie shouted, bolting upright and pressed herself against the cheap fiberglass.

"Sorry, I forgot."

They had only moved in a few weeks prior. It was all either of them could afford. The fifth floor, Upper East Side walk-up was inherited when a friend relocated to Germany. He'd spent the last few years auditioning without a single job offer. When he signed the lease over to them, defeat showed in his limbs, as well as in his eyes. Sophie had to beg her grandmother to help her with the rent, $350.00 a month each, until she could find a job. The studio became theirs and Sophie was catapulted into adulthood.

Chloe brought an old pullout sofa from home. It was in great shape with soft inviting cushions, they just had to overlook the hideous green corduroy. They kept it closed during the day and opened it before bed each night, placing all their pillows down the center in a long straight line. Sophie liked the closeness; she and Chloe could talk all night if they wanted – replaying the classes taken, teachers admired, gay boys they wished were straight, or they could drift off into their own reruns of the day.

"I need to get out anyway," Sophie said and turned off the water. She grabbed her towel from the hook on the back door. Chloe started brushing her teeth. Sophie looked over at her friend. She hated that she was always so envious; of her long straight blonde hair, her perfect body that looked like a sculpture, and worst of all, she could eat anything she wanted.

"Sure, I'll go to the kitchen," Chloe said, humming as she left.

And she was always in a stunning mood. Sophie dropped her towel and stepped on the scale. It read one hundred and ten pounds. Almost there, she thought, two more to lose. She wrapped herself again and padded out to the kitchen. She could see one stream of light hitting the brick building outside the tiny window, which was practically arms distance away. She dropped a piece of bread in the toaster just as the phone rang.

"I'll get it," Sophie shouted to Chloe, who was now in the other room, putting the sofa back together. Their pillows and blankets were tossed all over the floor.

"Hello," Sophie couldn't imagine who would call them so early in the morning.

"It's Jane."

Sophie would know her sister's voice even if she were in a crowded concert − it was impossible to mistake her raspy tone. She sounded like an old lady who had been smoking for sixty years.

"You have to cover for me tonight."

"Why?"

"I want to go over to Joe's house. His parents are gonna be out late and−"

"No! I'm not going to lie for you so you can have sex with your boyfriend. You're fifteen years old," Sophie practically screeched.

"And you're a prude."

"You're such a slut, Jane. Just cause you look like Nicole Kidman doesn't mean you have to act like -"

"Who the hell is that?"

"Never mind. I'm not helping you," Sophie hung up the phone.

Her stomach rumbled and her mind raced. Why did she always allow Jane to get under her skin? Why couldn't she have one sister she felt close to? She thought that she and Jane had a shot when Hannah went off to college in California, but Amy usurped her. Jane thought Amy was so cool getting in trouble for smoking pot and cutting school. Then when Amy left, Jane was absorbed her own social life, as if Sophie wasn't even there. It was still like she was the runt of the litter.

The toast popped out and landed on the counter. Sophie grabbed it and went to get dressed. She had ten minutes to throw on her clothes and head to the train.

"I'll meet you at Peridance," Chloe said while brushing her hair.

"You're not coming to ballet?" Sophie slid a black cotton dress over her tights and leotard. It landed mid-thigh.

"No, I want to try a different class. Tina's getting so snippy with me. I'm gonna go to Steps and then come down for Graham," Chloe said.

"See you there." Sophie lifted her bag, which was heavier than usual. She had a separate outfit for

Graham, two large water bottles, and three apples to hold her until dinner time.

The six train was packed. She spent the first several stops bobbing back and forth while holding one of the cold metal poles. After 42nd Street it cleared a bit and Sophie threw her body into the first seat that became vacant. She sat across from an impeccably dressed business man who looked around forty. He and Sophie made eye contact and then she rummaged through her bag for Dance Magazine. She flipped through the pages until she got to the classifieds. Sophie stretched her legs out for a moment and then re-crossed her thighs, her eyes landing straight ahead on the other side of seats. Sophie blinked a couple of times, startled. The same man held a newspaper in one hand across his lap, but slightly lifted, while his other hand held his very large erect penis. Sophie knew she should instantly look away, but she was mesmerized. She had never seen a grown man's penis before, well, except for when she was ten and walked in on her father getting out of the shower. In his modesty, he pulled the curtain closed and she rapidly exited the bathroom with very red cheeks. Sophie knew she should get up and move, but she couldn't stop staring. She felt her body getting warm. Her gaze broke when an old, heavy-set woman pushed into the seat next to Sophie. It was her stop and she ran to the doors, just in time to squeeze out.

***

Sitting on the carpet at Peridance, Sophie took a long drag of her cigarette. It was her fifth of the day and only ten a.m. one ballet class finished. She untied her pointe shoes, wrapped the satin ribbon around the heel end and placed them in her bag. She was worried about this agreement she made with Chloe to take Graham One.

"Sophie, come on. The doors open!" Sophie heard Chloe shout, as she walked over quickly. She dressed in all black as homage to Martha (Graham). Chloe leaned over and whispered, "Let's go in fast so we can sit right up front. I hear that if Debbie likes you, she'll ask you to dance in her workshops." Chloe always searched for an opportunity to be recognized and plucked into stardom. She felt no shame in complimenting any teacher that could propel her not yet happening career, an ability that both enthralled and repelled Sophie.

Sophie smashed her cigarette butt in the ashtray, already spilling over, and grabbed her bag. "I'm coming."

They walked into the studio and placed themselves front and center. No one else was there yet, just like Chloe wanted. Sophie went straight into a full split and laid her body down onto the floor in front of her. As soon as her head landed, she got a flash of the man on the train.

"Chloe, I have to tell you something," she whispered.

"Is it juicy?" Chloe lay down on her back, grabbed her ankle, and brought it toward her face.

Just as Sophie was about to tell her, a handful of dancers walked in and Chloe was instantly distracted. "Sophie," she whispered, "don't look yet, but that's Rebecca – the one with the plastic pants on – she's amaaazing. I saw her dancing with Donald Byrd a few months ago."

Sophie and Chloe simultaneously put their heads down to their respective places on the floor. Another couple of minutes and the door shut behind Debbie, the teacher. The tiny studio was now crammed with about twenty dancers in three staggered lines, which was customary. She didn't know any of them aside from Chloe, but knew they all held similar dreams, and they all wanted to be better than anyone else in the room.

"I can do this." Sophie chanted to herself, although she didn't believe it. *"This will be it,"* she thought, *"this will be the fit I have been waiting for."* She closed her eyes and took several deep breaths.

Debbie didn't follow the typical dancer mold. She was just shy of five feet with a "regular" body, which appeared enormous compared to the pubescent bodies around her. Debbie's blonde hair was cut short in a page-boy, in contrast to all the women in the room with buns tightly wound. And best yet, she wore loose-fitting sweats to cover her thirty something year old frame.

"Let's get started," Debbie said. She sat on the floor facing them, cued the pianist, and began the first exercise. Her short muscular legs were splayed with flexed feet and chubby toes that had as much expression as any other body part. Her arms mimicked her legs, but her hands were cupped. Her entire spine rounded between her limbs, as if a gigantic ball had been thrown to her middle. She raised her face to the ceiling in an expression of exuberant pain. Sophie longed to understand that feeling; she imitated each move, articulation, and nuance she witnessed. And as she arched her back to the ceiling and lifted her face, she saw the man from the train, but he had morphed into a hot twenty-year-old. She could practically taste his mouth.

"Wake up, girl," Debbie shouted toward her.

Sophie hadn't realized that they had moved into the next exercise. Now everything moved faster and faster; Debbie added twists, folds, and spirals. The accompanist played with more and more power to match Debbie's ferocity. Sophie was hooked.

"Pick up the pace people. You're dragging like old ladies," Debbie shouted while she clapped her hands.

An hour and a half later, Sophie, Chloe, and the rest of the dancers had pretzeled, slid, coiled, fell, and tumbled all around the room. As the temperature rose, their bodies perspired, and their breathing intensified into a hum of panting. She felt ecstatic, like all her years of ballet culminated in this moment, like a child becoming an adult. All the years she spent crafting her technique created the foundation to allow her to move abstractly and with a sense of freedom.

At eleven-forty-five a.m. Debbie opened the door. She thanked the dancers and her accompanist, and then walked over to Sophie, who had collapsed on her back with a gigantic sigh, while wiping the sweat from her face and bare arms. The studio smelled used and musty.

"Don't get so distracted. And come again tomorrow," Debbie said, staring down at her.

Sophie lifted up to her elbows and looked at Debbie. "I will, I mean I won't," Sophie rambled. "Yes, I'll be here, thanks," she said as a smile timidly formed.

"That was amazing!" Chloe said glowing. She had practically run over to where Sophie and Debbie were. She slung her bag over her shoulder and stood at Sophie's feet. "Thanks for class, Debbie."

"Sure, see you tomorrow," Debbie said, looking at Sophie, and walked out of the studio.

"Oh my God, she likes you!" Chloe said, giving Sophie's foot a nudge. "I mean, of course she would, look at you, you're perfect. And you killed the floorwork!"

"You think?"

"No doubt. I have to get to work, let's hash it out later," Chloe said. "Drinks at The Pub?"

"I wish I could. Family dinner."

CHAPTER SEVEN

Sophie ambled up the steps of her childhood home, a mug of hot tea in hand. The once plush carpet was now worn and smashed against the wood, having been trampled on for years. She passed Jane's room first, which used to be occupied by Hannah and Amy. The walls were covered in posters: Billy Idol wearing a black leather vest exposing his chest: Cyndi Lauper with her fluffy dyed pink hair and bangles up her forearms: and Prince, clad in purple, dark eyeliner and shadow accentuating his sensual brown eyes. And there was Jane splayed on her back, squeezing her body into a new pair of dark blue Jordache jeans, getting ready for a night with her boyfriend. Sophie watched her take a deep breath as she sucked in her teeny gut and zipped up.

"Do you have protection?"

Jane turned, "Bite me."

Knowing it would be impossible to convince Jane to alter her plans, she started for her bedroom but was caught by the image of her father in the den. He reclined on the L shaped sofa, asleep, with his legs dangling off the side, brown slippers on his feet. Sophie put her tea down on the floor and sat against the banister.

"Sarah, slow down! Sarah!"

He didn't need to say it loudly for Sophie to hear. His sleep remained a constant agitation since the accident. How could she expect to heal with him replaying the night her mom died over and over for ten years? As she got older her grandma encouraged her to keep trying to reach him. "He's in there," she repeated, perhaps as much for herself as her granddaughter. Sophie abandoned the tea and headed into the den. She sat beside him. At first the quiet was unnerving, but she succumbed, leaned back against the couch and closed her eyes. Her body was exhausted from the day and her thighs and back ached.

"Sophie, is that you?"

Her dad's voice startled her out of her doze. "It's me." A yawn escaped.

"I dreamt about you dancing." His voice was quiet, but lucid.

"You did?" Sophie smiled reflecting on the days' classes.

"Your mom loved all kinds of dance." He smiled timidly.

"Really?" Sophie longed to know everything she could about her mom. "Did you guys go to the ballet?"

"You went too. We took all of you to *The Nutcracker* every year. You don't remember?"

"No. Did I like it?"

"You fell asleep a lot, on my lap. It was such a lovely time," his voice drifted, "so long ago."

Sophie wanted to push him to say more, but knew he was getting flustered. His warning signs were like a flare on the highway; legs bouncing, feet tapping, breath shallow.

"Can you hand me that container on the side table, Sophie?"

She slid to the end of the couch to grab the bottle of pills he asked for.

"They help me relax." He unscrewed the top, pulled one out with his forefinger and swallowed it dry.

"I'm glad, Dad." She smiled apprehensively. "I have to get something in my room, be back soon."

He grabbed her hand and squeezed it just as she was about to rise. It was an infusion of parental affection she so rarely received. She held on tightly until his hand went slack.

She headed to her room, dying to light up. Gliding the window open as far as possible, she stuck her shoulders and head out into the warm, dry night. The first drag was perfection. She blew the smoke out in one long, languid exhale, wishing she remembered the nights she spent in the theater with her mom. She so rarely allowed herself to reminisce or dream. She imagined them hand in hand, bundled up in coats and scarves, racing up the stairs of Lincoln Center.

The thoughts swirled around her like the last inhale of the cigarette, nauseating her. She slid the window shut and went to the closet. She sat on the floor and skimmed her hands along the surface of a bin filled with her old pointe shoes. Most were pink, but a few had been dyed to fit the roles she played while growing up in the ballet scene; red for the Queen of Hearts, green for her role as Spanish in *The Nutcracker Suite*, tan for an Egyptian princess. The role she always coveted was Arabian, in *The Nutcracker* – a lanky, seductive, sinewy role that lushly moved about the stage evoking exoticism and sensuality.

Sophie pulled a pink pair from the pile, worn so thoroughly that the wood frame showed through the satin. Untying the ribbon, she reflected on all the hours spent in the studio over the past ten years, and the first time she had ever put on a pair of pointe shoes. She was twelve and had been waiting since the day she started classes. Her first teacher, Mrs. Reilly, wouldn't allow her to begin before that though, saying the bones in her feet had to develop and be ready or it would be dangerous. The moment she elevated to the tips of her toes was magical – her joy a natural anesthetic, keeping the pain in her feet and toes at bay that first day.

Although the ribbons were frayed, Sophie replaced her sneakers with the pointe shoes – quickly winding the ribbons around her ankles and into a tiny knot, tucking in the remainder of the material. She rose onto them, bumping into a few loose hangers. "Shit," she said and left the confinement of the closet. Out in the open she took first position, a slight knee bend, and then she lifted onto the tips of the shoes and began to move around her bedroom. The bare floors absorbed her weight and she glided across the spacious room in tiny measured steps. Her left arm extended to the side in a sweeping motion and her right raised high above her head. She looked toward her top fingers, stood still for a moment and smiled.

At her desk, she opened the top drawer and selected a cassette of Tchaikovsky's *The Nutcracker Suite*. She popped it into her player. It was already cued to the Arabian solo. The fact that it was never her part did not deter her from learning the entire 2.47 minute dance. Locked in her room as a teenager, she rehearsed it over and over again to choreography by Balanchine. She pretended she was on stage and sauntered across the floor, sweeping her arms out in front of her body with hips swaying side to side. Her mind morphed her jeans into genie pants -loose and transparent pink. Her T-shirt became a small top to match the pants with gold trim and exposed midriff.

Landing in front of her desk just as the music paused, Sophie spied a pair of scissors. She stood still, panting lightly, and reached over and grabbed them. The metal sheers met her skin between her ankle and the satin. With one snip they released her. She repeated the action on the other side. With opposite feet she pushed off each shoe and shoved them beneath her desk. Channeling performances she had seen at the Joyce Theater of Avant-garde modern choreographers, she shut the music off. She stood still, turned her legs and feet parallel. A deep breath in and staccato exhale signaling herself to move. She made a sharp shift with her ribcage to the left, and then languidly added a sway of her shoulders, head, and arm like she was laying herself along a table. Then a jump up with both feet toward her butt in coordination with another loud exhale. She reversed the movement to the right, imagining the sun against her face, neck, and chest. She landed quietly on the floor with her legs outstretched the opposite way. A roll to her back, which grew into a Graham contraction, like a slow-motion sit up, only her middle was curved in opposition to her arms, she pushed up slowly, placed her hands to the floor and balanced on one leg. The other reached toward the ceiling with a flexed foot. That leg began straight, but on each sharp exhale she bent and swayed it, forcing her torso to react like a willow tree in a soft breeze. With her head upside down, she faced her bedroom door where she saw her father standing, the door slightly ajar. She had been so immersed she didn't hear it open.

"That was beautiful."

Startled, she stood, chest lifting and releasing as she returned her breath to equilibrium. Her dad had only seen photos of dance concerts she had performed in, but he never came.

"Thanks."

"You remind me of your mother."

"Really?"

"Not the dance part, she had two left feet," a partial smile formed on his gaunt face, "but like you, she was reserved and driven."

I'm like my mom?

"Can you show me more?"

That would be impossible. The stage created a distance between the audience and performer, without it she felt exposed like she was standing naked in Times Square. With the house dark, the theater silent, except for the occasional cough or candy wrapper being opened, the magic began. A swell of music dictated a mood and Sophie's body followed suit. Her dad was asking for an intimacy beyond anything they had ever shared. And yet, he was asking. "Okay."

Sophie closed her eyes and imagined the setting. Placing her hands behind her back, she felt the heat of the lights across her chest, framing her in the spotlight. She swayed from hips to shoulders, side to side, channeling herself as a little girl, a whimsical smile and twinkle in her eyes. A step back with one foot at a time descending from toes to heel as her arms reached out in a circular motion, like she was gathering a bouquet of flowers. Tilting her head to the left and letting out a sigh, she looked down, her face registering a loss. The flowers had vanished and her arms were empty. She looked up to the ceiling with pleading eyes, her arms reached up manically as her legs stamped below her in an open stance. She took a large jump into the air and then slowly crumbled to the floor, her knees buckling and her eyes searching above. In a fury, she started grabbing in every direction, her body moving like a wild animal with rage in her eyes. With every reach she saw an image of her mom; the soft look on her face when she fell asleep in bed with Sophie as a small child, a wide laugh when Sophie tickled her, the last moment they looked at each other –it was an over the shoulder look while she mouthed "good night" to Sophie.

In her mind she heard drumming, a primal beat, one she had listened to often in the subways while guys played using only buckets, bare hands, and sticks. With each thump she said "Mom." Creating a rhythm. The sound mounted and she continued her erratic gestures on her hands and knees, scraping the floor with her fingernails. It sounded like her father was responding with 'Sarah,' but she was unsure if it was her imagination.

Standing back up she pounded her fists to her gut and ran, *would this be the time she regained her father's love,* a leap with both legs and she was on top of her bed. Using the momentum of the springs, she leapt toward the ceiling with both legs extended in front of her. Sophie's fingers reached for her toes flailing like a dying bird. She landed on the ground upright with her body shaking and her hair tossed around her face. Two taps to the chest with both hands, then she spread them up to her cheeks like rising bath water and covered her eyes, palms to the sockets. Slowly, she settled until her body was completely still.

Winded and relieved that she had shared movement with her dad for the first time, she said, "Dad, thank you." She dropped her arms by her sides, about to add, *for watching and inspiring me to be brave and take a risk*, but when she looked toward the door he was no longer there.

What if she had said no, like she originally wanted to? If she hadn't danced for him he might still be standing there. Was it too much? Was she too much?

"Sophie, let's go!" Jane screamed from her room.

CHAPTER EIGHT

"I'm leaving," Chloe shouted.

"Wait for me, I'm almost ready." Sophie threw her shoes in her bag, along with adhesive tape for modern classes. Debbie told her to wrap her feet as an aid for ripped calluses and splits between her toes.

"I have to go – I'm late."

"No, you're not, we still have-" Sophie heard the door slam and wondered why Chloe was in such a hurry to leave without her. It only took five more minutes and then Sophie was out the door as well.

The Upper East Side was buzzing and vibrant that Monday morning. Taxis, cars, and trucks hurried up First Avenue. Sophie felt a boost of energy as she headed west to the six train and downtown for class. She fell in love with Manhattan as a teenager, when she was accepted into a training program at The Joffrey Ballet. Instead of going to her local high school in Queens, she went to Professional Children's School. While her grandfather had reservations with the idea, her grandmother stepped in and reminded her how vital it is to follow a dream.

The set up gave Sophie the opportunity to dance all day; ballet, pointe, and partner classes. Joffrey was downtown and school by Lincoln Center. Sophie didn't care which part of town she was in, the city was like a beautiful orchestra, constantly tuning up in the pit. She found rhythm in the horns honking and followed the beats of people's boots on the pavement. The corner bodega was always open, the trains humming at any hour, buses passing over potholes and people racing, a purpose in their stride at any hour. Sophie felt success waited, if she just kept moving. After graduation, she auditioned for the Joffrey Ballet Company but didn't get accepted, so she heeded Chloe's advice and started taking classes around the downtown area.

As the elevator doors opened at Peridance, she dashed down the dimly lit hallway to studio one for her morning ballet class. She rushed to ensure her favorite spot. As she swiftly positioned herself at the barre, simultaneously pulling off her cotton dress, she collided into David, a soloist with American Ballet Theater.

"Morning," he mumbled with a crooked smile.

"Hi."

She perused the room not wanting to stare at him, sure she blushed. No Chloe.

The next ninety minutes allowed ample opportunity to fixate on David's flawless technique and body, which was chiseled to perfection, a Michelangelo in motion. When she arched her back with her head tilted to the side, she could peek at his chest. With every new exercise at the barre, he grew sweatier and Sophie could map out the structure of his torso as his white T-shirt clung to him.

The second half of class was for floor work. Each time she waited for her turn to go across with her group, she imagined dancing a duet with David. The one she had just seen performed at the Joyce Theater. As he leapt across the floor, Sophie pictured them climbing on each other's bodies. The music would be hypnotic with a pulsating rhythm for the duration of the fifteen-minute piece creating anticipation till she and David finally merged and enveloped one another. Sophie would take an open leg stance, leaving just enough room for David to slide through, offering his body as a resting place for hers. They would stay intimately intertwined for the remainder of the dance; rocking, swaying, embracing, and balanced on one another.

In the adagio section of class, the music grew more melodic and the movement matched with slow pivoting, long balances, and extended limbs. With one leg outstretched behind her in arabesque, she envisioned David placing his shoulder beneath her pelvis, holding her by the waist and raising Sophie toward the ceiling. She would hold a beat then travel down his torso till they met, chest to chest, and she could drench her face into his neck. She lingered in her fantasy until class ended.

A quick break between ballet and modern allowed for an apple and cigarette. Sophie threw her bag to the ground and put her plastic pants over her thighs to keep her muscles warm.

"Hi Sophie, how's it going?"

Sophie shook her legs up and down on the dingy blue carpet, another warming trick. Her fist pounded her thighs to assist.

"Hi Eric." Sophie dreaded seeing this guy day after day. He was the only straight one around and he repulsed her. His perspiration permeated the very small lounge area. His body was short and square, with legs that looked like they belonged to a wrestler, not a ballet dancer. To add insult to injury, his mediocre dancing did not inhibit his getting work. If women were a dime a dozen, men were diamonds in the ruff.

"I went to that audition for Heidi's company this weekend and got a six-month contract. Can you believe it?" When he grinned, his crooked teeth taunted Sophie. His sweat dripped down his nose and he didn't even wipe it.

Sophie tried to hide her disgust. "That's great."

"Women's auditions are today at three. You're going, right? They love girls with long legs and great feet." Eric blushed.

"I have a job interview today." Chloe had arranged for Sophie to meet the manager where she hosted. Sophie was nervous about working in a fast-paced restaurant with no experience. She stood, grabbed her bag and squashed her cigarette butt in the ashtray. "See you, Eric, my next class is starting."

During her next two classes, Sophie was completely distracted. All she could think about was Eric getting the gig with Heidi; pancake feet, no stretch, Eric. It infuriated Sophie, who could kick, lift, or place her legs in any direction to her ears. She could point her feet so far she broke most pointe shoes in two wears. Her balance outlasted most around her and she was a dynamo when airborne.

By the time her classes were over for the day, Sophie was so worked up that she ditched the job interview to go to the audition. She pulled out *Dance Magazine* and found the ad:

Female Dancers.

Between the ages of eighteen and twenty-five.

Six-month contract, touring the U.S. and possibly Europe.

123 Green Street.

2nd floor – Three p.m.

Sophie splashed some water on her face in the girl's room. *You can do it*. She dried her hands by smoothing out stray hairs form her bun, fixed a few bobby pins, and headed downtown.

When she arrived at the address, she was met with a line of women waiting for the same audition. The promise she had felt leaving her apartment that Monday morning dissipated on the crackling street, as she waited over a half hour just to reach the elevator.

She dropped her bag down on the cement with a thud. The girl in front of her turned, seeming perturbed by the noise. She regarded Sophie like she was a repulsive homeless guy and unabashedly checked her out from head to toe, her mouth puckered the whole time.

See something you like, Sophie wished she had the nerve to say aloud. Of course, she sized up the competition as well, just more subtly. She held her *Dance Magazine* as if fully engrossed, when in actuality she perused leg length and muscle structure, not to mention overall beauty. She needed to know how she measured up.

Smoking was the only thing to do over the next hour, while she waited and sedately made her way into the building, and finally into the home stretch... the hallway leading to the audition room. She was handed a white index card with the number 301 to pin to her red spaghetti leotard. As she fastened it, she caught a glimpse inside the audition room.

Sophie was crushed. Through the mirror she caught sight of Chloe, number 258, buoyant as she nailed a triple pirouette, and landed in a perfectly balanced ponche, her right leg lifted up to the ceiling, left fingers practically touching the floor.

Sophie felt sick. The mingling of one apple, multiple cigarettes, and betrayal swirled in her belly. Without a thought or care for all the time she had spent waiting, or the fact that she ditched a job interview to come, Sophie ran. She ran past the line of girls, knocking into a few with her giant ballet bag, past the elevator to the stairwell and down three flights to the street, where she threw up beside a brown Daschund who was mid-pee against a fire hydrant.

Sophie hailed the first taxi she saw.

"First and 74th Street, please," she said, throat dry with a sour taste. She put her head back against the black leather seat, which was held together by silver duct tape, and watched the city whizz by. The two back windows had been rolled down, bringing a much needed breeze. She watched all the people purposefully scurrying about, keeping pace or passing one another to get where they were going. The city mocked her.

Slamming the door upon exit, Sophie went straight to Tasti-D Light next door to her apartment. She ordered a pint of chocolate mixed with peanut butter and cradled it like a brand-new baby up all four flights to her apartment, her face a hot mess. She sat on the kitchen floor and finished the entire dessert in ten minutes flat. She had ruined her whole day: no audition, no job, and now her one hundred and eight pounds were compromised.

The only thing she could think to do was to call Hannah and beg for money.

"I'd like to help, Sophie. Really! But I'm already helping out Amy, since she moved in. She has all those acting classes and auditions…"

"But Hannah," Sophie tried not to sound as desperate as she felt.

"I'd like to help, Soph."

"You just said that!"

"I'm working like crazy this summer, saving up as much as I can. I start my classes again soon and med school is 24/7."

Sophie felt like she did when she stood in the bathroom begging for her nails to be polished.

"Uh huh." What a foolish notion, Sophie thought, why would she expect anything to change between her and her older sisters? They still banded together at her expense.

"Don't be like that, Sophie. You could move out here and live with us in California."

"You know I can't do that." She felt like a rotund balloon being pricked by a mischievous little boy, grimacing at her.

"Talk to Grandma and Grandpa. I'm sure you can figure something out with them."

And there was that fucking authoritative voice that Sophie despised. "Bye, Hannah." A bit of vomit re-surfaced in her mouth. Sophie swallowed it back down.

"Sorry, honey. Love you." The last two words were barely audible.

Sophie uncoiled the cord from around her shoulders and hung up the phone on the wall. Slumping onto the floor she imagined Hannah and Amy laid out on beach blankets, giggling and boy watching. The thought repeated for an hour like a skipping record, until she heard the turn of the key in the front door.

Chloe flew in, practically bouncing out of her skin. "I got a job today, Sophie!" She jumped up and down, hugging the paper bag in her hands. "I bought us Tasti-D Light to celebrate."

"Why didn't you tell me about the audition? I had to find out from stinky Eric." Sophie looked at her dearest friend with venom. She saw Chloe register the empty carton beside Sophie on the floor.

"Did you get in too?"

"NO! Would I be eating this shit if I got in?" Channeling Jane, she smacked the empty container across the kitchen floor, little drips sprinkling the linoleum like a Jackson Pollack.

***

It was a bitter fall and winter. Chloe packed an un-packed her bags, touring not only the U.S., but Europe as well. She returned to New York a few days here and there, bringing crap Sophie didn't want. Coffee mugs that read, I love – name the city. The T-shirts were even worse. Sophie felt taunted, like she was supposed to wear love for the cities she wouldn't be seeing. It poured salt in the wounds.

She took over Chloe's restaurant position for a few weeks, but standing all night and being leered at by middle-aged men disgusted her and exhausted her body. And she hated babysitting entitled kids who smugly said things like, "You're not the boss of me." Tail between her legs, she called her grandfather.

The first words out of his mouth were – "No handouts," accompanied by "Your parents always wanted their children to learn the value of money, and that's what you will finally do. You will work for me. I just fired a lousy receptionist. You'll take the night shift."

Dressed like a midtown banker, Sophie begrudgingly took the train uptown from Peridance and into the sound studio her grandfather founded. It was situated in Hell's kitchen, housed in a rectangular gray brick, windowless building, with gigantic gold lettering on both the front and side, reading GOLD SOUNDS. When she arrived at her new job, it was like walking into a foreign land; if her dance life was disproportionately female, the scales were tipped here. It was the first time she had ever stepped foot into his business.

"Hi Sophie. Welcome!" Laura, the daytime receptionist, said. She stayed late to show Sophie the ropes. They walked down the long quiet halls and into each room so Sophie could be introduced to the engineers. This was a world of testosterone. Pot-bellied men ran the booths, sitting in airless ten by ten rooms, staring at screens while moving little colored pegs up and down the sound boards. They spent twelve hours at a shot separating the sounds of a violin from an oboe, putting them on separate tracks, or each violin from

111

each other in search of the magical outcome that the world would later hear on an album or tape. Sophie's life was about expression through movement, the body as the instrument. These guys were all neck up.

It wasn't that Sophie was averse to making and delivering coffee or ordering dinners for the engineers and their clients, but the notion of being in such close proximity to her grandfather, day after day, that felt so crushing. She had moved out to make it on her own, only to be thrown back into the family fold.

"I see you're getting acquainted."

Sophie swerved to see her grandfather standing erect. He was clean shaven, with a pleasant smile.

"Yes, Mr. Gold. I was just showing Sophie around," Laura replied.

"Wonderful. Nice to see you all dressed up, Sophie."

"Thank you."

"You're in great hands. Laura knows everything and then some."

Laura's clear white complexion turned a shade of light pink. "Thank you, sir."

As soon as he left the desk area, Laura turned to Sophie and said in a hushed voice, "Your grandfather's really the best. He takes such good care of his employees."

***

Wrapped in a down coat and wool scarf one frigid night in December, Sophie opened the door to her apartment to find Chloe home, but not alone. Two suitcases sat open with dirty clothes and shoes spilling onto the kitchen floor.

"I'm so glad you're home," Chloe said, louder than necessary in their 400 square foot apartment.

The heat was on full blast. Sophie began to peel off her layers and hang them on the hooks behind the front door.

"Hi Sophie," a man's voice followed.

No way, thought Sophie. She knew that voice. It was eleven o'clock at night. She was bleary eyed and her body weary from classes and work. The last thing she needed was this. It only took three strides into the apartment to confirm what she heard and smelled. Sitting on the open bed was Chloe with Eric beside her, holding hands. They were practically naked, wearing only boxer shorts – both of them – and loose hanging T-shirts.

Chloe must have registered the look on Sophie's face and immediately scrambled off the bed to hug Sophie, who received the affection stiffly.

"I should have given you the heads up, I know."

"You think?" Sophie ripped off her wool sweater and threw it on the bed.

"I got you a present from Paris." Chloe stepped past Sophie to her suitcase.

Eric joined them. "How are you, Sophie?"

It felt impossible to be civil.

Chloe held out an Eiffel Tower the size of a pint of milk. Sophie looked at the gift, then her friend. "No thanks." She headed to the bathroom and locked the door. It was the only room left to retreat to. Roasting still, Sophie removed her turtleneck and leg warmers and carefully hung them over the towel rack. She splashed some water on her face and neck.

Over the next ten minutes, Sophie overheard whispering and smooching. Then the front door quietly opened and closed before footsteps shuffled over to the bathroom.

"Sophie," Chloe said.

Sophie could tell she was plastered to the door on the other side. She wanted to be happy for Chloe, but the envy was too thick. "Tell him to go home. I need to go to sleep."

"I already did. Please come out."

"You should go with him." Sophie crossed her arms over her chest. Even though Chloe couldn't see her, she wore her don't-fuck-with-me train face.

"I want to be here with you. I brought really great chocolate from the airport. We can sit on the kitchen floor, smoke and eat – catch up."

"There's nothing to talk about."

"You're sulking. Stop it! I'm not one of your sisters, Sophie. I'm not out to get you."

"You wanted that audition all for yourself. You didn't even want me to have a shot. You lied to me. We promised that we would tell each other everything!" Sophie screamed through the door. The air was hot and dank, but she refused to come out and face Chloe. She didn't want anything to compromise her momentum.

"Why does everyone have to take care of you? You could have figured that out for yourself. Don't blame me." Chloe's voice stayed collected and that pissed Sophie off more than anything. "If you auditioned, we could have both gotten into the company. Then we would be travelling all together. It's so much fun…"

Sophie could hear a sparkle in Chloe's voice. "I have no desire to hang out with you and Eric!"

"Fuck you, Sophie."

"Eric – what could possibly see in him?"

"Really? Should I be like you, pining for David? Pick a straight guy for once." This sentence rang out louder than the others.

This is too messy, Sophie thought, as she removed each article of clothing until she was in her underwear. She counted the bruises along her thighs. Some were fading away, just a hint of green left – others were fresh. The sliding and rolling on the floor in modern classes left her body looking like it was always in a state of battle. She grabbed a washcloth from under the sink and submerged it in cold water before covering her face.

Minutes later Sophie heard the door open and slam shut. She cautiously exited the bathroom and peered around. She was alone.

CHAPTER NINE

Different versions of the same argument ensued: from the January blizzard that buried cars along the curb, making the hoods look like a long line of colored umbrella tops – through spring when the daffodil and tulip buds began to emerge from their dirt beds. By summer their life-long friendship disintegrated into a frayed remnant of what it had been.

Close to midnight, Sophie padded her way into the living room, toothbrush hanging from her mouth. She pulled her side of the covers down to find a yellow Trojan condom wrapper. Chloe looked over the edge of her book, "Oops," she grabbed it and put it on her side table.

"You get that I sleep in this bed," Sophie's hand slammed down harder on the mattress than she intended, "the bed you and Eric use to slobber all over each other."

Chloe turned her eyes away from Sophie.

Their bodies were only a couple of feet apart, "Do you even clean the sheets after you have sex?"

"Of course, we do."

That was doubtful.

A truck could be heard from their front window thudding up 1st Avenue, pummeling along the concrete and metal slabs that acted as road band-aids.

"Eric and I want to move in together." Chloe's eyes twinkled like a pair of sapphire earrings.

Did she expect excitement? "You're moving out?" Her chest felt heavy.

Chloe folded her hands in her lap, "Could you?"

She knew they had a teetering friendship to date, but still – is this what Chloe really wanted? Sophie twirled her toothbrush around in her palm. "I don't understand your attraction to this guy."

Chloe sat up a little straighter, "You don't have to. He's my boyfriend."

Sophie uncrossed her legs, "You already told him he could move in, didn't you?"

The lack of response gave her the answer. "After everything we've been through?"

Chloe's eyes darted across the room. It was a swift kick in the gut. She grabbed her shorts from the floor and duffle sitting in the kitchen, which held her dance wear for the next day, and exited the apartment half dressed. She flew down the steps to the last landing and smack into Eric. Two large suitcases rested against the dirty cream colored hallway wall.

"I got kicked out of my place last night."

"The neighbor's dog pees in the hallway and a new crop of water bugs land every summer, but really –

mazel tov." It was immature to throw the jab, besides she knew this was coming, but it felt so satisfying.

After pulling on the shorts from her hand, she headed down to Hell's kitchen where her new friends Maurice and Steven lived. They just moved to New York since graduating from North Carolina School of the Arts and had immediately given her a key to their place after hearing tales of her roommate woes. She knew she would be welcome.

Arriving in front of their building at twelve-thirty a.m. Sophie found a homeless man sleeping on the stoop. Sophie didn't know what to do. She stood at the bottom of the staircase, stunned. After a few minutes, she convinced herself that she was brave enough to step over him. Sophie took out her keys and held them in a position to either defend herself or place them rapidly in the key hole. After deciding whether or not to run or tiptoe past the man, she settled on an in-between solution: a quiet, but rapid fire approach up the stairs and to the door, no hesitating. She took a wide stance over the belly of the guy, held her breath, her heart pounding so deep and fast her entire torso was on fire. She pushed the key as he began to grumble and turn to the other side. Sophie was so alarmed she left the key, ran back down and pulled out a cigarette. After ten minutes she tried again; a run up the stairs, a turn of the key, and a race up the three flights, with so much adrenaline pumping that she shook for the next hour.

***

"You have to live here with us. We can divide the rent equally." The three sat holding mugs of tea. "Take the bedroom, the living room has plenty of space for us," Maurice said, the smaller and more muscular of the couple.

Sophie looked into his hazel eyes and completely understood why Steven would fall in love with him. He was wholesome; with a clean-cut short haircut and dimples that accentuated his smile and perfect teeth. "Are you sure?" she asked, but only to be polite, because she couldn't think of anything more inviting. One more shift at Gold Sounds and she could afford the extra fifty dollars she needed to make the rent.

"We've been sleeping out here for the last week anyway – nestled in front of the faux-fireplace, pretending it's winter," Steven said. "I mean look at the crown molding and parquet floors," his hands swept in each direction as he spoke.

"You should get your realtors license." Maurice leaned over Sophie and kissed his boyfriend. "Come on, let's get you settled in." He pulled Sophie up from her seat on the futon and led her into her the small bedroom off the kitchen. It was perfect. There was a mattress on the floor and a small night table beside it. All she needed. She dropped her bag, then her body, exhausted and happy.

When she woke the next morning, the sun shone threw her window, a perfect orange sphere radiating summer heat and humidity. Sophie was already sweating as she climbed out of bed and released a huge yawn.

There was knock on the door.

"Come in."

Maurice poked his head and arm in to hand Sophie a cup of French roast, her favorite. "Breakfast awaits you in the kitchen, girl."

Sophie gave him a kiss on the cheek and took the mug. The aroma taunted her. She was dying to devour the breakfast he made, but rebuffed, "That's so sweet, but I'm really not a breakfast person, Maurice. I'll eat later."

"I've seen you later, Sophie, smoking your cigarettes and eating your granny smiths. You need nutrition, girl." They walked to the kitchen together. Maurice grabbed a piece of bacon from out of the frying pan. "I'm gonna make you and Steven a great dinner tonight."

"I have to work tonight till ten." Sophie looked at her watch. "In fact, I have to hurry and get in the shower." She took a gulp of her coffee and placed it in the sink.

"Ten it is. I'll pick you up and we can stroll down 10th Avenue in the sweltering New York heat and home for a wonderful meal." The bacon was gone by now and

Sophie could see Maurice pondering his menu as he washed the dishes.

"It's a date."

"Dance your teeny tiny fanny off today," Steven said groggily from the other side of a Japanese screen they had stretched out in front of the futon.

She loved his deep voice. He sounded like a radio DJ.

There was a stride in her step as she exited her apartment for the day. Her new living arrangements were divine. It was like having two surrogate boyfriends, but better. There was intimacy with no fear.

By the time three p.m. rolled around, Sophie arrived at work fatigued, but pumped. The first six hours of the day had been spent at a workshop with Avery Snow, the first in a series of four workshops she signed up for, each a week long. The work spawned out of the Graham and Alvin Ailey tradition, but the movement was denser than her predecessors, it was fast and sharp and circular. It required a power and athleticism still to be attained by Sophie. She refused to be deterred by a friendship crisis or squander any other audition opportunities.

Sophie dashed into the over air-conditioned sound studio humming and headed straight to the kitchen to check on the coffee and tea for all the rooms. Quickly she made her rounds, delivering hot beverages and taking dinner orders from the engineers and clients. The doors to each "cave," as Sophie liked to call them, were so heavy, she had to push with her entire body, until she heard the whooshing sound they made upon opening and the brush of air that was released. Each engineer quietly worked in his room, back to the door, fixated on the screen in front of them. They wore headphones while hunched over in deep concentration.

When she walked into the last studio, the largest one reserved for the biggest clients, Sophie found her grandfather sitting with the engineer and a few other men, all of a substantial age. Animated laughter filled the window-less room, until the sound of the closing door caused them to turn.

Her grandfather stood immediately, "Let me introduce you to my granddaughter." He wore a beautiful double-breasted navy-blue suit, even though the industry called for jeans and dilapidated T-shirts. He walked over and took her arm into a gentle hold. She fought the urge to slink away from his grasp.

"Hi," Sophie said politely. "I didn't mean to interrupt. I just wanted to see if you needed anything."

One of the men stood, pulled up his jeans and extended his hand. "I'm Bill. Great to meet any member of the Gold family," he said with a smile.

Really?

"Sophie, we've heard so much about you," said another, swiveling around in his chair. His thick gray mustache curved up at the ends as he spoke.

"I've known your granddad for years, young lady. I'm honored to finally meet you." The last man rose and offered his hand to Sophie.

She reciprocated.

"A firm grip, just like you, Rob," he turned toward her grandfather.

"She's a dancer, Ed." Her grandfather finally released Sophie's arm. "And seemingly talented too." He turned to Sophie and winked.

"We should get back to work. We'll let you know if we need something later, Sophie. Thank you." Her grandfather turned to the other men.

They all sat back down and in unison said, "Bye, Sophie."

Sophie left the room bewildered. She answered calls and delivered food orders as the night passed, but her mind kept returning to her grandfather's smile. It was pleasant. No, it was inviting.

As promised, Maurice waited outside at ten p.m. "Hello, my lady," he said, while curtsying.

Sophie exited the front door yawning, "A sight for sore eyes." The corners of her mouth lifted.

"I've been thinking. We need a party," he said, taking her hand.

"What?" She enjoyed the feel of his soft skin against her fingers and palm.

"A house-warming thing."

Sophie loved watching Maurice when he was excited. They may not have known each other long, but she already recognized how animated he grew with his ideas. His arms gesticulated and his face opened up like a sunrise.

"You know, we'll invite some people. A cute straight boy or two, hint, hint," he said, pushing his hip into hers and smiling like the Cheshire Cat. "You invite that fire bolt sister, Jane. I want to meet that one."

"I don't think I want to invite, Jane," Sophie said, her lips puckered. She wished she hadn't brought her family album to the apartment. Maurice saw it the day she moved in and immediately flipped through the pages. He stopped on a shot where Jane stood on the coffee table, syrup still on her cheeks from breakfast. She had her pajamas in hand, looking like she was going to throw them at their dad, as he took the photo. Her belly protruded with multiple pancake helpings. "Oh my, she's a pistol, isn't she?" Maurice had said.

"You must, you must! C'mon girl, let's go home and eat. Dinner is ready and so is Steven," he grinned.

Maurice grabbed Sophie's waist and pulled her in close. Sophie loved it. She smushed in as tightly as she could and laced her arm around his waist in return. She briefly rested her head against his shoulder. "All right, I'll invite her."

Over a lasagna dinner dripping with melted cheese, which she nibbled on, the three agreed that the party should be the following Saturday night. The boys stood over Sophie to ensure that she called Jane.

It took some convincing for her grandmother to allow it. "The neighborhood is so sketchy, Sophie, and you know how I feel about you living with those two men."

"They're gay, Grandma." Sophie stared at them and rolled her eyes.

"Are you sure, my sweet? I know about so-called gay guys. I knew one or two in my time."

Doubt it. She tried to picture her seventy-plus year-old grandma smoking a cigarette, shoulder to shoulder with Maurice or Steven. It seemed absurd.

"Grandma, they are in love with each other. They want nothing but friendship from me or any other girl for that matter." Sophie realized she felt a little disappointed by her last statement.

"And you'll meet her at the train station, right?"

"Yes, I promise."

It was settled.

Saturday night came and Maurice, Steven, and Sophie decorated the apartment with strings of pepper lights throughout the living room and her bedroom. They shopped at the local bodega for baguettes, cheese, grapes, and a six pack. They made the party a BYOB, because they spent all they could scrape together among the three of them already.

Jane arrived at the front door with her boyfriend, Joe, and a six pack. Sophie didn't feel good about lying to her grandma, but since Joe was invited too, she felt slightly off the hook. Even though it was a party, Sophie was casually dressed. The only attention she paid to her appearance was the number on the scale. Jeans and T-shirts were all she could afford anyway. When she saw Jane, she wasn't sure if she wanted to laugh or shut the door in her face. Jane wore a violet colored, bob-style wig, corset top that was black with fluorescent greens and pinks. She had black bracelets all the way up her arms and tight jean shorts that were so small they looked like underwear. The only part of Jane that was not overdone was her make up. She had one clean line of black eye liner and black mascara on that accentuated her green eyes.

"Come in, come in. You haaave to be Jane." Maurice went right over and kissed her on both cheeks. "I can't believe how much you two look alike, well except for the coloring." He stared at them back and forth. "And the style." He opened the door wider and Jane passed the threshold. "I'm Maurice. Have fun sweetie."

Joe looked pale, but managed a micro-movement upwards with his mouth. He, like Sophie, wore plain old jeans and a green cotton T-shirt. They were the last to arrive and Sophie wondered what they had been up to since the six o'clock call she received from her grandma, saying that Jane had left home.

At a steamy ninety-five degrees, the fans blew to assist the wide open windows. The crowd of mostly gay male dancers, all friends of Maurice and Steven, circulated the apartment. Sophie realized that after she cut off Chloe and Eric, she was pretty much a loner. Friends brought friends and by the ten p.m. the apartment pulsated like a packed rush-hour train, hot, and loud.

Sophie's room became as much a hang-out space as the living room. Couples kissed, people laughed vibrantly, and Jane flirted with everyone, even though Joe stood beside her every second looking stunned.

Sophie grew more and more anxious as the night went on. She smoked a pack, not knowing what else to do, especially without drinking anything but water. She tried a beer, but after a few sips, she felt nauseous. She feigned interest and said shy hellos to guests, but avoided small talk at all costs, which she found utterly boring and impossible to figure out. Jane got louder and more rambunctious; clearly having no problem with her alcohol intake. Sophie steered away from her sister, completely embarrassed by her behavior. Apparently, Joe shared her experience, as he finally left Jane's side and fell asleep on the futon in the living room. He carved himself a tiny space at the end, looking like he might fall off any second.

"Sophie, I want you to meet someone." Steven made his way through some guys and found Sophie sitting on the fire escape. "Sophie, this is John, a friend of a friend of a friend… straight, non-dancer." Steven swayed a little as he made the intro, "John, this is Sophie, dancer extraordinaire." Steven tripped over a plastic cup as he exited, holding the wall to catch his balance.

John climbed out and sat beside Sophie. He leaned back on the brick wall, appearing as if he longed for some super glue to hold him. His eyes shifted down at the metal slats.

They exchanged small smiles and glances.

"You know all these people?" John opened.

"None, except for Maurice and Steven."

"A little overwhelming, huh?" He pressed his shoulders back against the bricks and closed his eyes.

"I just needed a smoke." Sophie wavered, should she play it cool or go the honest route and admit she teetered on the edge of losing her mind, hating every moment of the evening so far until then.

"I'm afraid of heights." John tilted his head in her direction.

Sophie noticed his hands first. They were large and tan, very clean with perfectly manicured nails. The tighter he held the Budweiser can in his palm, the more his muscular forearms displayed slightly bulging veins.

"I don't really know how to do the small-talk thing." Sophie blurted. She glanced over at him again and realized he was at least a few years older than her.

"It goes like this, 'So where are you from?' You tell me, and I say, 'I'm from Boston. It's never this hot in

128

Boston.'" He took a deep breath. "You say, 'Do you have any brothers or sisters back home?' At which point I tell you that I have one brother, younger than me."

Sophie liked his deep voice and slow methodical explanation of how their conversation could be going.

"Sophie has three sisters, one dead mother, a comatose father, and she has never had a boyfriend." Jane stuck her head out the window, reeking of beer. Her wig was off and her orange curls were unleashed, cascading all over the windowsill.

John looked from Jane to Sophie, as if to say *really?*

"Excuse me," Sophie stepped over John, pushed Jane aside, and went straight for the exit, down the three flights, cursing under her breath. Just as she slammed the door of her building shut and plopped on the top step, she heard John's voice.

"You left these upstairs. I thought you might need one," John called from above holding her pack of Marlboro Lights.

Sophie turned her face up to the fire escape.

"I'll bring them down."

She watched him cautiously stand while still pressed to the bricks and then disappear through the window. She bit her nails and straightened her white T-shirt during the few minutes it took for him to descend and sit beside her. He handed her the pack.

"Thanks." Sophie pulled one out and lit up.

"One of your three sisters?"

"Yes."

"All true?"

"Yes." Sophie whispered.

John took Sophie's face into his hands, turning her toward him, and gave her one soft kiss on the mouth. "Let me know if you want to go out sometime." He stood and walked toward 9th Avenue.

Sophie watched him stroll down the block.

CHAPTER TEN

It took another hour of sitting on the stoop till guests finally meandered out. They passed Sophie on the steps like the strangers they were. By this point she had practically fallen asleep, leaning back against the hard cement and peering up at the dark gray night.

"I don't know why you have to be so prissy. They're just guys who like each other."

Sophie heard Jane before seeing her and quickly closed her eyes. As the front door to her building swung open, she heard Joe respond, "I don't think this is gonna work, Jane. I like you, but tonight…"

Their footsteps stopped beside her. "We should help your sister upstairs."

"No, she's fine. SOPHIE, WAKE UP. YOU'RE LOITERING."

Sophie opened her eyes and stared at her younger sister. "That was really considerate, thanks." She stood and brushed off the dirt from her backside. "Good night, Joe," she said while entering her building.

"Part-ee is over, girl," a very drunk and overly flamboyant red head said as Sophie climbed the last step to the fourth floor landing. He hugged the wall for a moment and leaned his slim hips against the chipping cream-colored paint.

"Are you okay? Do you want to come back in?" she asked.

"Fiiiiine," he waved a hand, nearly slapping Sophie in the face, and stumbled down.

She walked in to her apartment, which was littered with sleeping bodies draped over the futon and floor, tip-toed to her room and closed the door. Her comforter looked like it had been at a parade; she shook it and released napkins, crumbs, and empty plastic cups. When she went to turn her pillow over, concerned that someone or lots of someone's may have rested on it, or worse, she found a note:

John 212-644-3937
Call me sometime

He wrote it in a tight and angular script. With her head on the pillow, beaming with excitement, she held the ripped yellow piece of paper in her hand and tried to sleep. Two a.m. passed, then three, then four. Why did she always obsess? Either about her meals, her body fat, her perfect combination in class, or like tonight – John. She couldn't get the snap shots of each moment with him out of her mind. Over and over, she conjured the intensity in his eyes when he turned toward her on the fire-escape, or his forearms pulsating, and best of all, the moment when his full scarlet colored lips met hers. Would she be brave enough to call him?

After days of the same circling conversation, to call or not to call, Sophie dragged herself into the apartment, exhausted from the day, to find John sitting on the futon and Maurice at the stove. Another record breaking heat wave had hit the city, and sweat beaded down Sophie's torso as if she had just run the NYC marathon. Yet she had only travelled three blocks from the subway station to home. Her drenched tights clung to her legs, not to mention the jean shorts she had on top of them. She could not feel more unattractive as she glanced over at him, noticing that his eyes were blue, not brown, like she had remembered. Her hair, still pinned in a tight bun, clung to her scalp from perspiration.

"There you are," Maurice greeted her with a glass of wine.

"Hi, no – I don't –"Sophie's hand went up to refuse the glass, with her eyes still on John, a tentative smile forming. Maurice wrapped her slim, tan fingers around the chilled white, and slid her black Capezio bag off her left shoulder. He put it on the floor by the front door, and kissed her forehead.

"Have fun sweetheart. I have to get to work. Steven's already there." Then he whispered in her ear, "You deserve it." He grabbed his keys off the hook by the door and closed it carefully behind him.

John pulled on the bottom of his white linen shirt. "I wasn't sure you'd call."

The top two buttons were undone and Sophie, pausing to respond, used the moment to stare at his smooth chest. She took a few steps closer to him, glad to have the glass in hand, not only to cool her off, but to give her something to do. "It's nice to see you." Sophie was a novice, embarrassed by the only thing she could think to say.

John patted the cushion. "Want to sit next to me?"

"Would you mind terribly if I just did a quick rinse?" Sophie needed to collect herself.

"Sure."

She practically ran into her room for a robe and a change of clothes and then scurried into the bathroom, acutely aware of her proximity to John, and the fact that she still held her wine glass. Faucet on, she gulped half the glass to calm herself, laid it on the cover of the toilet bowl, and entered the shower. Her fingers scrubbed her scalp as she washed her hair. The shampoo cascaded down her back and legs and deposited straight into her sandaled feet, "Shit!" She squatted to unfasten them, feeling like an idiot.

Wrapped in a towel, she finished the wine, then shoved open the window as high as she could and placed her soggy sandals on the frame to air out. She stepped into a fresh pair of frayed jean shorts and slipped on a red V-neck tank top. This was one in a series of moments where she wished for a more feminine flare;

with a great wardrobe, painted toe nails and a smooth blow dry to press out her long brown waves. Instead, she took a deep breath, turned the knob and made her re-entrance. If only she had a remote to press freeze so she could spend the next few minutes studying John.

"Your roommates not only invited me over, but made us dinner. You could say it was the ultimate set up, but I have to admit that I begged them to let me come over so I could see you again."

"Really? Why?"

John took the wine glass from Sophie and placed it in on the "coffee table," a milk crate covered with a white cloth that Steven stole from the restaurant where he worked. "Because your lips haven't left mine since Saturday night." He moved his body closer to hers and touched the gold chain necklace sitting between her collar bones. His fingers lingered there.

"It was a gift." Just like the one from her mom, but she replaced it as a teenager when the original no longer fit. John moved even closer, still touching her, so close that she could hear the pattern of his breath.

Sophie waited a beat – for something. John moved his hand from her neck to her cheeks, lightly brushing her skin with his finger-tips. She swallowed in anticipation, feeling giddy. She felt like she'd had too much coffee, a rapid flutter invading her chest. And then his mouth touched hers. It took one second for Sophie to climb on his lap, the way she had fantasized, all inhibition gone. Her pelvis pressed for contact as she straddled him. Her wet hair dripped on both of them.

"Are you sure?" John said, moving her face back a few inches. "Should we slow down? He took hold of her hair and wrapped it in his fingers.

If Jane had been in front of her in that moment she would have slugged her. Why did she have to tell him she was a virgin? She shook her head no − she didn't want to slow down. Her body told her what she wanted and she was compelled to follow. She placed one hand at the nape of his neck and the other through his short dirty blonde hair. She started kissing him again, reflecting on all the trashy novels she had read and the descriptions of longing and hunger. It finally made sense, she felt like she wanted to eat this guy, with her teeth, her tongue and her hands, like he was the most decadent dessert she had ever tasted.

"Sophie," John said quietly, stroking her hair down her back. "Should we eat dinner?"

"No." She pushed her body closer to his.

He stood up and Sophie clung to him, her legs wrapped around his waist. "Wow, you're powerful," he said carrying her to the kitchen wall; a five foot wide area where mini fridge, stove, and sink were crammed between hideous brown cabinets that looked as old as the tenement building. They kissed with more urgency. He placed her on the edge of the counter where the sink was. She nearly fell in when he moved his hands from around her waist down her bare thighs. Instead, she slid into the pot on the stove and it banged into a canister of coffee on the counter.

"I can't believe you don't have a boyfriend," John came up for air, but kept his face only an inch from hers.

Sophie began to feel the effects of the wine, mingling with the heat and her excitement. It grew increasingly difficult to keep her eyes open or focused. She needed carbs. "What's that smell?"

"Check this out," he lifted the lid to a steaming pot of spaghetti sauce. "Al a Vodka. My Mom makes this too." He tilted his head to the side, "I'm not sure it ever smells this tempting though."

"Maurice is a crazy cook." She hopped down to the floor, now eye level with his shoulders. "Want to eat?"

"Sure." He smiled and she noticed that he had one dimple on the left side.

They sat on either end of the futon and twisted the perfectly cooked pasta around their forks. They ate without pause, glancing at each other and then back at their respective bowls. Each time she found another facet of him to note; he had a scar along his right eyebrow, freckles on his chest, perfectly straight white teeth, and his left eye brow raised when he gazed at her between bites.

"What was it like growing up with three sisters?"

She closed her eyes, thinking about her status among the four of them; her animosity and feeling of isolation, not to mention the distance she kept from each one of them. "Complicated." For once Sophie ate every morsel, her usually flat belly bulged by the end of the meal. She felt no choice but to slide down to the floor and lie flat. She un-fastened her top jean button and spread her arms straight out, like Jesus on the cross.

John brought their dishes to the sink. He pushed off his white Adidas sneakers and walked back toward her. When he got to her feet, he slid down on the floor, a playful smile forming. He leaned on one elbow and with his free hand began touching her exposed belly.

Sophie turned to him. Her hands began to shake.

He started kissing her neck, and then whispered in her ear, "Do you want me to stay?"

"Yes."

The moment his hand slid to her zipper, Sophie felt like she might be sick. "Sorry," she bolted up and ran into the bathroom. She slammed the door shut and lay down on the tile floor, the room spinning. There was no way she could vomit with John in the next room. She willed herself not to, but was incapable of moving an inch.

"Are you okay?"

A meek "fine" escaped her mouth. Then she must have blacked out, because thirty minutes passed before she woke, curled up in a ball. She unfurled, splashed some water on her face in the dark room and walked out. The living room was empty.

She had blown it.

Peeling off her clothes one article at a time, she used every profanity she could think of and plopped into her bed face down. She punched the wall a few times and kicked her legs against the bed until she exhausted herself and started drifting to sleep.

At midnight a tap on the front door caused her to stir. At first the sound faintly registered. It continued a few more times and she got up, threw on her knee length red cotton robe and headed to the door figuring Maurice and Steven forgot their keys.

"Hi," John held a ginger-ale, "Feeling better?" He offered her the can.

Sophie took his empty hand and walked him into her bedroom as she untied the robe and let it drop to the floor. Within seconds their bodies were bound to each other. His hands ran along her sides, and hers unfastened his shirt buttons while she kissed every exposed piece of skin. Her arms extended up to touch his hair and face. He tossed her over so that he could be on top, removed his shirt and threw it to the ground.

Sophie didn't know what to do next, part of her wanted to rip his pants off, the other hide under the covers – having never bared her body to a man before. What if she didn't measure up to his other girlfriends? Did he have other girlfriends? They hadn't even talked about anything yet. Should she just stop thinking?

She unfastened his pants and used her feet to slide them off, then wrapped her legs around his upper thighs. Her hands pulled him tightly to her until they were meshed. In that moment she felt like a foreigner in her own body, absorbing not only the sight of him, different from any of the dancers she knew − he was strong, but not perfectly defined, with unblemished white skin. Her hands travelled all over him. And when she burrowed her face into his neck, she released a moan, intoxicated by his scent. It took them a few awkward moments to find a mutual rhythm, but once discovered, they blended together like long-time lovers. Listening to the shift in his breath and feeling the speed of his body alter, she imagined that this was the missing link in her dancing – the action that would drive her to the next level in her craft.

They had a brief intermission to guzzle some water before he drizzled it over her middle and licked it off, spreading it over her chest and down her arms. Sophie's skin tingled; she wanted to laugh and cry simultaneously. When their bodies fused for a second time, her mind began climbing like a monkey from branch to branch. She experienced too many feelings at once for a man she barely knew. Her longing for him morphed into claustrophobia.

"You're incredible," John said. He rolled over to lie on his back, still holding her head with one hand.

Sophie's body hummed. "You need to go."

CHAPTER ELEVEN

After a restless night, Sophie slept till eleven a.m. She padded out to the kitchen in slippers and robe, grabbed her cigarettes and lighter and turned on the coffee pot. She found a note in Stevens's handwriting tacked to the fridge with a dildo magnet:

Hey Doll, Maurice and I decided spur of the moment to head to the Hamptons for a long weekend. Be back Monday night. Kisses.

Sophie plopped onto the futon. She had the apartment to herself all weekend and absolutely no plans. The answering machine blinked twice. She reached over and pressed the red button.

The robotic voice spoke:

"Friday – Ten p.m. – Hey Sophie, it's Hannah. Amy and I will be in New York this weekend. Hope we can see you. We'll be staying at the Marriot. Call you tomorrow."

This weekend? It was already this weekend – why didn't they call sooner?

"Friday – Ten-fifty p.m. – Hi Sophie, it's John."

Sophie pressed stop so she could catch her breath. It had been two weeks since she asked him to leave her bed. She had berated herself ever since. All the times she thought to call him, actually multiple times every day, evaporated in her embarrassment at kicking him out. He appeared so jarred when he put his clothes back on and left the room, he hadn't even looked back at her. She regretted the words as soon as they had left her lips.

Instead of listening to the rest of the message, Sophie dialed his number, which she had memorized day one. When he answered she felt the galloping of horses in her chest.

"Hello." His voice sounded like creamy hot chocolate on a snowy day.

"Hi." Before she could lose her nerve, she continued, rapid fire, "I have three sisters and grew up in Queens. Will you have dinner with me tonight?"

With adrenaline pumping Sophie prepared. Stop number one – the nail salon for her first pedicure. Little did she know how much cuticle pushing and cutting could both tickle and hurt. The foreign environment intrigued Sophie. She reclined in a leather lazy-boy like chair while a young Asian woman washed her feet, scrubbed her numerous callouses, and talked incessantly with her coworkers. They glanced at one another between incoherent phrases and continuously gigged, Sophie quite certain, at her expense. When the red polish was applied, all she could think about was how she and John would braid ankles so their feet could flirt.

Next stop was a run to the gourmet shop for dinner. She needed a solution to mask the fact that she had zero cooking skills. The shelves were stacked with glass jars filled with delicacies she couldn't pronounce or afford. Were they really going to eat anyway? For appearances' sake, she decided on grilled vegetables and lemon chicken, something not too messy that wouldn't get stuck in her teeth. On her way to the counter, she grabbed a couple of beers and prayed she had enough money to pay for all of what she carried in her arms.

She raced home to shower and change. She was stumped. A pile of T-shirts and jean shorts lay on the floor; how could she spruce up denim and cotton? She threw everything back into the closet in one big heap and went to the living room to raid the guys' armoire. They had style, and she and Steven were practically the same size. She put on a white linen shirt, wanting to pass it off as a dress, but that didn't quite work, so she belted it and put on shorts.

And then it was eight p.m. curtain time. Sophie adjusted and readjusted her hair, which flowed loosely down her back – hitting her pant line. She undid an extra button on the shirt and then redid it, not wanting expose too much flesh – yet. She made sure the beer felt cold. She worked super hard not to smoke, wanting to smell clean with minty fresh breath.

He was five minutes late: She paced.

He was seven minutes late: She tapped.

He was ten minutes late: She lit up on the fire escape.

She counted on the fresh air to dissolve some of the odor. Her nerves calmed after a couple of drags. She leaned back against the brick and closed her eyes. Halfway through her cigarette the intercom rang. As Sophie ducked her head to go inside, she registered eight-fifteen on the clock.

The four flights of stairs he had to climb gave her ample time to gargle mouth wash and fix her hair and clothes one last time. She heard the knock just as she shut off the bathroom light. *Deep breaths, Sophie* – she repeated walking to the door. Once opened, she grinned with more joy than she had felt for ages.

He spoke winded, "I'm sorry I'm late, I missed your stop."

Sophie stared at him enamored by his beauty. His shoulders were broad and angular under his blue polo shirt. The color accentuated his eyes and square jawline. She couldn't wait to have sex with him again, the urgent kind, straight to business.

They stared at each other for several seconds. John clearly had another agenda. He reached for her hands first and ran his along the tips of her fingers. The space between their bodies grew electric. When he got to her thumbs Sophie pulled him into her apartment. He placed both palms on her cheeks and brushed his mouth over hers, barely making contact. The sensation caused heat along the small of her back. She closed her eyes anticipating the next kiss. Instead, his mouth covered her ear, "You smell so good." He licked her earlobe and then kissed her neck as he glided his hands around her lower back.

Her usual instincts to control a situation deferred. She succumbed, allowing him to travel around her body like a tourist in a new country. She didn't care that the front door remained open or that they barely knew each other. He had the ability to transport her instantly away from her racing mind.

John pushed the door closed with one foot and pressed Sophie against the nearest wall, covering every inch of her. His fingers drifted along her collar bones provoking a slew of sex words in her head: throbbing, vibrating, pulsate, quiver. They were all invited to the party.

"I want to know everything about you," he whispered, as his palms slid into the back of her shorts.

Lower back, tailbone, front of the hips, waist. She named all the parts he visited, barely able to handle the anticipation of what he would do next.

The tip of his teeth and tongue tugged on the top button of her white shirt. Sophie's chest involuntarily leaned toward his. *Rip my clothes off.* He didn't. *Fuck me.* He kissed the bare spaces of her skin. Each time she reached to touch him or return a kiss, he gently took both her hands in his and whispered no. His exploration continued in a thorough and provoking pattern. Every new area he covered lit her up like a firefly on a pitch black night.

Round two, mission style in her bed, convinced Sophie that John was the next best thing after movement. She would never be able to resist this guy. Their bodies were still intertwined when he asked, "What made you start dancing?"

She wrapped her arms around his back seeing herself in the garden the day of her mom's funeral. "My friend Chloe was going." She kissed him and didn't let go.

They woke up in the middle of the night and raided the refrigerator. Sitting on the kitchen floor, they devoured the chicken and veggies, using the open fridge for light. When they were done, John grabbed a beer and led Sophie back to her room. They crawled under the covers.

"Why did you kick me out?"

The room stood dark.

Self-preservation? Too much potential happiness? "I just got scared."

"I'm the least scary guy around, Sophie. I'm getting my masters in literature – I read the classics in my down time." His fingertips ran up and down her arms.
Sophie only read *Dance Magazine* and juvenile romance novels. "Where do you live?" She lit a large white candle on her bedside table.

"Morningside Heights. I'm going to Columbia."

Master's program, Sophie calculated his age; he had to be at least twenty-two, if not older.

He opened the can and offered it to Sophie, who shook her head no. "Do your sisters dance too?"

She laid her head in his lap while he drank. "No," thank God.

"What does it feel like?"

"What?"

"Dancing?"

No one had ever asked her that before nor had she reflected on how she would find the words to match the sensations. She slid off him and pulled the covers over her body and face for a moment and closed her eyes, *it's a portal for my pain*, she thought. "It's a sanctuary."

John joined her underneath. "My brother and I were both baseball players. I loved it. I got up early every morning to throw with my dad before school."

Sophie looked at John and smiled. "You must have been so cute."

"I'll show you a picture sometime. My brother also played, at my parents' insistence."

Her hands ran along his belly. "He was better than you, wasn't he?"

"Not just better, he'd be in the majors right now if he hadn't blown out his knee last season."

Sophie couldn't imagine her life without dance. "That's crushing."

"He took off this year from college to travel and figure out his next move. I miss him – I wish you could meet."

"Me too."

"What about your sisters?" He reached over Sophie to put the can on the floor. She took the opportunity to slide below him.

"What about them?" she said softly.

"Are they artists also?"

She pulled him down to her, "Can we stop talking?"

The answering machine clicked on just as Sophie and John came out of the shower the next morning.

"Soph – it's Hannah. Are you home?"

Steam billowed out and into the living room. Sophie held her towel at her chest. John was right behind her. "Do you need to get that?"

"No."

"Meet us for a drink tonight?" Hannah's voice sounded uncharacteristically cheery. Why were they here anyway?

"Sure?" John removed the towel from his waist and used it to dry his hair.

God, he's so hot. "It's just my sister."

"We'll only be here till Monday night. The Mars Bar at seven."

John pulled Sophie toward him and grabbed the top of her towel with his teeth. "Where do they live?"

She turned her back to him, how could she explain her relationship with her siblings was nothing like his with his brother. "L.A. Want some coffee?"

"Yes." He kissed her shoulders as she reached for the pot and turned on the water. "When did you see her last?"

She flipped on the switch and leaned against the Formica. "Them actually, Hannah and Amy. They always come as a pair. I think last summer." She felt lightheaded when he moved closer to her, so close not even a piece of paper could fit between them.

They took their mugs and sat on the futon. Sophie admired how comfortable he was sitting there naked.

"I'd love to meet them sometime."

She tugged her towel tighter around her body. Her sisters brought out the worst in Sophie. She didn't want to expose that part of her life to John, who she had such intense feelings for already. It could ruin the perfect time they shared. Taking a sip of coffee to avoid eye contact she thought – absolutely not. She would keep that part of her life private. "Sure, next time. But for now, I want you all to myself."

When early evening arrived, Sophie felt an ache in her gut that he would leave and she would have to go meet her sisters. John crouched down to tie his second shoe and Sophie thought she might cry.

"I'll call you tomorrow," he stood and hugged her tightly. As the door shut, her phone rang. As usual, she let the machine pick up.

"It's Hannah. I'm so sorry to do this, but we have to head to Queens. Jane needs some help. Next time, I guess."

Barefoot and half dressed, Sophie flew out the door and yelled down the stairs, "JOHN – JOHN!"

He was two landings below.

**

Over Labor Day weekend, a month into their relationship, John's parents, Beverly and George, visited the city while Maurice and Steven headed back to the Hamptons.

"Thanks for inviting me to dinner with your folks tonight," Sophie said removing a pair of small gold loop earrings John had given her the previous week. "Do you think they liked me?" It was difficult not to feel insecure. They had taken her out to Le Colonial, an upscale French Vietnamese restaurant. The décor reminded her of a movie set, with gigantic palm trees in large white clay pots and shutter-like doors leading to the bathrooms. She had never been in such a fancy place nor eaten anything with lotus root or oxtail broth. On the walk over John had prepared her; Bev adored her role as stay-at-home mom when they grew up. She had poured herself into her domesticity. While she looked

150

like a modern-day June Cleaver, she had a wicked sense of humor and love for the arts. George practiced law, which meant he worked round the clock, even on vacation.

John removed his wallet from his back pocket and placed it on her nightstand. "Are you kidding? I think my mom always wanted to be a ballerina." He stepped out of his dark blue jeans. "She took my brother and me to *The Nutcracker* for years until we revolted. Secretly, I loved it." He sauntered over to her and held on tightly, burying his face in her neck, "I'm in awe of what you do, Sophie. And so are they."

She loved the feel of his body against hers. "Good. Cause I really liked them. They're both so funny, and clearly so proud of you. Does that feel amazing?"

He pulled back and stared in her eyes, "I'm sorry. I should have told them about your mom."

"It's fine. I'm used to it." But Sophie never got used to saying that her mom died. She encountered the same look every time, no matter how many years passed; a blend of pity and curiosity. She knew John's mom wanted to ask what happened but was too polite. "I loved the story your mom told about you and your brother in the bathtub."

"That was so embarrassing."

She pushed her hip into his, "No! It was adorable." She laced her hands into his and lifted her face toward his mouth.

"Did any of your sisters ever dare you to put poop in the tub?"

They both started laughing. It amazed her that he could he be both sexy and funny at the same time. "Tell me another story?"

John pulled off his shirt, "Your turn."

"I just have to go to the bathroom."

Sophie sat on the toilet wondering what topic she could bring up to steer their conversation in another direction. She had nothing. He and his family got along famously. How could she compare stories? Leaving her dress on the ground, she headed back to the bedroom in her underwear. John was equally dressed.

She instantly reached for the rim of his Calvin's, "You've got the best ass." With one hand on each butt cheek, she walked him backward to the bed and pushed him down. One corner of his mouth lifted as he watched her remove her green lace bra. With the bottoms still on, she carefully climbed on him, into a perfect landing, pelvis to pelvis. He pulled her shoulders back from his and looked at her. "Do you really like me, Sophie or are you just using me for sex?"

The air in her bedroom hung dense with moisture. She had two floor fans blowing on high.

"Are you joking or serious?" She tried to move toward his mouth.

"There's a barrier between us I don't understand. You won't ever talk to me about your family." He pushed himself up and leaned on the wall. Sophie sat up on him.

"Because they're not like yours."

"So? They're not supposed to be. You just met my parents and I've called my brother numerous times to talk about you. Why don't you do the same?"

His inquiries made her feel like a patient on the operating table and he – the doctor standing above, masked and ready to assess the damage. What did he expect to find, hunched over – scalpel in hand, magnifying glasses strapped around his head? Once he finished his inspection, she would be left with stiches to heal. Or worse, what if he sliced her open and found her insides rotten and never sewed her back up again, just ran away?

"Why does everyone always want to know about my tragic family? Does that make me more interesting?" Sophie got off the bed, grabbed her tank top and stood up, frantic for her lighter. Too tired to filter her thoughts before they came out, she lit a cigarette as fast as she could. "Is that it? Is that what you like about me?" She looked at John, who was in the same position, but she could see his jaw pulsing. "It's always the same, people drawn to the accident on the sidewalk, gawking at other people's pain, they can't peel their eyes away even though someone's whole life is about to explode." She didn't realize that between drags her voice continued to escalate to a scream, tears pouring down her cheeks. "Shards of glass are everywhere, splayed out on the street from the windows and windshields, and those fucking people keeping staring." She pulled on her shorts. "The fucking glass gets everywhere, inside the crevices of the sidewalk, into the gutters, under the car wheels."

She butted the cigarette out and was about to light another. "That's me, John, I am one teeny tiny piece of fucking glass in the gutter. Are you sure, are you sure," she choked on the saliva in her mouth, "you want to talk?" Her body was on fire, she slammed the door and went to the bathroom.

Sophie sat on the tile floor for the next half hour shaking. She had revealed more to him than anyone else – ever. And she was certain he would flee as a result. The heat permeated the five by eight room, but she couldn't put a halt to the shivering. She grabbed every towel off the rack and covered herself from head to toe. Her mind ran in a visual loop; picturing their family car being pummeled by an on-coming truck and her mom lying on the side of the road. Even though no one dared to ever tell her exactly how and what happened, this was the dream Sophie had had over the last ten years. The doorknob turned and John stood there in his red Calvin Klein's. As upset as she was, she couldn't help being turned on by the sight of him.

"I don't know, Sophie," he sat beside her and reached inside the towels to find her hands.

"It's okay, John. I wouldn't want to be with me after that." She pushed her hands between her thighs wishing she could rewind the past hour.

He found them with his right hand and held on tightly, "I don't know how you've held that inside." He kissed her cheek. "No one should have to carry those feelings for so long."

Her body tempo slowed down. "You still want to be with me?"

"Of course, I do. Let's go back to bed. I'll warm you up." He lifted her off the floor, making sure not to let her lose any of her multiple towels.

Once nestled in together, John stroked Sophie's hair. Her eyes lulled with his touch.

"How about coming with me to Boston next weekend?"

"I'd love that." She fell asleep beside him.

CHAPTER TWELVE

Rain pelted the side of the train and slid down the windows, reminding Sophie of worms wiggling into the dirt and burrowing for safety. She mimicked them by curling up in John's lap while he slept, as the end of the long ride to Boston approached. The tempo of John's belly expanding and contracting with every breath comforted her. She wished his even breath could communicate with her own jagged and choppy rhythm. Taking this trip felt like a leap of faith, one she had made impulsively after he treated her with so much affection. Now she had doubts crawling around her, like imaginary ants she wanted to flick off her skin. What was she thinking, an entire weekend with his parents? And now wouldn't his expectation for her to do the same increase?

John yawned and looked at his watch. "We should be there in a few minutes." He leaned down to kiss her and said, "How ya doing?"

She had been awake the entire ride in a whirl of worry. What did she have in common with John and his family? They had raised two boys, without drama, and sent them off to Ivy League schools. "Good, I slept a bit too."

"I have a great day planned for us. We can have a quick coffee with my folks and then head into the city."

Sophie smiled. She willed brevity and said, "Sounds great."

They exited the train and John led her through the crowd. "I want to make a quick detour."

Sophie glanced around dumfounded. "What's with the baseball caps and jerseys?"

"You're in Boston, babe. Home of the Red Sox."

John slowed down as they landed in front of Barbara's Bestsellers. "This is one of my favorite places. I come here every time I'm in the station." He leaned over one of the wooden bookshelves and sniffed. "Everything about a book is right, the smell – the feel of the pages in your hand. Just like you."

Sophie wrapped her arms around his waist and leaned on his back, "You're such a romantic."

They walked out of South Station to find Beverly and George Reed waving by the curb side, leaning against their immaculate black Mercedes. Bev wore a pair of white linen shorts and a blouse, with Jackie O sunglasses, and George, cigar in hand, sported a short-sleeve button-down blue shirt and khakis. Sophie straightened her rumpled white T-shirt and tugged on the edges of her jean shorts. John took her hand and squeezed it.

He and his parents embraced. The air, about ten degrees cooler than New York, gave her a chill. She

157

craved a cigarette. Could she sneak away for just a few minutes?

Before she could contemplate it further, George pulled her into a big bear hug. "We're so glad you could visit us," he said.

Sophie stood stiffly – it was like being surrounded by a flannel blanket.

Bev nudged at his arm. "George, you're suffocating her."

Once they pulled away from the curb, Bev turned toward John and Sophie in the back seat, "Are you ready for the audition?"

Sophie's stomach tightened. She looked from Bev to John, "What audition?"

"You didn't tell her John?"

He looked at his mother sheepishly. "I've been reading for classes all week, I totally forgot."

"Oh dear!" She did an about-face and then around again, "We're on the board of Boston Modern. Do you know it?"

Sophie wondered why John hadn't mentioned this. How could he forget? "Yes. I just saw them at the Joyce. They were stunning."

"They're having closed auditions today. One of the dancers is injured and they're about to start their season. I got you a spot."

Holy shit, Sophie thought, this was the opportunity of a lifetime. The Sunday *New York Times* had just written a feature article on them with great praise for the founder/director. And *Dance Magazine* came out a few weeks previously with a huge spread, covering the pages with photos of each dancer around the streets of Boston. "Bev, I don't know what to say − this is amazing. They haven't held an audition for two years." No one had ever given Sophie a chance like this.

"Let's pop by Capezio. I'm guessing you didn't bring anything with you. George, drop us on Newbury Street."

George swerved the car to the right, then left, cutting off drivers who were cutting off him. "Sure. I have to go to the office for a few hours, so I'll drop the three of you and meet you back at the house for dinner."

Sophie's nerves rose. She calculated how much she could spend on one outfit, not really having the extra income for new dance wear. She knew her credit card was maxed out after purchasing ballet slippers last week. It would be too obvious to pull out her wallet and count her bills.

"I really appreciate that you did this for Sophie, Mom, but we have a lot of plans for the weekend. We were going to hit the Harbor this afternoon."

"And you can later, dear." Bev pointed out the window. "George, double park there." He made a sharp turn and stopped as directed.

Sophie exited the car dizzy.

"Oh my, you're as white as a sheet, dear. Let's get you some food first."

"Mom – give us a minute."

John pulled Sophie over to the front of a shop with large glass windows, selling men's graphic T-shirts. He placed his hand along her face and stroked her cheek, "Is this okay with you? I didn't think you would want a job outside of New York – or because my parents have a connection."

"John, this is the hottest modern company around right now. I don't get why you didn't tell me, so I could be prepared."

"I thought you wanted to make it on your own – your terms. Not with family interference."

"I appreciate that, but this – this is a gift. I would never be able to have this shot otherwise." Sophie could see some version of upset in his eyes, "The audition will only take an hour." She kissed him softly and quietly added, "The rest of the weekend will be about us." She held his hand which still lingered on her face.

Bev came up beside them. "Sorry to intrude, but we have to get going so Sophie won't be tardy." Bev's soft, nail-polished hand took Sophie's. "Come dear, you're going to love Boston. It's just like New York."

They walked a few steps and sat at an outside café. Sophie absorbed her surroundings.

"It's like being in SoHo, wouldn't you say?"

Bev reminded Sophie of an exuberant teenager.

"Mom, this is nothing like SoHo."

Nor Hell's Kitchen, from Sophie's estimation. Everyone that passed was white and well dressed.

"You must be starving. They have a lovely lunch here."

The waitress, a young pale-skinned girl with crystal blue eyes, stood above the three of them. "What'da ya havin?" she asked with a thick Boston accent.

"Fish and chips please," John muttered.

"Coffee and the number one special. Sophie?" Bev gave her a warm smile.

Sophie immediately understood John's confidence, always having a mom in his corner. How would her life have been different if her mom had stayed alive? "I'm not really hungry. Just a coffee please."

"And one rum cake. Please bring that with the coffee first." Bev winked at Sophie, "We'll share."

Once the waitress returned with their first items, Bev leaned on her elbows, hands clasped and faced Sophie. "I'm dying to know what made you start dancing?"

Sophie glanced from John to Bev. "My mom died when I was eight." She wondered how she let that out so easily, but continued as fluidly. "At her funeral my friend Chloe came over and encouraged me to go to ballet with her. She said it would be fun and, more importantly, distracting."

Bev poured milk and cream in her coffee. "And did you love it instantly?" She slid the plate in front of Sophie. "Here, try the rum cake. Put some meat on those bones."

Would her mom have said that too? Sophie smiled. "I felt at home."

Sophie fiddled with her napkin, twisting it in her lap, perusing a group of preppy young men passing. Wanting to switch gears she asked, "What was John like when he was little?" She often wondered this at night while he slept beside her, snoring.

Bev smirked at her son while twirling her gold wedding band, "Much like he is now, determined to succeed at every turn. It doesn't surprise me that he would be so smitten with you." She took a bite of her tuna sandwich followed by a sip of ice water that had one lemon wedge perfectly positioned on the edge.

Sophie took the moment to reach for John's hand under the table. She stroked his fingers, then laid her palm on his thigh.

Bev wiped the corners of her mouth with her napkin and placed it back in her lap. "I hear you have three sisters."

"Mom, why don't we talk about something else."

He's protecting me, Sophie thought. "I do."

"I have two. It can be quite trying at times, even now that we are of a certain age. There are still a lot of petty jealousies and old harbored angers."

"Bev, I'm really happy to be here. Thank you for inviting me." Sophie dug her fork into the cake and took a large bite. Maybe it would be nice to live in Boston.

At the Capezio store, Sophie searched the racks for the bare essentials; black leotard and tights, while Bev kept handing the sales girl piles of dance wear for Sophie to try on. John meandered behind, mindlessly brushing his hand along the hangers.

Sophie stopped in front of him. "Are you okay?"

"Fine."

She didn't believe him. He had been stewing since the car. "By three o'clock, I'm all yours," she hummed in his ear and strolled into the dressing room, hoping he watched her go in.

Everything fit like it was sewn just for her, but she settled on the original outfit she picked out. Prior to paying, she stopped in front of the register to tie her white converse.

Bev grabbed the load from inside the dressing room and the items beside Sophie and handed them to the cashier.

"Bev, I only need the one."

Bev winked at her. "It's fun to have a girl around."

No one had ever doted on her like this. If only John could be as enthusiastic. She didn't understand what bothered him so much.

As they sauntered out and over to the audition, bags by their sides, Bev glanced over at Sophie, "Are all your sisters as beautiful and talented as you?"

Sophie's face flushed. "My sister Hannah is in med school, Amy is an actor, and Jane still lives at home and goes to high school. Yours?"

Sophie felt like they were weaving a basket together.

"My older sister is a lawyer, my younger one – let's just say she has troubles." She stopped in front of a building that looked like a warehouse just by the water's edge. "Here you are. Merde! Isn't that what you dancers say?"

"Yes. Beverly, thank you, for everything today…"

She waved her hand in front of her and then gave Sophie a kiss on the cheek. "Enjoy yourself."

Sophie pulled John toward her by the edges of his shirt. "John," she slid her hands inside his.

He moved closer so their foreheads touched.

Sophie placed his hands on her hips, and swayed them side to side. "Be happy for me." She kissed his neck. "Please."

A tiny space between their mouths gave John room to answer, "I am."

Once John and Bev were off in the distance Sophie used her remaining ten minutes to smoke and shed her concern that John felt upset about the audition. She needed to make a clean entrance.

Dwight Thomas, the founder and artistic director, was in the studio when Sophie walked in. His shiny bald head shimmered under the overhead lights and his horn-rimmed glasses accentuated his deep brown eyes and rich black skin. He met her half way and kissed her on both cheeks. "You must be Sophie Gold."

"It's a real honor to meet you." She felt glad she didn't tear up in embarrassment.

"Let's do this girl," he took her hand and led her toward a young man. "This is Matthew. You'll do a series of phrases together from my new piece. You have thirty minutes to learn the material." He left the room.

With no time to spiral into self-doubt or intimidation, Sophie followed Matthew as he faced the mirror and instantly began marking the work for her. The movement reminded her of barefoot ballet with a pop-culture twist.

After thirty minutes elapsed Matthew placed her down from the last lift. "You got this."

When Dwight returned, Sophie wiped the sweat dripping from her brow, smiled at her partner and they began.

Dwight clapped his hands midway. "This is not going to work."

Sophie nearly dropped out of Matthew's arms. He looked as taken aback as she felt.

Dwight sauntered over to them in a turned out stance. He placed one hand on each of their bellies, "There is nooo chemistry. You're supposed to be lovers. This is pubescent." He turned and walked back to the front mirror. "Make it raw! Again!"

Sophie knew raw, it inhabited her like fleas on a dog. It kept her up at night.

She and Matthew, a tall white man with his brown straight hair in a low ponytail and piercing blue eyes, gave each other a nod.

A stamp of Matthew's foot signaled them. He grabbed her waist. Sophie lifted to the balls of her feet and arched back till her head skimmed the floor. She thought of the first night she and John had sex and her breath deepened audibly. Her arms reached for Matthew's chest; *if only John could embrace this possibility*, and then back to the ground. She shifted her weight into her arms so her legs could wrap Matthew around his neck. Sophie clasped with her full force so she could release her arms as he swayed her body side to side, her hair sweeping the floor. Matthew released a staccato "HA" as he lifted Sophie and pulled her onto his left shoulder. They moved across the studio as Sophie glided down and around his torso and legs, leading them into a running sequence in every direction, as if they had lost one another. Sophie ran frantically with the thought of losing John, eyes searching every crevice of the room until she leapt sideways facing Matthew doing the same. *I'm in love with him.*

Back to back they stood, statuesque from hips to heels, with torsos undulating. Sophie placed one arm at a time around Matthew's waist, then a leg at a time, her chest lifted and her face to the ceiling. She let out a cry. It was more primal than Matthew had directed her, but came straight from the gut.

"Enough." Dwight called.

It only took a few minutes for Sophie to grab her bag, run down the stairs, and jump straight into John's arms. He held a rose in one hand. "I'm sorry about earlier. And not telling you…and…"

Sophie kissed him firmly on the mouth. "I got the job."

Her excitement deteriorated over the day. John's apology disintegrated once she had delivered the news. He retreated and moped while insisting he wasn't angry. They walked around town barely speaking. When they hit the Harp in Bar, the place he had talked about on several occasions, where bar-room brawls were common place, they just sat nursing beers and people watching.

"You wanted me to turn down the job?"

John peeled the label off the glass bottle. "Of course not."

"So why are you so upset?"

"I'm not."

Her insides twisted up like a rag being rung out. "You've said a handful of words to me since the audition."

"Did it matter? You and my mom had plenty to talk about."

The prism had turned to a side of John Sophie had never experienced. "You're mad because I like your mom? Wasn't that what you wanted?"

He placed his hands on his temples. "Of course."

Across from them a young couple slobbered all over each other. They kissed so deeply they looked like they would swallow one another.

"I have a headache, Sophie. Do you mind if we leave?

Yes, I mind, Sophie thought. *I want the John I know, the one that wanted to share his family and hometown with me.* "Okay." She tried not to sound as disappointed as she felt. It was like being in an intricate web, sticky at every turn. She slid her chair closer to John and placed her legs on his. One last ditch effort, "What do you want to do tomorrow?"

John removed her legs gently and stood, placing his hand in his pocket and fished out his keys. "I don't know yet, Sophie."

She walked behind him and through the front door he held open. "Did I do something?"

Once outside he paused. "I'm crazy for you Sophie and now I'm going to lose you to my parents and Boston."

Sophie peered up to the sky that looked airbrushed and confected with stars. "Is that why you didn't tell me about the job?"

"I didn't think you'd want to be away from New York."

"You said that already and I don't buy it. It's only a three month contract."

"And what if you don't want to come back?"

Monday late morning the Amtrak train from Boston to New York deposited John and Sophie at Penn Station. He had spent the entire ride reading a stack of papers and she, *Ballet Shoes*, a book that Bev gave her. John pecked her on the cheek and rushed uptown to Columbia. Sophie stood on the platform waiting for the one train to stop. The doors opened and commuters pushed into her on every side. The feel of their bodies barely registered. Would anyone, other than Bev and George, be happy for her that she was now a member of a renowned dance company?

"Move your fuckin' ass bitch!"

On any other day the verbal attack would have alarmed her, instead it became her lightbulb moment. A turn of the heels and she headed to the E train. What if her three month contract got extended for a year? Or more? Her dad would want to know that. Wouldn't he? She had three days left in New York, to pack, and to the thaw the ice with John, while learning four pieces of choreography off VHS recorded rehearsals. There was no time to dawdle. Forty-five minutes later she was in Queens.

"What are you doing here?"

Jane's voice boomed from the dining room, not the voice Sophie wanted to hear. She had avoided Jane all summer, since the party, furious with her. Sophie headed in anyway. She found her grandma doing a crossword puzzle and Jane huddled over a textbook. "I came to see dad."

She had just spent two days in a luxurious house in Massachusetts which made her childhood home seem shabby and outdated. Nothing had changed in the last ten years.

Her grandma took off her reading glasses and looked up at Sophie. "This is an unusual surprise," she said. "Don't you have class and work today?"

"That's what I came to see Dad about."

"I think he's in the den taking a little cat nap. Would you like some coffee or tea?"

"Coffee please, black."

Her grandmother stood and moved toward the kitchen. "How's your grandfather doing?"

"What do you mean, Grandma, he lives here with you?"

Jane gave a snort. "That's what you think." She raised her eyebrows when Sophie looked over.

Her grandma called from the next room, "He's working so hard on that documentary project that he's been staying late at the studio, sometimes sleeping there if necessary."

"There's no space to sleep at the studio, Grandma. It's a bunch of tiny rooms with lots of equipment." Sophie was perplexed. "You've been there, right?"

Her grandma stuck her head through the archway between the kitchen and dining room. "Yes, yes, but his office has space, and he has a friend nearby." And back she went like a turtle in its shell.

Jane scooted next to Sophie, who stood by the dining room table.

"Told you!" Jane waved her smug flag high. "What are you doing here anyway? I haven't seen you since that monumental party. Did you hook up with that hot guy or what?"

"Shut up, Jane."

"Oh Jesus, Sophie. Are you still mad at me? Get over it." She twirled her waves into a French twist and clipped it up. "I'm so glad summer is almost over."

"How's summer school, Jane? Still have time to see Joe?" Sophie wanted to kick her in the shins.

"Actually, it was great. And now I get to help Grandma pack up some odds and ends. She thinks Dad and I can do just fine on our own now. Like that's a surprise. And she said," Jane air-quoted, which Sophie despised, "she and Grandpa have their own lives and it's time they get to it." Another smug smile made Sophie sorry she even made the trip to Queens. "What do you think that means, huh? I'm telling you, Sophie. This family is like a slow-motion train wreck."

Jane's analogy made Sophie's stomach churn. She went to the kitchen to grab her coffee and headed up the stairs to the den. Her grandmother loomed there, and upon seeing Sophie in the doorway said, "Sam, you must be so excited for this unexpected visit." She smoothed her son's hair, as if he was a young boy.

"Could we be alone, Grandma?"

"Of course," she scurried out of the room looking misplaced.

Her father sat reclined, in brown slacks and T-shirt, watching *Jeopardy*.

"You look nice, Dad." Sophie sat as close as she could to him. She took a deep breath, luxuriating in the fact that her father's scent had never changed. He used the same aftershave since she was a kid.

He glanced at Sophie and then back to the screen. "You too."

"Is this a re-run?"

Her dad's eyes stayed with the set. "Your grandmother records it for me."

After their niceties, Sophie spurted it all out. "I got a job, Dad. It's with this amazing modern choreographer in Boston."

Her dad mumbled to himself. "Who was Jimmy Carter?"

Sophie pummeled forward anyway. "It's a three month contract and I'll be living really close to John's family. They're super nice." Was he even listening? "John's my boyfriend, Dad."

"I'm glad to hear that."

"But he's mad at me, he wants me to stay in New York – this is so – so – unfair." Sophie didn't know if she wanted to scream or cry. She bit her fingernails instead.

Her dad took hold of her hand and placed it on his leg. "It's okay, Sophie."

"But it's not. I really like him and –" she took in his profile. He always looked like a fragile bird.

"What is Cliff Clavin?"

"Dad, are you even listening?"

"Don't worry so much." He looked at her for a brief moment. "Life hits you with unexpected circumstances."

"What if he doesn't want to wait for me or be my boyfriend any more?" She stopped, feeling the build-up of tears. She hadn't told anyone in her family about John. "But if I go, John's parents said I can go to their house whenever I want, spend weekends. You would like them."

Several minutes passed. They listened to the old-fashioned wooden clock tick and the voice of Alex Trebek signing off for the night.

"Go, Sarah. It's okay, you can let go. I'm right here." His voice drifted, as he closed his eyes.

Sophie stood and tip-toed out of the room. She turned back around to face her father. "Dad – I'm not Sarah. It's Sophie." She needed an indication that her future mattered to him.

He opened his eyes, but they appeared vacant.

"I'm your daughter, why can't you see me? Why can't you give me – *Something*?"

"Who is Madonna?"

Teeth clenched, Sophie exited.

Jane's body was draped against the hallway wall, black rubber bangles climbing up her arms; eyeliner and mascara thick around her eyes. "Give it a rest already, Sophie. You're never gonna get what you want."

With more resolve and confidence than she had ever felt Sophie glared at Jane, as if she was confronting all three of her sisters, "Watch me."

CHAPTER THIRTEEN

1998

The New York sky appeared even more radiant than Sophie remembered it. It could be the vantage point. Ten years earlier her view stood obstructed by the red bricks of a neighboring building. Now, she dwelled on the tenth floor of 420 Riverside Drive. This perspective showed tree tops and the Hudson River, and when she leaned at just the right angle the George Washington Bridge made an appearance. Maybe ten years away from the city created a false sense of memory, like a dimly lit room. If she kept her focus outward, she could avoid the disarray surrounding her; open cardboard boxes spilling over with a decade of living – hers and John's. She left New York a girl and at twenty-eight came back a woman.

Her long fingers pulled open the drawer of a red lacquer side table, and she removed a silver cigarette case. The first smoke of the day was always the most satisfying, and this one even more so. She had dwindled down to five a day, each week she smoked one less after promising John she would quit.

It was five a.m. Unable to sleep, she curled up on her off-white living room sectional and tucked her sinewy legs beneath her. How had a three-month contract with Boston Modern, one suitcase, and a few hundred dollars in hand evolved into a ten year prolific career, enough money to live, and a marriage proposal from John, who had followed her from New York once he finished his masters? Now it was she who followed him, migrating back to New York for his dream job, teaching literature at Columbia University.

Sophie peered out the naked window as she took a long drag. Her right hand clutched the cigarette while her left twirled her engagement ring around and around. It was a simple one-carat diamond, sitting in the center of a sterling-silver band, an heirloom that belonged to John's paternal grandmother. She wondered how her father would take the news of her upcoming nuptials. It didn't feel right to tell him on the phone; she wanted to be face to face. Would her marriage to John imply a stability that created expectation − visits and family dinners? It was simpler to maintain distance when there were 190 miles between them and she could choose when to pop in and out from JFK Airport between tours.

The matter at hand: another day of emptying boxes and finding where and how to organize her new home. Just one week prior she and John had loaded up their studio apartment in the South End of Boston into a U-Haul and drove down to Manhattan. Staring at the water lulled

Sophie's concerns about work. She had been dancing with Boston Modern since age eighteen and finding a gig in the New York daunted her. Dwight put in some calls to colleagues, she scavenged through ads and called friends to find out what jobs might be available in New York, but the scene was dry. Money might not be an issue, but sanity certainly was. Sophie didn't want to rely on John and his family, as generous as they were.

"We've got it all, Soph," John said. He stood above her, red plaid pajama pants on, shirtless. "This view is amazing isn't it?"

She studied her fiancé, noting a few wrinkles around his eyes and strands of premature gray at his temple. "Yes, it is professor. What are you doing up so early?"

John's hand reached for Sophie's. "Spending time with you."

They walked down the hall and into the bedroom. It only took a couple of moments for them to drop their pajamas and race into bed together.

Sophie slid her hands along his chest, admiring the results of all his gym hours. "Let's elope."

"What?"

"Just you and me. Wouldn't that be romantic?"

John rolled Sophie over onto her back and pushed up onto his elbows. "I think we would disappoint a lot of people, don't you?"

Scanning through her family rolodex, Sophie considered the bunch; aside from weekly calls with her dad, and occasional ones with her grandmother, she and her sisters were estranged. The people she would hurt most would be John's family. "What if we flew down to some island and had the ceremony on the beach – at sunset. Your family could meet us afterwards to celebrate."

Their eyes locked for several moments. Had she disappointed him even mentioning the idea? She could tell by the pulse of his jaw that he was agitated.

"We can't avoid our families meeting any longer Sophie. Or you seeing yours."

She used her legs to draw his body closer to hers. "You're right."

That was all the encouragement he needed.

As the sun illuminated their bare bodies spread across the duvet, the phone rang. It was just nine a.m. Groggy, John rolled over and looked at the clock on his side table. "I'm gonna be late. Can you get it?"

"Sure." Sophie watched him leave their bed and walk naked into the master bath. How had they become so domestic? She grabbed her nightgown from the floor and padded down the hall to turn on the coffee pot. She forgot all about the ringing, which stopped just as she entered the kitchen.

Not wanting to spend another day unloading dishes and glassware, Sophie skimmed her mind for studios to take a morning ballet class. Listening to the gurgle of the coffee as it dripped, she startled when John stepped behind her and kissed her neck. "I love that you don't have a travel agenda. What are you going to do today?"

"I don't know yet — attack all this," she said, gesturing at the pile of boxes shoved against the cabinets.

"That sounds like a plan. I'll be home around seven."

Once he left, Sophie felt a surge of panic. What if he didn't come back? What if something happened to him on his way to Columbia or back home? What if that was the last time she saw him? She knew it was far-fetched – just like the dozens of other times the same thoughts had overcome her — creeping in like rising flood water, exposing her vulnerability. But she stood at the door and told herself that it was enough, and she should get to work. She didn't understand how she could travel the world without a single concern, but when John left their home, nightmarish thoughts invaded.

She ripped the tape off the nearest box and pulled out the dishes wrapped in newspaper. She had found the set of China from Bev and George: ivory plates, cups, and saucers featuring a gold band. Wanting to find the ceramic bowls she brought back from Turkey the previous year, Sophie abandoned the china and tore through the next box.

The phone rang again. This time Sophie answered it.

"Sophie, this is Lloyd Jenkins, manager of The Blank Company."

She knew exactly who he was. The Blank Company was the hottest modern dance company in New York. Sophie thought the name was ridiculous when she first learned of them, but with further investigation she discovered that they named themselves after their motto. New choreographers had the chance to come and pick their dancers, and to create new and innovative pieces. They were all the blank slate, each artist, thus the name was spawned.

"I'd like to invite you to an open audition today. Can you be available at noon?"

If she could have opened her wings and flapped downtown, she would have been there already. There would be no time for class − a quick warm up at home would have to suffice. With her nightgown still on, Sophie began to do a barre holding on to the kitchen island for the next thirty minutes.

At eleven, she slammed the door, flew down ten flights of stairs and into the lobby, humming Madonna's *Ray of Light*.

She hollered '"Good morning"' to the doorman upon exiting and moved along Riverside Drive at a clip. She forgot how balmy August in the city was. The heat and humidity made her dress cling to her waist. Perspiration dripped from her neck to her belly button.

At 110th Street, she raced down the steps, with a New Yorker's fervor, through the turnstile and to the platform of the one train, still humming. She had impeccable timing. It just took a moment for the one train to arrive, idling in front of her feet and the doors to slide open. The rush-hour traffic was long gone by eleven a.m. on a Monday morning, and Sophie immediately found a seat. The last time she had been in the city, a few years prior, everything she needed sat in a small proximity to the theater where she performed. It was remarkable to her how clean the car was, no hint of graffiti or trash littering the floor and seats. For the entire thirty-minute ride, no one walked through begging, and she wasn't interrupted from reading by teenagers dancing to rap music along the poles or mariachi bands playing for the duration of one stop. It made the ride pleasant, almost soothing; nothing like her experience in the late Eighties.

It was no different when she stepped out on Houston Street, like New York had been polished. She sped along the three-block walk, mouth agape, taking in the new high-end stores in SoHo and glass-front restaurants with outdoor seating, buzzing with hipsters. She and John would have to come back downtown together and stroll around.

Once at her destination, she headed up the three flights of a beautiful loft building where The Blank Company rehearsed. She knew they had major contributors allowing for not only the immaculate rehearsal space, but a tour schedule that lasted a full forty weeks. Boston Modern had about thirty weeks of work a year, and that was considerable in her industry. This would be the perfect transition.

"Sophie, please come in."

She turned to the left where a man stood with extended hand. "I'm Lloyd."

He was nothing of what she had envisioned. Instead, she shook hands with a fifty-something-year-old, slightly balding, barring a few strands across the top of his head and a tiny ponytail at the nape of his neck. His glasses were perched right above his nostrils, so his blue eyes could peer above the rim. "What a pleasure to meet you. I am a great fan."

She detected a bit of a mid-west accent. "Thank you. I'm so thrilled you called."

Lloyd ushered her around, gesturing toward the studio they would meet back in after she changed, the lounge, and lastly, the dressing room. It was empty as the company was in transition; the last group of choreographers and dancers had finished their tour and the new crop waited to be formed. It only took a couple of moments to climb into her dancewear before Sophie found her way back to Studio 1.

There, perched front and center, clipboard in hand sat Chloe. Sophie paused before continuing to introduce herself to the line of people seated on fold-up chairs. Chloe bounced up immediately and gave Sophie a gigantic hug. "I am so glad you were free to come. This is such a gift."

"I had no idea – "

"I wanted it to be a surprise. I'm the choreographer."

Chloe hadn't changed a bit; she was as skinny and buoyant as ever. She looked like she might propel out of the room with all the exuberance she exuded. Sophie, on the other hand, had to eke out a polite smile. All her old feelings of anger and resentment swelled, but rather than run, like she would have ten years ago, she mustered up her courage and said, "It's a great surprise, Chloe. I'm so happy to be here."

After introductions were made between Sophie and the board members, they got down to work. Chloe demonstrated – Sophie absorbed. The phrases were lyrical, with long sensual movements, circular gesturing, reminding Sophie of both Lar Lubovitch and Twyla Tharp: luxurious and powerful.

Having not chosen the music or male partner yet allowed for some collaboration between the old friends. Once the board nodded their approval to Chloe, they cleared out, leaving them alone.

"I wasn't sure you'd come if you knew it was me who wanted you."

Sophie gazed at her old friend, hands on knees panting from the previous hour of work. "I may not have." She smiled genuinely this time. "But I'm so glad I did."

They sat on the floor for the rest of the afternoon getting reacquainted; cities lived in, boyfriends passed, dance, dance and more dance. Sophie couldn't believe

Chloe's list of conquests. "Honey, you move through boyfriends like a hungry girl digging through a pint of Ben and Jerry's."

"I have to, there's always something wrong with them; hands too big, nose to small, too much hair on their chest. The last guy I took home removed his shirt and the smell – oh my God," Chloe held her nose and made the face of a woman who just got caught in toilet stall with feces flowing out of the bowl.

They laughed until their sides ached. "I have to go home. You should come over soon and meet John."

"I have to tell you, Sophie. I never thought you'd get married."

I didn't either, she thought.

Wanting to experience all the new food in her neighborhood, Sophie stopped at Ollie's on 116th Street and picked up pan-fried dumplings, general 'Tso's chicken, and sauteed mixed vegetables for dinner. The aroma taunted her the two blocks home – she was ravenous.

John stood at the door, a stack of papers in hand. "Your sister's here," he said in a low tone.

She hadn't even walked through the threshold yet. "Jane?"

"Hannah. She called this afternoon."

The sheen of the day disintegrated in that second. Sophie pushed through the entrance and peered into the living room. So many years had passed since they saw each other.

"She lives in New York now, a few blocks away. She's an ER doctor."

Sophie's heartbeat raced. "I don't know if I can do this."

John took the take-out bag from Sophie and placed it on a long wrought-iron table beside the door. "Sure, you can – come in. I'm going to go to the library so you can be alone."

Sophie grabbed John's arm. "NO! Please don't do that. Stay – be a buffer."

"I believe in you, Sophie. You got this."

Sophie entered her home, like an interloper, and seated herself across from Hannah. They sheepishly smiled at one another before speaking, hands in laps, mirror images.

"You know my apartment is really too big. It's just me and Pepper, my Siamese," Hannah scratched her head. "I couldn't decide where to live, close to St. Lukes Hospital for simplicity, or the East Side – so I could get away at the end of the shift."

Sophie wrapped both hands around the Japanese tea cup, one of four Sophie had carefully wrapped in tissue paper, then her clothing as extra cushioning, before tucking it her suitcase. In each city she visited, she brought back something for their home. Sophie could smell the aroma of Jasmine tea, John and her favorite.

"But proximity won," Hannah said.

"You have no body fat," Sophie blurted, looking at how Hannah's scrubs were practically hanging off her frame. She couldn't believe what she had just said, or how her sister's physique pissed her off. When they were teenagers, Hannah could eat whatever she wanted and remain not only thin, but sculpted, with little effort. Sophie however, had to spend hours at class and rehearsal, and stay conscious of all her intake to keep her physique. Hannah was exactly how she had imagined her over the years. She even had the streaks of blonde running through her hair, from year-round sun. "Sorry, that was awkward."

"I still run a lot," Hannah said, continuing to look at her cup, her shoulders rounded forward.

"John had to go back to work. You met?"

"Yes, when I walked in." Hannah tapped her clogs lightly on the floor, in a slow even rhythm.

"Right."

Hannah looked up, and Sophie registered the circles under her eyes. "I thought it might be nice to talk− "

Sophie interrupted, "You know John and I just moved in here a week ago. He got a job at Columbia − a dream of his." She tucked her lower legs beneath her and pushed her body into the corner of the couch.

"It's a great apartment, Sophie. You seem really happy." She rubbed her eyes. "And do you have work too?" She placed her cup on the glass coffee table and looked up with a serious demeanor.

The gesture reminded Sophie of the "mother" Hannah had always pretended to be, but fell short of. "Yes, I just got a gig today." There hadn't been time to share the news with John, but here she was with Hannah, downplaying her exuberance. She reached over and opened the drawer, retrieving her pack of Marlboro Lights. "Do you mind?"

Hannah shook her head no.

"So, you came to New York for work?" Sophie asked. The first drag was always the best, the deep breath in and the long flow of smoke as it cascaded out with the exhale. She wondered what life would be like without a cigarette, what would replace the awkward moments like this?

"I missed being close to Dad and everyone."

Sophie doubted that, but she couldn't deny the weariness in Hannah's face, like she hadn't slept for years. "Everyone?"

"I know you think we were awful to you, Sophie." Hannah covered her face with both hands and took a deep breath. "But we were just kids. And we lost our mother too."

"Dad told me you got married a couple of years ago."

Hannah lifted her left hand toward Sophie.

Gardening hands, Sophie thought. *Just like mom.* Then with a blink, she registered the white line on Hannah's ring finger. "Oh. John and I just got engaged," Sophie wished she hadn't said that.

"That's wonderful, Sophie."

"How can you say that? You're divorced." Sophie jumped up and took the final drag. It should have been her last cigarette of the day, but with Hannah not just visiting, but living in a tiny radius of Sophie's world, she might need an extra week. Or possibly two. "I'll be right back." Was she going to run into her at Westside Market now, and at the Abbey Bar? Was she supposed to invite her for dinner and holidays now? Would that be so bad? She went into the kitchen, dropped the cigarette butt in the sink, and splashed some water on her face.

"Sophie," Hannah leaned on the counter beside her, "I know this is strange, after so many years, but – "

"Why are you here?" Sophie wiped her face with the closest towel she could find. It was one she had picked out in France, on tour, with small yellow flowers. It reminded her of the marigolds in her childhood garden. Flowers her dad had ripped out over the years. Why was she messing this up?

"We're sisters. And now neighbors." Hannah's voice was low.

Sophie had heard stories of sisters living next door and never speaking. Is that what she wanted? Here they were, and Hannah held the olive branch. "And does that remove the wounds?"

"We all have wounds, Sophie. I don't really know which you're speaking of." Hannah leaned against the cabinets and crossed her arms.

"It doesn't matter. Do you need some more tea?" Not waiting for an answer, Sophie turned the kettle on.

"I'm fine, thanks." Hannah walked over to Sophie's side of the counter and touched her shoulder. "Can we just move on from here?"

Sophie slid her body away and opened the refrigerator, looked inside and closed it again. "Can you excuse me for a sec?"

Needing an escape hatch, she went down the hall and into her bathroom. When she looked in the mirror, she didn't see the woman she now was – the woman who traveled the globe and commanded an audience of thousands. No, the reflection showed her a little girl, and the voices of her sisters behind her echoing: We don't have time for you Sophie, go away Sophie, not now Sophie, you're so strange.

There was a knock on her open bedroom door. "Can I come in?"

Sophie took a deep breath and entered the bedroom. "Sure."

Hannah's back leaned against the door with her arms folded against her chest, "I have to go to work pretty soon, I didn't mean to upset you. I just thought..."

"What did you think? You'd show up here after all these years and we'd be buddies? You don't know anything about me. You never have." Even though it was a record-high temperature outside and the only cooling mechanism in her apartment were open windows, not having had time to buy air conditioners yet, Sophie was freezing. Her body began to shake with a chill. She tore open her closet and pulled the nearest jacket off the hanger and threw it on.

"What do you know? Did you call me? Did you visit Amy and me – ever?" Hannah's voice remained calm. "When you performed in L.A., did you call us? Did you tell us you were there or invite us to a show? We only found out by looking at your review in the paper." Hannah took a breath. "I don't have time for this martyr thing you do, Sophie."

"No, of course you don't." Sophie turned and looked directly at her sister. She mustered up all her years of performing and imagined Hannah as a stranger sitting in a dark theater. She straightened up her spine, pulled her shoulders back and held her hands behind her.

"Jane says –"

"Jane! Jane? This is about Jane?" Sophie flew around Hannah to the living room. She lit another cigarette and looked at the river. The water was choppy, cutting in little waves. One red tug moved through, pulling its garbage. "I can't fucking believe this," she muttered to herself. "Why didn't they just come all together?" Sophie continued mumbling between drags, "Why is this bothering me so much? I'm a fucking grown up." Hannah's clogs clunked on the floorboards. Sophie stiffened.

"Grandma and Grandpa split."

"I'm well aware of that, Hannah. Let's talk about you. Do you visit Dad or call him on a regular basis? Or sit there when he's only partially coherent and you're trying to figure out the puzzle of who he is? Or sometimes he doesn't say anything at all. Did you know that?"

Sophie had waited years, for Hannah to show up, for Hannah to find her. Sometimes she even had the fantasy of having a relationship with all her sisters – a good one – but now all she felt was contempt. She looked at her watch. "You're going to be late for work. Thanks for dropping by." Sophie's head throbbed.

Hannah crept slowly toward the door and stopped just as she was about to reach for the knob. *Don't stop,* Sophie thought, *just keep going.*

"You are so incredibly righteous, Sophie." Sophie watched her demeanor shift, as Hannah stood her full height. "You don't know anything about any of us. When was the last time you spoke to Amy?"

"I don't know." Sophie hated to admit she had no recollection of any phone calls with Amy, not since she had followed Hannah to California.

"Right," Hannah smirked, sighed, and shook her head simultaneously. "Sophie, you have spent the last ten years judging us based on shit from when we were kids."

Sophie knew she wasn't a kid any more, but she felt the beginning of a cower that only Hannah and Amy could cultivate.

"Do you have any idea what a mess Amy is?" Hannah's entire face squished up. She looked constipated.

"God, I need an aspirin," Sophie trudged away from her sister toward the bathroom. She needed to regroup for a moment. But, of course, Hannah followed on her heels. Sophie could hear each step, but refused to turn.

"Amy has eaten up every inch of what little money she has had; snorted it, drank it, lost it, gambled it."

Sophie stopped mid-step and faced her sister.

"Don't say a single word," Hannah spat, staring at Sophie. "I have no marriage because of Amy. You're not the only one who felt pain, Sophie, who lost her parents. Where were you when Amy called from some seedy apartment with another vacuous guy? Did you look for Amy on Hollywood Blvd? Or better yet, in the bars she frequents in the midday, mourning the fact that another call-back disintegrated into nothing. You've dealt with you, Sophie. As you do best; your body, your applause, your boyfriend. You abandoned us."

Sophie popped the top of the aspirin bottle and swallowed a pill without water. "You're one to talk. You ran to L.A. first chance you got, leaving us here to fend for ourselves. And you haven't looked back for a second."

"Did you ever wonder why we left you out, Sophie?"

Sophie imagined the last moments of watching Hannah run at a track meet, as she pulled up past the line of runners who had been inches in front of her. She waited until the very end to grab every bit of momentum before going for the finish. It was her signature move, every race. She always won.

"Who got the last hug before bed? Or the special present before her actual birthday? No, let me rephrase that, who got the last present Mom gave to any of us?"

Sophie thought of the heart necklace, with the S on it. She had it in a special box that she took out and wore only on her birthday each year. Was Hannah right? Had she imagined a paranoid scenario all these years when they were actually envious of her?

"You're right, Sophie. I'm gonna be late," Hannah swiftly spun on her heels.

"Don't you dare," Sophie chased in front of Hannah, meeting her eye to eye. "You don't get the last word this time. You don't get to waltz back in here and do that dictatorial thing you've always done." Her body shook slightly. "Did you invite me to your graduations? Your wedding? I found out you were getting married from Grandma." Sophie felt so venomous that she had to pause, afraid of the words that spewed out.

There had been no lights on in the living room, it had been such a sunny day, but now it neared eight p.m. and darkness infused the space between them. Sophie quietly turned the knob to her front door and opened it.

The hallway light was blinding. Hannah followed the cue and exited.

CHAPTER FOURTEEN

The Chinese take-out stood on the counter untouched as Sophie ripped through the unopened boxes surrounding her in the kitchen. How dare John invite Hannah into their home without her permission? She tore tape and threw bubble wrap and newspaper on the floor. She knew John meant well and must have been jazzed to finally meet a family member of hers, to know they truly existed. But it was a betrayal of their trust. She frantically searched to find the platter she bought in Amsterdam a few months ago. She needed to be surrounded by her own memories, ones unshared by anyone else. Instead, she found two large blue and white plates from Tokyo depicting a Japanese landscape, four Turkish bowls with rich clay colored designs, and a ceramic pitcher from Venice.

The particular piece she scoured the boxes for had been purchased her last afternoon in Amsterdam, on her final tour with Boston Modern. What had begun as a gorgeous spring day ruptured into a hard and fast thunderstorm. The rain charged down, rocking house boats on the canals and bowing tree branches over car hoods. She was caught off guard, no raincoat or umbrella for coverage, even though she had been warned of rain by her Dutch company member, Mirco. Sophie ran for cover inside a corner bar and ordered a coffee. She sat alone, just as she preferred, and watched the multiple bikers pass. Rain didn't deter them. She admired the people, their solid bone structure and towering heights as if reflections of their no-nonsense and hardy demeanor.

Sophie nursed her coffee, pleased with the Dutch platter she would bestow upon John as a gift. He had loved the Japanese plates so much, and this platter too showed the classic blue and white design, with windmill, water, and billowing clouds in the sky.

Just as she began to lose the wet chill in her bones, the door to the bar swung open, bringing in drenched American tourists, a mother and her daughter. Taking the seats beside Sophie they ordered two hot chocolates. The mother, who Sophie guessed was around her age, maybe a few years older, removed her raincoat and sweater and used it to towel dry her daughter, of around six.

"Amelia," the mother spoke. "What's that Dutch word we learned yesterday for cozy?"

"Che – zell-ich," the girl said slowly, with the meticulous guttural tones Sophie had been listening to all week.

"Oh yes!" The mom slapped her thighs. "Such a funny word."

Curious, Sophie continued listening to the interaction. She barely remembered anything about her own mother any more.

"Mama?"

"Yes, Amelia?"

The little girl took a sip of her hot chocolate and mustached her upper lip with the whipped cream. "Robbie said everyone dies. Is that true?" She licked the cream off with her tongue.

"Your brother," the mom began.

Sophie could see the mom shaking her head through her peripheral vision.

"Are you gonna die, Mama?"

"Not for a long time."

Sophie turned her head in time to see the mother place a kiss on her daughter's forehead. She felt a hit of emotions she had not expected. Sophie placed two Dutch guilder coins on the table, grabbed her shopping bag, and practically tripped over the chair legs as she sped out, tears streaming down her cheeks. She sprinted back to the hotel. The girls' question rung in her head. She pictured her eyes wide, accentuated by the wet hair that framed her face. Wasn't every mundane goodbye possibly the last? She never said goodbye to John when they left each other, only have a great day. That one simple word altered her life forever.

By the time John walked in their apartment an hour later, Sophie sat on the kitchen floor in the dark, a mess surrounding her. Before he even stepped foot into the room, she started, "How could you do that to me?"

"Why are you sitting in the dark, Soph?"

Sophie pressed her teeth together. "How could you invite Hannah here without asking me?"

John flipped the light switch on. The ceiling fan spun. "I thought you'd be happy to see each other after the initial discomfort." John opened the bag of take-out and began removing containers. "I'm famished."

The light blinded Sophie for the first moments. She needed to smoke. "Discomfort is a paper cut, John. This is a deep gash."

"So, you want to get it infected or can we stitch it up already?"

"Infected."

John laughed. "You're really stubborn, Ms. Gold." He crouched down, moved the stray hairs away from Sophie's eyes and cheeks and pulled her into an embrace.

Sophie could barely look at him, let alone reciprocate. Squirming away, she took a deep drag, then, used the first cigarette to light another.

"Maybe some magic will break the spell when you become Mrs. Reed."

The words sounded so old fashioned when they bounced across the room, leaving a palpable pause. "Why don't you take me seriously?"

"You don't want to change your name?" John asked.

"Everyone in the industry knows me as Sophie Gold, but I was talking about my sister."

John stood. "I can't believe we haven't talked about this yet. What about when we have kids?"

Sophie still wasn't sure she wanted children. Pregnancy seemed an interminable period of body morphing and sacrifice, and then what? Was she supposed to stay home and play housewife? "Did you know no one in Boston Modern is married – I'll be the first? And Hannah is divorced. I don't think she was married more than a couple of years – my grandparents just split too."

John slammed his hands on the counter, which knocked the dumplings into the sink. "Goddammit, Sophie. Do you want to have kids with me?"

"I don't know. Stop pressuring me." Sophie's voice cracked with last word. She envisioned the little girl in the Dutch cafe. Being a parent was an enormous responsibility. Was she ready for that? Sometimes she felt like an idling car in the left lane, cars honking as they sped past her.

"I want to be a family," John said in a faint tone, staring into the sink.

"We are."

"*No*, we're a couple. I want a house spilling with fights and laughter," he turned toward her, "and a drooling dog."

The visual made Sophie's toes clench and her stomach ache. The implication was loud and messy.

"You know I'm not going to be a wife like your mother is, right?"

John grabbed a beer from the fridge. "This isn't Oedipus Rex."

"I got a job today. I start rehearsals tomorrow." The way she said it sounded like a punishment.

About to take a sip from the bottle, John paused with it at his lips. He stared at her. "Really?"

Did she want to hurt him? "You're disappointed?"

"I just thought we'd have some time to settle in before you were off and going again."

This was the fight that repeated between them like a tumbleweed in the desert. "You have a job John – you were gone all day."

"And then I come home."

Sophie tucked her knees to her chest and wrapped her arms around her shins. "I always come home."

John placed his beer on the counter. Sophie saw him take in the clutter of her paraphernalia. "I wonder sometimes where you prefer sleeping, here with me or your Motel room."

"That's ridiculous," Sophie said, standing to face him.

"Is it?" His gaze held both the question and a puncture wound to the heart.

He left the room, pulling at his tie with one hand and lifting his light blue button- down shirt out of his jeans with the other.

Alone in the kitchen, she pondered the question. She did love traveling and the quiet plane rides bringing her to new destinations where her senses were flooded with new experiences. Listening to the sounds of different languages and tasting new foods were stimulating, but the performances were always the highlight; a bare stage, black house before her, and a world to create − nothing fulfilled her more.

With a deep sigh she headed to the bathroom to get ready for bed. Sophie bent over the sink and splashed some water on her face. Using her wet hands to cool off her neck, front and back, she looked through the mirror. Behind her on the wall John had a hung a photograph taken of Sophie in her early years at Boston Modern. Even though he argued with her about her travel, she knew he stayed her biggest fan. The article had been called, "Behind the scenes," a look at multiple dancers when they're off stage. Sophie declined an interview, but agreed to be photographed. Half her face was in full stage make-up; false eyelashes, thick black liner surrounding her eyes so the audience could more easily view her expressions, powder and shadow creating more extreme contours of her bone structure. The other side was bare. She reached up and took turns covering each side.

With her nightgown on, she made her way to bed. When she got in on her side, the one closer to the window, John opened his eyes. "Your sister is not what I expected."

"I thought you were asleep." Sophie turned toward him. She would play along, knowing she had probably over-reacted to everything John said since he walked in. "What did you expect?"

"A lioness… a blonde warrior goddess spitting fire." He turned on his bedside light. "At least a female Thor – the way you have always intimated she is."

Sophie's hand smoothed out her side of the comforter. "And?"

"She was more like a kitten with a broken paw."

"Hannah?" Sophie had to admit, she did appear ragged.

"I tried really hard to hate her – for you – but, I couldn't. She elicited pity in me. I think she's been through a lot, Sophie."

"Why are you so empathetic? It makes me look bad." She kissed her fiancé on the shoulder. Anytime her lips met his skin goosebumps tingled. "Good night."

He kissed her forehead. "There's always more below the surface."

Just as he reached to shut off his light, Sophie reached over his body and grabbed his arm. "Please don't invite my family here again without asking me."

"Okay. I'm asking. Can we please invite your family over this weekend? I'd like to finally meet the rest of them."

It was as if everything she had just said to him evaporated in the narrow space between their distressed faces. "I have non-stop rehearsals starting tomorrow, John. We only have three weeks till opening night."

"And then?"

"I didn't get the tour schedule yet."

John sprung upright, his back hit the headboard. "I thought when we decided to move back to New York this would stop."

Now she sat and stared at him. Was he for real? "You thought I would stop dancing?"

"NO Sophie, but I thought we would integrate your family into us."

"Why?"

The pause between them felt endless. Sophie listened to the rain pelting and the footsteps of their upstairs neighbor. She heard every move of the clock hands ticking away the time they didn't speak.

John spoke in a whisper, "I want to be a good husband."

Their bodies lay back to back now. "You will be."

"NO!" he shouted.

She turned her right shoulder and head in his direction, "What?"

"I'm not asking any more." With a quick flip, his eyes penetrated hers, "We're getting married. We're gonna start our own family one day. I can't do that without knowing yours."

The rest of her body turned. Her finger stabbed the air between them – she closed her mouth just in time – before the words – you're my worst nightmare – leapt from her lips. A build-up of tears followed, the kind that sits just below the surface, stinging her nose and cheeks. She could ruin it all in that moment. Walk away and be free. Relationships were sloppy and filled with unbearable disappointments. Fights repeated in a monotonous loop and caused more misery than harmony. The truth – peace came from a dark stage and a full house.

***

Light flooded the studio through the enormous windows. Sophie faced east to absorb as much sun as she could, pulling her tights higher over her leotard and folding the elastic down over her hips. She wrapped tape around the balls of her feet, which had gotten softer during the weeks off between homes and cities. She had a few cracks between her toes that were a nuisance, but knew the discomfort would dissipate once she got moving.

Chloe stood at the door. Her cheeks glowed like she had brought the sun with her. "Hey, good morning. I'll be in in a sec so we can warm up together."

Sophie peered up at her friend from her floor position. "I'm so glad to see you."

"Ooooh, you look like a wreck," Chloe said with concern in her voice.

Sophie had been up all night, just like the past few, swimming in thoughts of John and Hannah. She had fought with both of them to no resolve. She had thought the worst possible thing about him. Usually when she and John argued they made up immediately, but his time it lingered like musty air. Their hours at home together felt more functional than connected.

"I'm bringing you a coffee," Chloe said. "Be right back."

"Thanks," Sophie hollered as she stood and walked to the barre. She placed one leg up and stretched the entirety of her body over, holding onto her foot as she pointed it to its fullest. A few deep breaths gave her suppleness, her muscles relaxed and her mind quieted down.

Chloe traipsed back in, mug in hand. "Black, right?"

"Perfect." Sophie took multiple sips. "I needed this, I ran out of the house before John woke up."

"Still fighting?"

Sophie switched sides. "Not talking is more like it."

Chloe leaned on the barre facing Sophie. "What's he like?"

Sophie picked her head up from her ankle and then stood upright. "Easy-going, great with people, really handsome." The list made her feel the weight of her own struggles. "Very patient." Maybe I'm being irrational about the whole thing, Sophie thought.

"He sounds kind of perfect. Tendus?"

Sophie put down the mug. She and Chloe faced the barre together. They began; one leg at a time extending in each direction, front, side, and back. Their feet slid along the floor until they reached their maximum points.

"Are you lonely?" Sophie asked, while doing a port de bras, back arched to the ceiling and her face turned to the right side where her arm was raised.

"Not really. My own agenda keeps me quite occupied."

Sophie reflected on the minimal amount of time she had lived alone, when Chloe and Eric were on tour and before she moved in with Steven and Maurice. Aside from the quick pizza dinners and empty fridge she kept, she couldn't remember what that felt like any more, having spent her formative years intertwined with John.

They stopped their small chat during the rest of their barre work, synchronizing their movements. After a lifetime of ballet class, the sequencing sat deep in their bones. Moving to the center of the room they worked through a series of petite allegro, making their jumps tight and quick.

"Break?" Chloe asked.

At the water-fountain, Sophie took a long slow stream of water. She lifted her head and said, "He's a glass-half-full guy."

Even though Sophie had picked up a conversation from an hour before, Chloe was right there with her. "I get it. He's the honey in your tea."

***

Ascending the stairs at 96^{th,} Street Sophie felt the burn in her thighs. The afternoon had been spent finishing her half of a duet she would dance with Scott. They would meet for the first time the next day. It had been some time since Sophie danced with a new partner, a thought both exciting and daunting. They had to move like lovers, understanding all the nuances of each other's bodies: strengths and physical cues had to become second nature. If that didn't materialize, both the emotional power of the piece and their physical safety were at risk. They had to glide with both precision and fluidity, in unison. With only a few weeks till opening night, that was a task. And for Sophie, Chloe's piece felt like she had walked into warm Caribbean water, one step inviting the next, until she was submerged. The chemistry needed to be just right.

Sophie strolled along Riverside Park, wanting a breath of fresh air and the scenic view up to 114th Street. The walk gave her the opportunity to visualize phrases of movement and occasionally mark them with her hands as well. The edges of evening light mingled with the vivid blue sky like soft jazz on the radio. She passed kids and parents soaking up their last moments in the sandbox or on the swing, runners with dogs of all sizes sprinting along -tongues hanging out, but she barely noticed any of it because she was deeply concentrated in her work.

At 112th Street, she sat on a bench to scrutinize a complicated lift. She had to run to Scott and jump sideways onto his back – the simple action, then curl into him so she could make her way down his legs to the floor, while her legs fluttered around like butterfly wings – the challenge.

"Soph," a man's voice shouted. "*Sophie…*"

It took a few booming calls for Sophie to register her name. She turned to her left and there stood John. Rather, there jogged John, in place, with Hannah at his side. Perplexed, she furrowed her brow.

"We ran into each other about twenty minutes ago along the promenade," John huffed. Sophie knew he didn't have the stamina that Hannah must have. He was more an occasional Sunday jogger. The Hannah she knew could run miles upon miles.

"Hi Sophie," Hannah said.

Sophie took in her black lycra shorts and matching crop top. Her muscles rippled as she evened out her breath. She looked like an Olympic athlete. A tried, "Hi" eked out of Sophie as she stared back and forth between John and Hannah. Didn't he understand that he was supposed to be on her side?

"Sophie, your sister just told me the most amazing story about the ER," John said. He put his hand out, as if to say wait a sec, and took a large gulp of water from the bottle he held. "A little boy came in with a possible concussion -"

She knew this storytelling method of his. She was meant to say, 'And what happened?' She wouldn't bite.

"He fell four flights – off a banister – and get this…" John glanced at Hannah, "you tell the rest."

"He landed on an empty box, completely fine. Not a scratch," Hannah finished.

John took another swig of water while Sophie looked at her sister. Hannah smiled sheepishly. "He was a beautiful little boy. I think the parents were more in shock then he was."

John wiped the sweat from his forehead as Hannah swayed back and forth, and Sophie fantasized about karate-chopping them both in the groin.

"John told me you're performing in a couple of weeks," Hannah said. She folded her arms at her ribs. "If it's okay with you, I'd like to come."

"Sure," Sophie replied. She'd be a monster if she said no.

"I should go, I have a midnight shift and need a quick nap. Great to run into you," Hannah said, then added. "Both." She raced off.

Sophie watched her glide away, her blonde ponytail swinging back and forth with her perfect stride. Her long legs carried her across the street and into the distance.

Sophie turned to John. "Why didn't you pretend you didn't see her?"

"Why would I do that?"

CHAPTER FIFTEEN

"These sequins are scratching my stomach," Sophie murmured to Scott, her partner, who hovered above her body in a push up position. He was several inches longer than she, and shades darker. She watched his ribcage fan open and closed while they waited on the dark stage. Their partnership created a perfect union. If Chloe's choreography was the canvas, they were the brush strokes. They were the last on the program. Three other choreographers had already gone and the audience buzzed in front of them. Sophie could hear the occasional cough and sneeze of restless watchers.

They had a deal, tic-tacs before they took position. Sophie enjoyed the minty air between them. "Lie still baby – we're almost in flight," Scott whispered, a phrase he had been saying during rehearsal all week. Sophie smiled. She was ready. "By the way, I saw your fiancé out there." The lights went on and the cello began its song.

"I wasn't sure he would show." The rehearsal weeks were so dense that Sophie took the opportunity to focus only on the work; coming home late and going straight into the shower and bed. She fell asleep while rehearsing the piece in her mind, going over the most arduous lifts and phrases. She knew there was a reporter from the *Times* in the audience.

"Oh honey, did you two love birds bicker last night?"

He teased her about the purity of her relationship. Most dancers climbed in and out of each other's beds, especially on tour, but Sophie stayed faithful. She preferred a warm bath and a good book, even though the thought of a new conquest occasionally enticed her.

"More like weeks of silence. Here we go."

As the curtain lifted, a pink light circled them like a womb. The space between Sophie and Scott's bodies decreased as the light expanded across the entire stage, the hue melting to a warm orange. A lone cellist sat at the far left behind them, embracing her instrument. Their only music. They were immersed.

The first notes held deep, rich tones, reminding Sophie of warm tears streaming down the sides of her cheeks, while lying in bed. Her arms reached for her partner. Her legs laced around his torso as he swept them up to a standing position. She clung on as Scott thrust his arms out and took an open leg stance.

Her inner dialogue began,

I do want to marry John.

She and Scott separated so they could do a phrase of small jumps in unison.

Maybe I can be a mother.

She flew into Scott's arms and he lifted her overhead, her legs extended to hip height in opposite directions, her torso and arms swaying side to side. Scott held Sophie by the thighs and with a press upward she went airborne for a moment before he caught her, and they landed in an embrace.

Why do I keep pushing him away?

The music paused. They repeated the phrase faster and faster several more times.

"Why do I do this? I don't think I can do this.

Sophie chased Scott across the stage and grabbed him by the waist. Their bodies smacked belly to belly. They collapsed to their backs and landed feet to feet. Scott stiffened, arms outstretched with palms up and legs pasted together. Sophie scrambled to her side and curled into a fetal position, arms bound around her shins and rocked in an even rhythm for ten counts of music and then unfurled, her hands clutching her dress as she pulled it overhead and threw it onto Scott without making eye contact, exposing her bare back and legs. Scott's left arm reached for the material and offered it back to his partner. Sophie's right hand rubbed her thigh, scratching the skin with her nails before reaching to take hold of the red sequined dress. She stroked her cheek against the material over and over while her torso undulated.

The stage went black.

When the orange hue returned so did Sophie and Scott, shuffling toward each other, arms hanging by their sides, palms facing each other, shoulders lifted creating concave chests. Heel – toe – heel –toe – twenty

212

rhythmic paces. When there was no space left to traipse, their heads collapsed on the other's shoulders.

The stage was silent but for the sound of their coordinated breath. They glistened with sweat.

Applause...

Standing ovation...

When the lights rose for their second bow, Sophie searched the balcony for John. She had left his ticket on the fridge, underneath a magnet that held a photo of them, taken in a photo booth when they first met. They kissed as the camera snapped a row of black and white pictures. She meant it as a peace offering. He stood beside his neighboring audience members, in full applause, but she could see the solemn expression on his face, even from the distance. "He's still mad at me," she whispered to Scott, while taking his hand. They took one final bow.

"Oooh, I would not want to be you tonight," Scott mumbled before they returned upright. They faced the audience. With sternums lifted, they smiled and then exited.

Once backstage, they gave each other a tight embrace. "It's so safe out there," Sophie said, her head against his collar bones, eyes on the stage.

Scott gave an extra squeeze.

Chloe scurried over. "I only have a few notes, but that was magical. I knew it would be." She hugged both of them. "Come guys, people are waiting in the lobby to see you."

Scott handed Sophie a glass of cheap champagne she wouldn't drink, kissed her cheek and went to greet a few board members who ogled them. This was not the part of performing that she enjoyed. The lobby was crowded with audience members chattering and critiquing the performance they just saw. People clamored to talk with her. "Thank you so much, I'm so glad you enjoyed the performance." If she said that one more time, Sophie thought she would burst. She imagined a fire escape and a first kiss. She longed to make up with John.

And where was he? And Hannah for that matter? She had left a ticket with the doorman of her building the night before. She scanned the reception area. Her gaze halted when it hit the bathroom line located below the staircase leading to the theater. Waiting on a notoriously long queue swayed a woman with a pile of orange curls, holding hands with a little girl, in a pink tulle skirt. It didn't matter if their backs were turned, Sophie would know Jane anywhere. A flash of the baby announcement that had turned up two years prior came to mind. It wasn't like the usual shot of just the baby, but a family portrait with Jane, her husband, Paul, and their delicate baby girl who weighed 7lbs 2oz. They named her after their mother. It shocked Sophie that Jane was the first Gold girl to have a child. Sophie watched mother and toddler taking small steps forward, Sarah hopping from foot to foot while chatting to herself. Sophie threw half the glass of bubbly down her throat and contemplated walking over. Her feet, no longer performing, stood leaden.

Sophie shook her head several times. Of course, Hannah would forfeit her ticket and tell Jane to come in her place.

John purred in her ear, "Look how cute our niece is. We could have a little ballerina too." He wrapped his arms around Sophie's waist and kissed her neck.

She alternated between wanting to slap him across the face and hug him as tightly as possible.

"Okay, you two," Chloe said, her timing impeccable. "You must be John. I've heard so much about you." She smiled while extending her hand to him. "It's time to get dressed for the gala. I have to steal her away."

"I'm coming," Sophie said. But before stepping away from John she turned toward the bathroom line. Jane and Sarah had disappeared through the door. "Can you make sure they wait for me? I'll be really quick."

He kissed her. It was the first one they had shared for weeks and it held all the unspoken words; I'm sorry, I love you, I forgive you.

When Sophie stepped into the dressing room it vibrated with activity. Everyone sipped from plastic cups while they stripped off their costumes and wiped off layers of make-up.

"I thought I was going to drop you on that last lift," Scott said, as he came up behind Sophie. "Your body was so slick." He paraded around in his red bikini thong.

"I know. I sweated like crazy tonight. This costume is so heavy." Scott helped her peel down the dress, so she could step out more easily, and hang it on the rack. "I think we nailed it though, right?" Sophie hated how doubt crept in so quickly. "Was Polinsky in the house?"

"I hope so, this was a night to review." Scott peered at her through the mirror, as Sophie began to pull off her false eye lashes. "We nailed it."

Sophie envied his bravado.

"Blah, blah, you two – it's time to party!" Martin, another performer, walked over swinging his costume, as he made his way toward the showers, naked. His piece was a Trocadero-esque comedy that turned midway into the darker realities of the gay underworld. He both choreographed and danced in it, with three other men. Their meticulous pointe work could easily match any female ballet dancer. Martin was notorious for his quick remarks and uncomfortable jabs, be it about his own sex life, jagged family relations or, his latest love, the scandal with Monica Lewinsky and President Clinton. He got a lot of mileage out of that one.

Sophie cleaned up rapidly, as promised, and headed out to the reception area to find her family.

"Where's Jane?" Sophie asked John, trying not to sound too enthusiastic. After her interlude with Hannah, she thought it might actually be nice to start something again with Jane. Maybe she could make-up for the mess of years behind her?

"She apologized for leaving, she really wanted to stay, but her daughter had a terrible tantrum. She said she'll call you tomorrow."

"Sarah was smaller than I imagined."

"You've thought about them?" John smirked.

"Maybe once or twice," she said and took his hand, walking him toward the stage door. She had missed him, the comfort of his palm against her own and the secure feeling he had been bringing her since they met.

"The bus is waiting, Soph. We have to get to the gala. What are you doing?"

She looked back at him and put her finger to her lips, admiring his starched white shirt and black blazer, and winked. They passed the crew who were in full force clean- up mode, moving lights and pulling wires. Sophie led him along a narrow path, behind the stage, where the dancers ran back and forth between movements. When they were midway, listening to the guys talking in front of them, she moved her body to the wall. John followed, a smile beginning to form. She had shared this fantasy with him, when they were first together. Resting her back along the concrete, she moved his body closer, lifted her cocktail dress with one hand, and unzipped his jeans with the other. "Soph, when you dance…" She wrapped her first leg around his waist and then hoisted herself up to add the next. Sophie looped her arms under his and around to hold his shoulders as he entered her. He in turn, grabbed her ass.She bit her bottom lip with more ferocity than

217

intended. He licked the drip of blood that emerged and tightened his grip.

**

Time was limited; it had been difficult to get out of the house. John buzzed around her like a bee to honey. He grabbed her for one last kiss and hug so many times she almost missed her window to visit her dad before her flight. She needed to make a detour before going to JFK Airport, to leave for her first tour with The Blank Slate. It had been months since Sophie had seen her father. As the taxi drove up in front and Sophie paid her fare, she rehearsed the multiple topics she wanted to discuss with him.

She put her head toward the partition and spoke to the driver. "Can you wait for fifteen minutes? I'll pay you double. Then straight to the airport?"

He shook his head in response, without turning. "Fifteen minutes, that's it ma-an," he said in a thick Caribbean accent.

"Great!" She grabbed her bag from the seat and fled around the side of the house. It was a mild September day. Her dad would surely be sitting in the garden on a chaise. The roses on path to the back reminded Sophie of young children, in assorted stages of growth. Some were completely open and others in various stages of bloom, each one vying for their place in the sun.

"When you were little, you always went that way, through the thorns," her dad pointed in her direction. "The other girls went to the other side, where the path is clear."

"I like the flowers, Dad." Sophie felt relieved that he was having a good day. Maybe if she told him she was getting married it would keep his spirits up.

"The thorns don't bite you?" he looked up at her from his seat, his eyes blinking several times in a row.

"They do," she said, kissing him hello and pulling over a chair. "I'm going to Cincinnati today."

"Don't forget your belt. Fasten your seat belt."

"I always do." Sophie had missed him. Even with his ticks and quirks, she still had him. "Dad, Hannah came to see me." She started slowly, unsure of the ground beneath.

"That's nice. I'm glad you girls are getting along now."

She was surprised by the clarity in his voice. "Was she here?" Sophie always waited for signs of recovery or normalcy from him, knowing he had become increasingly more agoraphobic since Jane had gone to college seven years ago.

"On the phone," his voice dimmed. He began pulling on his shorts.

She wanted to tell him about her engagement, but instead blurted out, "Why did Grandma and Grandpa split?"

"That's not true, Sarah. Focus on the road, my parents are fine." He stood up and looked at the house.

Crap, Sophie thought, she hadn't intended to rile him, but followed the trail. "I thought you were driving Dad," she tried to put her arm around him, but he squirmed away.

"I should have been driving, Sarah. I told you I was fine to drive." He began shouting at the house.

The taxi horn honked. She knew it had only been a few minutes since she got there, why was the driver pressing her already? "Dad?"

"You have to let this go, Sarah. My parents don't want a divorce."

She pulled in the scent of the roses. "It's okay, Dad. Everything is okay." It seemed ludicrous to Sophie to utter those words to a man who had been tortured for the last twenty years, but it was the phrase that she had been told so many times, by both her grandmother and herself. Did she really believe it?

"It's not okay, Sarah. Stop hounding me about my parents. It's like I'm supposed to give them permission to separate. How can I do that?" His voice trailed off, "How can I do that?" he ended quietly, appearing deflated.

"You don't have to do anything," Sophie heard another honk and wanted to scream from the pressure she felt and the discomfort her father's ranting caused.

"Eyes on the road! Eyes on the road." His voice escalated into a shout, like an unexpected boom of thunder.

Sophie longed to hold his hand or crawl into his arms. She wanted her father to tell her everything would be okay, that marriages work and people don't always die, and she could forgive her sisters. Unconditional love existed for real.

Her father punched his thighs repeatedly with clenched fists. "I'm not always like this."

"I know."

"NO – you don't," he yelled while looking directly at her.

"Dad?"

"I always get this way when you come here. Don't come here any more!" He turned away from her and walked up the stairs toward the back door, pulling on his hair.

Could he really mean that? She yearned for John's parents and visits that were unencumbered, as she made her way to the front of her childhood home, to a bare curb. Her nerves were frayed.

"Your taxi left," a familiar voice called.

Sophie turned to find Mrs. Long, watering her very dry lawn. "You're not supposed to water during the day, but what the hell." She had a full head of white hair, in a pixie. Sophie wondered if her mom would have let all her hair grow gray.

"But, I hadn't paid yet," Sophie noticed the multiple wrinkles along her forehead and around her eyes and mouth, finding them very striking. She was jealous that Mrs. Long was able to age while her mother was permanently fixed in time. She found difficult to conjure an image of her mother without pulling out old photographs.

"I took care of it, Sophie. Come, I'll give you a ride."

"I have to go to the airport, Mrs. Long." It had been many years since Sophie had seen her.

She hustled up the grass and pulled open the screen door, "I know sweetie, Chloe just called me from there. Let me grab my keys."

Sophie watched her place one foot against the wooden rim and lift off the keys. She remembered how they always laid on the hook, to the left. Would Mrs. Long and her mom have remained tight friends? Would her parents still be living in their house? John's parents already began migrating to Florida for the bitter months. Sophie missed them.

"Got 'em," she called and motioned for Sophie to come toward her car parked in the driveway.

Sophie smiled. "I really appreciate it." They opened their respective doors and popped in.

"He has some good days too, you know," she started the ignition, "and please call me Martha."

Sophie hesitated. Did she really want to have this conversation with Martha? "Does he?"

"Sometimes we sit in the garden together. I bring some tea or bake some muffins. We talk. Your dad's been a great friend to me this past year, since Mr. Long's death." She sighed, "But, mostly we like to chat about our girls, you four of course, and my Chloe."

"She's incredibly talented. I'm thrilled we're working together."

"She is, isn't she?" Her wide smile lifted her cheeks.

"Sorry to have missed you at the performance, I had to dash out that night."

"Not to worry. Your dance was flawless. I read a beautiful review in the *Times* about you this past weekend." She turned toward Sophie for just a moment and then looked back at the road, driving steady with the speed limit.

Sophie watched the younger drivers whizz by. As usual, she would not read the review. She never did. And she always declined interviews, like this time.

"Sasha Polinsky is a tough reviewer. I've been reading her for years," Martha continued.

Two more exits, Sophie thought. "Well, I have a really special partner, Scott. And then there's your daughter -" Sophie veered around the compliment.

"Chloe pushed to get the review – you know her ambition. She's determined to be the next Pina Bausch." Martha cut her off. "There was one line that I really loved. What was it? Hmm… Oh yes, 'Sophie Gold demonstrates emotions that usually take a lifetime to inhabit.'"

Sophie blushed. She never knew how to receive a compliment.

They looked at one another for a brief moment.

"I've embarrassed you. I'm so sorry."

"No." Sophie paused, "I just haven't read it yet."

"Really?"

"It's in my bag, but I don't like to look before I finish a tour. It throws me off." She pointed toward the exit for the airport. "We're here," she said, sighing.

"Well, that was quick." Martha put her signal on to exit. "How's your little niece?"

"I don't know, Martha, we've never met," Sophie admitted, feeling ashamed.

"O,"

She stammered, "I travel a lot." She began to nibble on the cuticles of her right thumb. "Has she been to my dad's?" Sophie knew her sister and niece spent time there. They only lived ten minutes from each other. And she spied a pail and shovel splayed on the back lawn with familiarity.

"Jane brings her often. Your Dad lights up when they come. He calls her little S." Martha's hands, no longer chubby, but still bronze from the summer sun, held the steering wheel at two and ten. She dove into a spot smack in the center of departures. She turned toward Sophie, "Well, dear…"

"What happened that night?" For twenty years, Sophie had created scenarios about the night of her parents' accident. Her dad's periodic rants helped her put some pieces together, but she was still never sure what was real and what was imaginary.

Martha put on her hazards and sat back against her seat. "Your Dad I and have become close friends. We talk a lot, but I think this is for him to discuss with you."

"Please, Martha. I don't' think my dad is capable."

"That may be true. I'm sorry, dear."

Sophie registered Martha's apologetic smile. She felt an impulse to jump from the car. She placed her hand on the door handle but didn't move.

"I know this is none of my business, Sophie, but what you girls are waiting for? You could have each other. You each sneak visits with your dad, and maybe…"

"I wish it were that simple," Sophie pushed down on the metal handle. "Thank you for the ride."

"It is that simple," Martha grabbed her arm and pulled Sophie into a hug. Sophie could feel the warmth of her body, the same permeating affection from when she was eight. "You're a lot like her, Sophie. She would be so proud of you."

Sophie smiled, but her eyes frowned. "I don't even remember her any more." She returned the hug and exited the car.

As she maneuvered through the airport, pulling her single bag, she fought the urge to cry, feeling the tingling of tears right below her skin: Tears of exasperation at another missed opportunity to understand anything.

Tears of anger at her father for leaving them all and choosing to disappear in his grief.

Tears of regret for never forgiving her mother for leaving her.

CHAPTER SIXTEEN

"Hurry, Sophie. They already called for final boarding." Chloe stood at the gate, tapping her ticket against the counter faster than the fluttering wings of a honeybee. "Everyone else is on the plane. Where have you been?" Her other hand clasped the handle of her bright red-roll on bag with clenched fingers.

Sophie bounded toward Chloe and the airline man waiting beside the check- in. He tore her ticket and gave them a syrupy smile. "In thirty seconds, we would have closed the gate. You just made it. Enjoy your flight ladies." Sophie wished she could puncture his protruding chest.

"You have a very pleasant day, sir," Chloe mirrored his face and sarcastic intonation. She turned to Sophie. "What the hell happened to you? You're usually here an hour before all of us." Not waiting for an answer, she raced down the corridor toward the door of the plane in her red converse sneakers. Sophie didn't attempt to catch-up. That would just ignite further interrogation. She moved at an even pace, relishing a few moments in solitude.

As she trekked down the aisle of the plane, to the last row, her bag bumped random arms and legs sticking out. She barely noticed. Her mind kept replaying the conversations she had with her father and Martha. Every relationship in her life perplexed her.

The twelve company members on the tour of The Blank Company were scattered around the back of the plane. As she passed the 30th row, Scott directed his gaze at her from his window seat. "Honey, you really need to read this review." Sophie registered a look on his face that she hadn't seen before, a mixture of pride sprinkled with pity.

"Okay," she replied meekly, knowing she wouldn't.

Once nestled into her seat, Sophie let out an enormous yawn and closed her eyes. She felt like she had already been travelling for days.

Thirty minutes later, she woke to the voice of a female flight attendant. "Due to a small pocket of turbulence, the captain has put on the seatbelt sign, please return to your seats."

Sophie startled, not realizing that she had fallen asleep before the plane had taken off. Normally she buckled up for the flight with CD player on and reviewed choreography. The player sat on her lap, the ear phones and wires laced around her legs and dangled at her feet. Her dozing had been like a restless night sleep, as she puzzled the little she knew about her family past and present: Her parents had barely fought when her mom was alive, but after she died, her dad often screamed at her. She and her sisters had spent years being mad at each other for the same thing apparently, and her grandparents who made it through fifty years of marriage were now separated. Relationships made no sense. People always said things they didn't really mean, masking their true feelings behind lies and partial truths. At least she had movement. And movement was pure.

There was a chill in the cabin air. Sophie reached below her seat and dug through her bag for the sweatshirt sitting at the bottom. She thought about what Martha had said about her sisters. Was she right? Severing her ties over ten years hadn't dampened the ache inside; in fact, it had worsened.

As the plane began to bump around, cries erupted across the aisle where a mom sat, traveling alone with her two children. She stroked the hair and face of her shrieking daughter, who Sophie assumed was around three years old. Her delicate little fingers cupped her ears and mucus streamed down from her nose and onto her top lip. Her older sister sat on the other side, sleeping through it all. Sophie didn't mind the crying. She felt the urge to pick up the girl and cradle her. She thought about Jane. She would call her when she got home from the tour and arrange a visit. Maybe she and Jane could find a connection through Sarah. Sophie looked across the aisle. The mom, despite the call to stay in seats, had taken her daughter onto her lap and rocked her, singing in her ear, in a whisper. Sophie wished she could hear the song. The girl kept crying and her mom kept singing.

Sophie continued to watch, doubtful that she could provide enough of anything for another person. She could barely sustain herself. And how could she keep dancing with kids at home?

The little girl's hand drooped and landed on her mom's arm. Her hair was matted to her head and the woman began to push back each strand.

There was a *bing* and the seat belt sign turned off. The voice returned, "You are free to move about the cabin."

Sophie placed her headphones on, ready to review the piece she would be performing. She clicked play. Instead of visualizing the start position, Jane appeared as vividly as if she were standing in the aisle, hands on hips like she always did as a kid. "Told you! Told you they hated each other," taunting her even in the sky. Maybe she had always been right about their grandparents.

"Sophie,"

She felt a nudge on her shoulder.

"I'm so sorry," Martin said, both hands on his narrow hips.

Sophie opened her eyes, "Oh my God, is the review that bad?" This was why she never read them. They were subjective. The thought of someone sizing her up for the world to read made her feel sick and doubtful. It had to be vile if Martin wasn't dissecting it into a fun fest.

"No, girl – it is out of this world," his arms waved around him, "You should read it this instant." The serious tone coming from Martin worried Sophie. "I meant about your family. You poor thing! I never knew," he looked distraught as he leaned down and kissed the top of her head.

"My family?" Sophie turned from Martin to Sonia, another company member who sat a row in front of her. They both held the same sad and apologetic smile.

"Excuse me." Sophie unbuckled her seatbelt and walked toward Chloe on the other side of the plane. She rounded the bathrooms and bent over her friend, "What are they talking about?"

Chloe pulled off her left earplug. "This is the funniest movie, are you watching?"

"Why is everyone looking at me strangely? What did that review say?"

Chloe moved over to the window and motioned to Sophie, "Sit down beside me, honey."

"What did Polinsky say?" she asked, not really wanting the answer.

"The truth." Chloe grabbed Sophie's hand. "Read the review. It's beautiful and honest."

With great reservation, Sophie returned to her seat, registering little peeks toward her from each member of her company, except Jennifer, who always took a valium before flying. She was dead to the world for the next four hours.

Some of the most passionate artists I have ever encountered in my thirty years as a critic have lived through some version of profound loss. Sophie Gold is no exception.

Sophie's hands shook as she held the paper. While she always refrained from reading them, John would cut them out and hand them to her each time. Sophie graciously received them, but immediately placed them in an envelope, folded over many times, and put them in her purse. She had a zip lock bag that held them all.

A tragic accident when she was a mere eight years of age took the life of her mother, and subsequently propelled her father into severe PTSD. Perhaps this explains the constant urgency in her movement and the ability to stay in full command of her audience at all times.

Sophie pushed up the shade of her window. The clouds were robust and pressed against one another. She felt like a mouse whose leg was stuck in a trap. She wanted to gnaw it off and run. Sophie ripped off her buckle again and stormed over to Chloe. "You told her about me! And now every fucking person on this plane knows that I've been motherless since I'm eight and that my dad is a freak." She couldn't contain her voice as it bellowed through the cabin.

"Honey, do you really think no one knew anything about you?" Chloe moved over again. "You're the only one who never goes home to their family for the holidays or talks about them. Hell, you barely talk about

John." Chloe took a sip of her coke. "Go back to your seat, finish the article. You'll be pleased."

In the backdrop of the present day modern-dance scene, where text and video often give the audience a vehicle to get inside the story of the choreographer, the setting is bare bones.

The mood is set by the haunting cry of Bernard Smith's cello as it begins, Elgar's Cello Concerto in E Minor. Sophie Gold and Scott Matthews begin what swells immediately into a lover's battle. Their bodies push and collide in almost darkness, after they emerge out of a soft pink light that encircles them at the start of their journey together. The piece, "Flight", is a fifteen-minute interlude as these two stage lovers capture the give and take of life's most intimate of relationships. Ms. Gold taunts him, encourages him, invites him in to her body, then envelopes him with her slight ballerina frame.

I've been an admirer of Ms. Gold since 1990, when she made her NY debut with Boston Modern. While still honing her craft back then, she already knew how to use more than just her incredible flexibility to pull an audience in to the experience on stage. She draws you into her web and holds you from start to finish. She can permeate longing and detachment, she can mold her body with the pliability of clay, she can move from languid to staccato in a moment's breath. There are no blemishes in her craft.

When the cello intermittently halts, at what could be called inopportune moments, even the sound of Ms. Gold's breath has a purpose and creates a growing and frantic need for her lover on the opposite side of the stage. She scrambles to reclaim Mr. Matthews in darkness, but we can see her body slide and caress the floor rapidly to reach her prey. And while she repeats the same sequence moving toward him, each time Ms. Gold finds a nuance and expression to change to the experience for her audience members.

What I find most exciting to watch is that she moves as though her skin were transparent.

Unable to read further, Sophie pushed the call button for the flight attendant and ordered a beer. She ached for a cigarette. Chloe appeared at her side a moment later. "You can't drink that, you know we have tech rehearsal at seven tonight," she reached for the plastic cup.

"Don't take it." She leaned her head onto Chloe's shoulder. "I feel like a child who just found out the tooth fairy and Santa are adult fabrications." Sophie lowered her voice for the last part, not wanting to spoil anything for the kids beside her.

"I don't understand."

"The magic is gone." Sophie took a sip of her beer and spit it back out, hating the bitterness. "Why does John drink this stuff?"

"You just got a beautiful review, no − spotlight, and now your magic is gone? That doesn't make any sense."

"You never get it. You grew up in a neat little package with your mom and dad doting on you."

"Nobody's family is a neat package with a bow. At some point you're going to have to move on and realize how much you do have, not just the deficit."

The older little girl across the way woke up and watched them. "Are you dancers?" she asked with a grin. "I saw the *Nutcracker* this year with my mommy and daddy."

"We are. Did you like it?" Chloe inquired.

Her mom smiled as well. "She's a big fan. Sorry to interrupt."

Turning away from the children, Sophie spat, "She called me vulnerable."

"That's not negative, Sophie," Chloe answered. "No problem," she said in the other direction.

Sophie zipped up her sweatshirt and put her hood on. "Yes, it is."

"How do you think the white swan would be to watch if she wasn't vulnerable?"

"That's different. This isn't ballet."

Chloe crossed her arms. "You can't be for real."

"She called me transparent." Sophie tried another attempt at the beer, worried she wouldn't make it through the flight without a cigarette soon.

"She implied that you reveal yourself and that makes you more interesting to watch," Chloe replied, agitated.

"Don't get mad at me, you did this," Sophie snarled.

"Sasha Polinsky is the most acclaimed dance critic. She adores you. What is your problem?"

The plane lurched and the bell went back on, signaling everyone back to their seats to buckle up. "Everyone knows my business now. How dense can you be?" Sophie couldn't contain the sharpness in her voice.

"I wish I could get away from you right now, but I'm stuck here, so I'm gonna let you have it." Chloe turned to Sophie, who did not reciprocate. "You have an opportunity here. You can perceive this as another miserable disappointment or you can realize that you are at the top of your game, with a hunk of a guy beside you." Chloe took the beer out of Sophie's hand and gulped down half of it. "You have been pushing since we were kids to get everything you want and before anyone else, playing as if you were a lost and wounded animal."

Aside from John, Chloe had been her most intimate relationship and still she couldn't explain… her life as a dancer was all she trusted. It had been the only safe place since she was eight. What began as an outlet for loss quickly morphed into her greatest asset. And Polinsky exposed the irony of her life. Her loss was her gold.

Sophie watched Chloe finish the beer through her periphery. She rummaged through her bag on the floor, while her seatbelt cut into her belly, and found a cigarette. If she couldn't smoke it, she would at least hold it.

"I'm sick of it. I gave you this gig because you're an amazing dancer, the best I've ever known, and you're spitting in my face right now."

"This isn't about you, Chloe. You always make things about you; your company, your boyfriends, your choreography. I don't want to talk to you any more. I need some rest before we land." Sophie had no intention of sleeping, but this was always the part of an argument where she gagged. If she went any further, she risked spilling from the river that was kept dammed.

With eyes closed, she moved her rage from Chloe to John. If she had purchased one of those big clunky cell phones like he had suggested, she could call him as soon as she landed. He read the review. He should have warned her about this one. Were the other reviews about her the same? Her mind began to play tricks on her, she would see herself taking a bow and then the audience turned into clowns, with wide open exaggerated red mouths laughing, while pointing at her on stage. And then they morphed into adults with sour faces shaking their heads, as if to say "'poor thing'" or "'that poor girl lost her mother'" or "'oh she was so young − did you hear about her father'", the list of possibilities was endless. This was exactly what Sophie wanted to protect − this was why she loved the stage, until now. Now it was spoiled. Now it was ruined. How could John not have protected her?

Finally, the plane bumped along the runway as it landed and came to a halt. At the gate, Sophie watched as Chloe obtained her luggage from the overhead bin, quickly fled down the aisle, and exited. Sophie waited till the plane was completely empty, then rose, tossed her bag over her shoulder, and sauntered toward the exit. She stopped at the bathroom, pushed open the accordion door with her hip and pulled out the bag with all her reviews. She tossed it in the trash.

CHAPTER SEVENTEEN

Immune to the residue of dirt and urine, Sophie sat on the bathroom floor of Chicago's Dulles airport. She didn't care that the line for the women's room extended out the door. It didn't matter that the rest of the dancers boarded a bus to the Marriot Hotel and would be wondering what had happened to her. She burst like a rain cloud that had been threatening for days. Tears and mucous seemed to be competing down her face and along her chin. She didn't wipe any of it away. She wanted to feel the mess of it. Everything was ruined.

After her parents' car accident, Sophie tried to integrate with the other kids in her neighborhood and at school, going through the motions of riding her bike, playing jump rope, and hanging from the monkey bars. While other kids giggled with genuine delight, immune to how loss gnaws on your insides, Sophie struggled. She lost her scaffolding and without it she was always vulnerable, like walking around with an open cut.

She buried that wound in her body: the arch of her foot, the lift of her chest, the carriage of her shoulders. Every major and minor moment in her childhood was poured into her career. When she lost a tooth and no one noticed she could grand jette her feelings out. When all the other kids in her class had their parents at the school play and she had to be satisfied with sisters and grandparents, she nailed a triple pirouette. When all her sisters played hide and seek and they told her to get lost, she took an extra ballet class and perfected her extension. Her dance world was silent and allowed all the inner turmoil to be morphed into physicality. She was in charge of her body, her precision, her creativity, her power. Sasha Polinsky exposed the pearl in her oyster.

Sophie placed her head on her bent knees. Her belly ached from the coughing that followed the tears. She nearly choked a few times. Her nose was so clogged her breath became labored. Every time it seemed the stream stopped, another round of crying began. The stoic stance she manifested over the years cracked wide open.

Periodically, a woman in the stall beside her would knock quietly and inquire if she was okay or needed anything. Sophie said 'fine', each time, clearly an absurd response. It took a couple of hours before she stood. Her legs wobbled like a newborn foe straining with the weight of its body for the first time. With shoulders slumped, Sophie drifted over to the nearest ticket counter with a coke in hand.

"And where will you be travelling today?" A young woman, whose name tag read Marcie, asked.

Sophie zipped her sweatshirt to the top and pulled the hood on, embarrassed by her red, swollen face, "Boston," she blurted.

240

She took the soonest flight possible, which was delayed twice due to lightning, then made her way to the water taxi. The fresh air and the spray of water on her face, which she usually loved on her trips to Boston, felt like miniscule daggers. Sophie sat wedged between business men and women. She assumed they were traveling home to their families, and that depressed her even more. They had a purpose. She had no plan.

As soon as the water taxi docked, she nearly ran the entire way to George and Beverly's.

For four nights, she laid in John's childhood bedroom with insomnia. The only remnants of him were in the single closet, where small pencil marks indicated his measurements, starting at the age of five and ceasing at the age of eighteen when he left for college. Aside from that, Beverly had taken the opportunity to create a modern guest room, where her sons could come and visit.

Their house felt more like home than her house in Queens had for most of her life. Bev cultivated an atmosphere Sophie liked to imagine her mother would have done as well. Sometimes the aroma of Bev's cooking permeated the rooms and infused her senses with a sensory memory she couldn't quite grasp. She pretended her mom had cooked instead of Bev, who made herself available and included Sophie in everything, handing her a spatula to assist in the kitchen, placing napkins in her hand to help set the table… all while chatting about the day or future plans. She always asked Sophie her opinion about politics which Sophie barely followed, art they went to together, earrings to match her outfit. In her childhood home, they had fended for themselves. The tension thick, waiting for an episode from her father or a late night argument between her grandparents when they thought all the kids were sleeping.

The first time Sophie was a guest in the Reed home, John described his old room. It had powder blue walls to match his eyes. The theme was baseball; sheets, pillowcases, and stick-on molding with bats and balls surrounded the baseboards. He had two stuffed animals, both dogs, that he kept wrapped in a red and white striped blanket that sat by his pillow. The shelves were covered with books, comics, classics, sports, and the latest novels. He read each night until George came in and forced him to shut off his bedside lamp. It was all so Norman Rockwell, and Sophie was instantly envious from the description.

When the phone rang on Monday at eight a.m. her fifth day holed up, Sophie knew it was John. He called every morning before walking over to campus for his first class.

"Are you coming home soon, Sophie?" His voice sounded like a bad cocktail, a mixture of melancholy and resentment.

"My ankle's really a mess. Maybe in a week?" Sophie stared at her un-injured feet, propped on pillows. Everything had changed in the course of a few days.

There was a knock on the door. Bev sauntered in with a coffee in hand, just like she had every morning since her arrival. She loved the consistency of Bev − it explained John. All she needed was Bev and George right now, doting on her.

She had read an article recently in the *Times* that described how loss can lie dormant in one's body until a person is ready to face the emotions attached. Was that happening to her? Had she not properly grieved for her mom? Was she in crisis? She had certainly never felt this unable to cope, like her body was caught in an undertow.

"Your mom's at the door, can I call you later?"

"Will you?" John hung up before she could answer.

She placed the phone on the bed beside her, "John's on his way to class."

"Good morning honey, do you want me give a ring to the doctor today? It might be good for someone to check out your ankle so you can meet your tour, right?" Bev had on a pair of white knee length linen shorts and scoop neck cotton T-shirt. She wore brown leather sandals that exposed her red toe nail polish. And as always, she had on a gold chain-link necklace with one round diamond at the end, the size of a pea.

"I just need a couple more days of rest." Sophie pushed herself up to sit and rearranged her gauze wrapped ankle on the pillows. She always carried her own first-aid kit on tours, plenty of band aids, Neosporin, arnica, gauze, and lots of tape to wrap her feet. "Chloe's dancing my part and I'm sure it's really great with her and…"

"Okay, you rest then. I brought you some trashy magazines and a new novel John recommended." She sat down at the end of the bed. "Maybe later we can hop you out to the car and go for lunch? It's a beautiful day and Boston Common is having a concert."

"That sounds great," but Sophie knew she would not leave the confines of her room yet. It had been days already, and she was too settled in her down comforter and soft Egyptian cotton sheets. The windows let in a constant breeze, coupled with the matte chrome ceiling fan. She couldn't remember a time when she had been away from dancing this long and yet her body was in utter fatigue.

Bev handed Sophie a copy of *People* magazine, *Us*, and *Modern Bride*. "There's a beautiful dress on page ten – it would look gorgeous on you."

Sophie thought Bev was a natural beauty. She had barely changed since the pictures Sophie saw all over the house. They had the staircase photos that Sophie had only seen in movies. Each step or two held family portraits throughout the years, and even though Bev was now close to sixty, she carried the same vibrant look throughout her decades.

"How long have you and George been married?" Sophie thought of the black and white mantel photo of their wedding. Bev had an enormous smile, as she held George by the waist and her head tilted against his. She had a form fitted dress with long sleeves and a heart-shaped bodice. And Sophie's favorite touch, long white gloves that covered her arms up to her elbows.

"Oh honey, we got married when we were babies. I was twenty and he was twenty-one. Things were different then." Bev shook her head.

"Do you wish you had done it differently?" Sophie stared at Bev, as if she held all the answers she needed.

"Some years, honey, but not overall." She patted Sophie's unwrapped foot. "Are you having cold feet?"

"No." She lied. Nothing about her identity felt authentic now. She didn't know what she wanted or who she was, just that she couldn't go back to anything that existed before.

"The day George and I got married, I remember wondering if I could go the rest of my life without ever kissing another boy, but I zipped up my white satin dress and pulled down my veil and thought, 'Beverly Ann – everything is changeable. Just do it.' Who knew that would become a Nike slogan?"

"I love those ads." Sophie imagined running along a California road, with the valley below her, striding in her white Nike's. But that image quickly turned to her running into Hannah, and she had to blink, like she had a bug on the windshield and needed to wipe it away.

"OK! See you later, rest well. I'll bring you a tray of breakfast before I go."

"Thank you for everything."

"It's nothing." Bev blew Sophie a kiss and left the room, almost closing the door behind her. She poked her head back in. "By the way, I asked John to come home Friday night after his classes. I'm sure you're dying to see each other."

Her heart did a gallop in response. Was she ready to face him? She flipped through the pages of *Modern Bride* hoping to ease her anxiety. But every woman shimmered in white with a gigantic smile that was as sparkly as their dresses and accoutrement. She tossed it on the floor.

The day her mom died she had encouraged Sophie to mend the fence with her sisters and not give up on the potential of their relationship. Would her mom be encouraging her right now to push ahead, or like Bev, creating a haven to lick her wounds before her next move?

She turned toward the tulips on the dresser.

Bev re-entered the room. "You know what I love about those pink beauties?"

Sophie gave an encouraging smile.

"They take the shape of the vase they're in. They can stand up right for the duration of their lives, or fold and sway as they accommodate their environment." She handed Sophie a tray with fruit and a croissant, then kissed the top of her head. "George is playing golf with friends, so the house is all yours, dear. Maybe sit in the garden for a bit with your book. The sun will feel good on your face." Bev moved toward the door.

"I think I will." Did she deserve this kindness from Bev?

With a half turn, Bev said, "When John was a little boy, he met his best friend, Christopher. For years they played all the games Chris chose; marbles, basketball, chess. It didn't matter to him if John liked them, he didn't even ask. I encouraged John to tell Chris how he felt. I explained that friends listen to each other and care about one another's feelings."

"Did he do it?" Sophie took the bait.

"It took John till the age of twelve to finally request what he wanted, a baseball game in our backyard. He had planned out all the bases and had two mitts ready."

"And?" Sophie scooted higher on the bed.

"Chris said no. He didn't like baseball."

Sophie sat soberly.

"I love you dearly, but John is my son."

The sound of a ringing phone startled Sophie from her late-morning nap. When it didn't let up, she reached an arm out of the comforter, "Hello, this is the Reed residence," Sophie spoke in her most polite and measured voice.

"What the fuck were you thinking? Do you think you can just run away because some person exposed your big life secret? You are such an incredible child. Ankle my ass, get yourself back on a plane and meet us in Washington tomorrow." No one but Chloe would be so brazen. "You got your respite, now grow up, you have a responsibility to all of us."

"No!" Sophie said, with more conviction than she had rehearsed. She had been waiting for this call.

"We've been friends for more than twenty years. You cannot do this, not just because I will come there and drag you out of your bed, but because you can't walk away from this."

"No!"

Anticipating the call from Chloe, she practiced her one word answer for days, imagining herself on the witness stand. She would not incriminate herself. But years of friendship got the best of her. "Chloe, I love you and your work is amazing. I can even understand why you gave that interview," Sophie's voice trailed off, "I wish you could understand me. I guess I don't fully either. I'm not coming back."

Sophie hung up.

She went to the garden and sat on a lounge chair. The pool glistened with the sun overhead, burning like a hot August day in New York, even though it was mid-September. Sophie peeled off her cardigan sweater and then un-wrapped her ankle. The water called to her. She dipped her toes in and splashed droplets along the hot pavement before diving in. Once submerged, arms and legs pressing her along the bottom, the silence underwater pulled her back to a night months after her mother's funeral. Late one evening, Amy crawled in bed beside her. Sophie pretended to be asleep. Amy reached an arm across Sophie's side and whispered in her ear, "I'm sorry, I want to be your friend, but I have to stick with Hannah. We're gonna be okay, you'll see. Dad won't let anything happen to us." She placed a peck on Sophie's cheek and snuck back out of the room. Once she was gone, Sophie cried and smiled simultaneously. The interaction was so fleeting that by the next morning it was as if she had dreamed the whole thing. As usual, Amy was glued to Hannah's side, being terrible. What if Sophie was complicit? Had she ever tried to make amends? Could she forgive?

Sophie continued to ponder this as she wandered around Bev and George's house late that night, unable to sleep. Her fingers drifted along the walls, feeling the texture of wallpaper on her skin. Is this how her dad spent his life, aimlessly repeating the minutia in his head, the way she was in hers? She replayed arguments between her and John about marriage, kids, and her traveling. She flashed images of Jane and Hannah. She saw every word written about her as if she had clipped out the newspaper article and scattered it in her mind. It all taunted her. Would someone else be feeling on top of their game? Why couldn't she? Everything swirled around her as if she sat on a merry-go-round looking out.

She imagined John racing around Columbia teaching classes, writing in the library, and marking papers at home on the couch, always so content.

When the old grandfather clock on the upstairs landing struck eight each evening, Sophie saw the curtain go up in all the cities the tour would hit; Chicago, Santa Fe, San Francisco, and Seattle.

Then there were her sisters. She and Hannah had an opportunity to repair their relationship, but she blew it. Jane and her little girl were just a hand's reach away and she let them slip through her fingers. And what about Amy? Had Hannah exaggerated or was Amy really struggling with addiction?

Sophie stepped into the den in a haze of thoughts.

"Want a drink?" John sat on a deep brown leather couch. He held a thick glass filled with scotch. Sophie startled when she heard his voice in the dark room. Her heart started thumping. Was it already Friday? John switched on a dim light which sat on a large mahogany desk. No, only Wednesday.

"What are you doing here?"

It was almost one o'clock in the morning and Sophie had been had padded down the wooden stairs in a terrycloth robe, covering her pink cotton pajamas, trying to decide if she wanted tea or a glass of milk.

"Ankle's looking good," he said bitterly.

"It feels better," Sophie replied sheepishly.

John stirred the ice in his glass with his finger and then took a long slow sip. "Were you planning on telling me?"

Sophie sat down on the leather love seat across from John and pulled the tie of her robe tighter around her waist, twisting the ends between her fingers.

"We're done Sophie. We can't pretend any more that we are enough for each other," he shook his head.

"John -"

"NO – just let me finish. That mysterious, beautiful woman I met is gone. I'm tired of this. You don't want to marry me, you never have. I've been blind for the last ten years."

"That's not true, John."

"When you go on tour Sophie, do you miss me? Do you think about me or us during the course of your day?"

Sophie's hands trembled at the question. Their first years together she couldn't get enough of him, she thought about him incessantly; when they were apart as well as when they were right beside each other. She would think about what he said, how he said it, the expression on his face, the smell of his aftershave, the feel of his hands. She had forgotten that yearning that dwelled deep inside. When did that stop? When was it replaced with taking him for granted and being resentful of his needs?

"Of course, I do," she said after several minutes.

"Our crazy desire for each other can't sustain this relationship any more. We're not kids and I don't want to fix you or change you. It's not fair to either of us. You need to leave this house. You have a family, Sophie. This one is mine."

"It's one in the morning."

"Call a cab, stay in a hotel. I don't care, but you're not welcome here any more."

The resolve in John's face terrified Sophie. He emoted only detachment. Not at all the John she knew. When she stood, her legs almost buckled under her, the rush of blood draining from her head. She steadied herself by holding the arm of the couch.

She headed out of the room knowing she deserved his subdued wrath, that it must have cost him greatly to stand up to her like that. He deserved something she would never give him. When her foot hit the first step, she turned and trekked back to John.

"Remember the night I came home after the performance at Boston Theater and I had fallen on stage?"

John sat stoic.

"You knew there were no words to alleviate how I felt, so you drew me a bath with exactly one cup of Epson salt and gave me a mug of peppermint tea." She twisted off her engagement ring and placed it in his hand, which she held tightly. "I've never been able to reciprocate." She kissed his mouth for the last time. "I'm sorry."

The door closed quietly behind her. The street was disturbingly dark and empty. When the taxi drove off bringing her once again to the airport, Sophie didn't know where she was headed that night, at two a.m. with just one suitcase in hand.

CHAPTER EIGHTEEN

2008

The phone call came Friday morning, just as Sophie had stepped out her front door with a steaming mug of black coffee and a newly lit cigarette in hand; same thing she did each day since she moved in. It was a perfect Pasadena day with a slight chill in the morning air that would soon dissipate from the warmth of the sun. Sitting on the front steps gave her time to meditate on what lay ahead of her. She began this ritual when her sister, Amy, moved in only a month after Sophie arrived in L.A., shaken from her called-off engagement to John and the decision to truncate her dance career. She was emotionally strung out – Amy was literally strung out on the cocktail of drugs she consumed.

Her rash decision to go west fulfilled the criteria of being as far from the East Coast as possible. Putting three thousand miles between her past and present life satisfied her. Sophie had always been curious about where Hannah and Amy had lived, having seen photos of gorgeous mountains and perfect beaches with surfers in colorful suits. Ten years later she considered herself a California girl with just a hint of New Yorker lying dormant. The mountains called to her each morning. She replaced dance wear for good hiking boots, she tossed away her bobby pins, and leotards and invested in shorts; linens, cotton, and her favorite lycra active wear. She plunged into the lifestyle immediately. The sun seemed to absorb her pain slowly over the days, weeks, months… years.

"Soph?"

"Jane? I was going to call you on my way to Whole Foods in a few hours." She perused the outside of her home, admiring the Lemonade Berry shrubs she had planted. The name had attracted her when the florist suggested them, but she ended up admiring the rose-pink flowers seated in the middle of beautiful deep green leathery leaves most.

"Did you get the call?"

Maybe she should add a couple more next spring she thought, while taking a drag. "No. What's going on?" Sophie noted a hint of distress in Jane's voice.

"Grandpa died last night." Jane's speech was labored, with a crack between words. "I cried all night. I had to sleep in the den so I wouldn't wake Paul."

Sophie could hear her blowing her nose. "Of course, you couldn't sleep. What happened?" She lay back on her lawn, feeling the tickle and pricks of the blades, tears hitting the surface, trying to conjure the image of her grandfather in his bed. Instead, she saw Jane and her grandfather sitting on the porch together, at Jane's house, during her last visit to Queens. They were on the swing, holding hands, as close as ever. With a deep sigh, she pressed her eyes together and blotted the moisture on her cheeks with the back of her hands. She regretted not calling him the previous week as she had intended.

"Sarah, I'm on the phone – just give me a minute. Sorry Sophie, she's hounding me to go shopping." There was a pause. "I'm telling you, twelve is the age of narcissism – it doesn't matter what else is going on as long as Sarah's needs are met," Jane said. "She's like a glue stick, following me room to room with her desires and complaints."

Sophie knew that even though Jane often complained about Sarah, she was Jane's greatest love. "I don't know any other details yet. Hannah called me, so I called you. Can you come out today? Grandma wants to bury him this weekend." Jane muttered, "Sarah, give me a few minutes...I can't take her hounding me, not today."

Sophie liked to picture Jane as they spoke each Friday, their sister date, her flaming orange hair, now tamed by a straight iron, shaking her head at Sarah in warning. "I'll see what I can do. How's Grandma?"

"Shaken – sorry Sophie, I have to go. Text me, I'll be at rehearsal with Sarah after we shop. She got a solo in the workshop performances coming up. You know how much she wants you there, right?"

"I really want to come too." Sophie was so proud of her niece. They bonded over the phone, spending endless hours discussing every bit of ballet minutia since Sarah became a student at The School of American Ballet.

"Should we tell Amy?" Jane said.

"I'll try. She hasn't called me for weeks since we talked about her going back to rehab."

"Me either. Why doesn't this ever feel better?"

"Because we keep waiting for a different outcome. She told me she works at a café now. Seems farfetched to me, but I'll go over there and see."

"Good luck. Text me with your flight info and one of us will come to the airport, okay?"

"Yep," Sophie responded, more to herself, knowing that Jane had already pressed end. Their lives were as disparate as two could be. Jane became a mom at twenty-three and hadn't worked a day outside the home. She doted on her husband and daughter. The sassiest of the Gold bunch had become the most domesticated, replicating the old black and white episodes of *Leave it to Beaver*.

And there Sophie was, sitting in the California sun, perpetually single, petting her two German shepherds, as they wagged their tails upon exiting the front door.

"Come here guys," she wrapped her arms around them and they licked the tears that fell as she blinked. She wished she had seen her grandfather during her summer visit, but he had been in Italy. He seemed so healthy still, a spritely ninety-year-old engaged in his business and still traveling a couple of times a year.

She stubbed out her smoke on the cement step and uncoiled the hose to water her lawn. There were a few things to take care of before heading to New York. Just as she placed the sprinkler strategically to hit not only the grass, but shrubs and flowers too, her neighbor came out with her three-month-old baby in hand.

"Morning."

Their houses were a couple of feet apart from one another, Sophie's yellow bungalow beside their white one. In the driveway between was Sophie's used Mazda Miata.

With the sleeve of her sweatshirt, she wiped her nose and eyes quickly then turned. "Hi Lucy, how did Valentina sleep last night?" Sophie found this baby thing intriguing – the long sleepless nights, the forever feeding. All the mothers she knew grumbled with exhaustion, but their tenderness and attachment appealed to Sophie. The way Lucy stroked her baby's feet without a thought, or kissed the top of her head while talking about her level of fatigue and lack of adult stimulation.

"I got four full hours in a row. What was I thinking, having a baby by myself?"

Sophie walked over and looked into Lucy's arms. Valentina's tiny lips cooed while her large brown eyes stared up at the pale blue sky. "She's so beautiful. Can I hold her?"

"Please!"

Sophie swayed side to side, staring into the baby's face. "It's magical." She needed the hit of a baby's oxytocin before trying to get a hold of Amy and flying out to her family.

"I saw your commercial again yesterday. I counted ten times while I watched Boston Legal," Lucy said.

Sophie blushed. It was her second national commercial. It was never her intention to go into acting, but when she first moved to California, she met Amy at all her auditions. At the time, it seemed to give Amy a boost in confidence to have her there. The last audition Amy ever went to, she arrived completely wasted, nodding off to sleep, after sluggishly rambling to Sophie about the amazing party she went to in Venice the previous night. Just as her name was called, her head bobbed down to her chest and she began to snore. Sophie stood up trying to find an excuse for her sister and hoping to reschedule with the casting woman standing before her. The very seasoned, no- nonsense blonde said, "You're the exact look we want. Come in and read a few lines." While hesitant, not wanting to hurt Amy, she followed. After eating up her savings on the move and having a string of low-paying jobs, she was broke and had nothing to lose.

"You are so hilarious. I crack up with every new commercial that comes out, not to mention the irony of you being the spokeswoman for Wendy's. You're the antithesis in every way, shape, and form. Literally," Lucy added, "I mean, look at you."

"You're totally embarrassing me," Sophie said. She would never have expected to be able to act, let alone be comedic. And Lucy was right – the hiking kept her great shape. Sophie placed baby Val back in her mother's arms. "I'll see you ladies later. I have to fly to New York tonight."

"Got another job?"

"No, some family stuff. How about I babysit when I'm back so you can have a day off?"

"It's a date." Lucy released a great yawn as she padded back into her house in her slippered feet.

In record time, Sophie threw on shorts, T-shirt, and sneaks, booked her red-eye flight out of LAX, drove to Home Depot to order mirrors for her back room, and parked in the lot of Huntington Gardens, where Amy had said she worked the last time they spoke. Sophie turned off the engine, nervous about what she might encounter with her sister. She pulled out her wallet to look at the picture she put in there a few years prior, when Amy kept disappearing for days on end, only to reappear and act as if nothing had happened. She needed an image of Amy when her body still had flesh on it and cheeks that were pink and full. The one she chose was idyllic: Amy on her first day at UCLA, taken by Hannah who was a junior. The breeze tossed her hair partially across her smiling face. She desperately wished for that Amy to return.

After a few deep breaths, she got out of the car and took the path that led her through the North Vista and

Camellias. A path she and Amy walked many times before, during periods of sobriety. Keeping active helped Amy with cravings. Could this mean she wasn't using right now? Sophie inhaled the aroma from the lush pink Japanese flowers and picked up the pace to The Tea House. The outdoor seating area was packed with people of every age, computers open, tea cups at the ready. Sophie peered in, but there was no sign of Amy behind the register. She entered knowing any outcome was possible.

"I'm looking for Amy Gold," Sophie said apologetically to the barrister when it was her turn on line.

"She hasn't been working here for a couple of weeks," the girl said dryly without looking up.

Sophie noted her nose ring, multiple tattoos, and rich red lips. "Any idea where she went to work?" A futile question, Sophie knew.

"Nah, sorry."

Sorry – that was the word she usually heard in reference to Amy.

The girl looked up just as Sophie was about to move on. "You're the woman from the Wendy's commercials. I love those."

"Thanks." Sophie didn't have time for this burst of recognition.

"You might find her in the woods just a few feet behind us." She lowered her voice, "I let her keep her employee pass. I feel bad for her, you know?"

Sophie headed there at a clip, agitated about another wild-goose chase for her elusive sister. She had barely processed her grandfather's death and was now distracted by her search for Amy. The sky was a perfect steely blue, and the smell of roses nearby eased some tension.

There she sat, huddled on the ground, taking a deep inhale. Just as Sophie took her last step over, Amy looked up. "Hey, what a'ya doin here?" she asked, quickly hiding a joint behind her back.

Sophie sat down, noting the dark circles under her sister's eyes. "Looking for you."

"I'm sorry." Amy's lips turned down a bit. She looked like a small child. "That job didn't work out."

"It's okay, honey," Sophie gave her older sister a big hug, registering how brittle she felt. Her collarbones protruded through her cotton shirt.

"Your skin is so moist, Sophie. And look at your hair. Wow." Sophie felt uncomfortable when Amy began to touch her cheeks and smooth the top of her head with her spindly fingers.

"I haven't seen you for a while. Do you need anything?"

"Don't give me anything. I told you that." Amy crossed her arms and began to rock side to side. "I'm fine." She pulled her black sleeves lower down on her arms, but they only covered her elbows.

"Are you using?"

"Just a little weed here and there, nothing else." Amy stood and shifted her feet like she was playing basketball.

"Amy," Sophie reached for her hand, wanting to pull her arms straight and inspect for tracks, "I need to talk with you. Can we find a bench to sit on?"

"I got to move a little," Amy shielded her face from the sun. "I'm so proud of you, Sophie. You have such a good life."

"Would you come to New York with me tonight?" Sophie looked at her sister, feeling sad. Her hair pulled into a tight, stringy, ponytail made her eyes bulge. Not to mention the bands of black tattoos around her forearms that accentuated her pasty white skin. She looked like a wild cat cartoon with jagged whiskers and frazzled fur.

"NO," Amy shook her head like the mere thought was a threat.

"Grandpa died. It's his funeral this weekend. I can pay for your ticket."

"I have too much going on this weekend. And Grandpa, he's not – I can't go there. Do you have a smoke?"

Sophie lit a cigarette and passed it over.

"You would see Grandma, Dad... Hannah and the kids -"

"Jane says Dad's much better now."

"You could be to, Amy. Dad's gone to therapy for years. Let me take you."

"I tell all my friends about my sisters – you were such an awesome dancer and now, you have all these commercials I see on TV. So cool! And what about the amazing Jane who can bake anything in a moment's notice, and Hannah taking care of all the crazy shit that happens to people in the middle of the night – concussions, gunshot wounds… New York is not a safe place."

Sophie watched Amy suck down a long drag of her cigarette, fling it to the ground, and stamp it out with her big black boots. "We're all in God's favor, Sophie."

"Are we?"

***

Exhausted, Sophie stepped into the jetway after the six-hour flight from LAX to JFK. There wasn't one moment that she slept. She watched movies she had heard were great, but her mind kept harping on Amy. Should she abandon her and let her sink, or help her swim? All the experts in rehabs had told her, no one can help an addict. They have to want to help themselves. It takes individual will to get better. She needed Jane to discuss all the particulars and was happy she'd be picking her up so they would have time to talk.

But when she headed out of the baggage terminal area, she found her ex- fiancé waiting for her.

"You look beautiful, Sophie," John said.

Sophie thought that statement ludicrous. Even after ten years it was hard to stomach the reality that her ex-fiancé and sister had married each other. An ultimate betrayal. And yet, when she saw him each time she visited New York, she still felt a spark. It angered and disgusted her. The potential Sophie had felt to mend things with Hannah were severed when she found out she had started dating John shortly after Sophie moved to California. Jane called her with the news. Apparently, John and Hannah kept running into each other while jogging in the park. Why they didn't just nod and move on still flabbergasted Sophie. And how neither had been forthright with her... the betrayal nearly sent her over the edge. If she hadn't had a mission to save Amy, who she'd been vigilantly trying to help clean up, driving her to rehab, going to AA together, she likely would have used similar vices. Why the fuck did Jane send John to pick her up?

"That's kind," Sophie replied. She had just flown all night in what amounted to pajamas, having felt compelled to wear the "I love NY" T-shirt and sweats from Sarah. While certainly not fashionable, the outfit made it easy to maneuver her still lanky body around the tiny coach seat.

Her carry on was compressed with sweaters, the ugliest UGG winter boots she had ever seen, but could be barefoot in, and the hat and mittens her grandmother knitted and sent her for Hanukkah, forgetting that Southern California weather never called for such attire.

"I could have taken a taxi." His sky-blue eyes were as captivating as always. Maybe more so now that he had a configuration of lines fanning out toward his temples. She clutched her purse, thinking of the collection of emergency helpers she had packed once she had her flight confirmation; Valium, Ambian, *Peace is Every Step*, by Thich Nhat Hanh. It was her version of a binky. "Where's Hannah?"

"Waiting at the funeral home with Jane. They didn't want to pick anything out without you." He smiled. "I'm sorry for your loss, Soph."

She had left behind a perfect eighty-degree sun-filled Pasadena day, knowing that she would be met with a February cold so bitter that she'd want to hibernate like a large brown bear.

"Thank you." They stood facing each other. People pushed past them ready to hit the New York streets. John fidgeted with his keys and Sophie began perusing the tourists speaking in all their foreign tongues.

She had pondered loss all night, while on the plane. There had been so many in her life; her mom, dad, Amy, and now her grandfather. She had collected losses like some gather stamps or rare butterflies. Squished up in her coach seat, she had ruminated about each one. They came to her like movie clips, in real life order:

Her mother – After a few years of therapy, Sophie began to have memories of being with her mom again. Her favorite, being cuddled up under the covers, Sophie holding a flashlight, as her mother read from *Little*

Women. Her mom whispered one chapter a night, after Jane began snoring. Sophie could almost smell her mother's breath with the remnants of warm milk and two ginger cookies she ate before bed. She imagined the crumbs that were from her dinner roll on the plane as remnants of cookies from her mom, and brushed them off her blue sleeping blanket with a smile on her face.

Her father, before the accident, standing at the dining room table, as he often did before he sat for dinner. He would hold his drink, one scotch a night, and begin babbling to their mother about his latest case – using what Sophie had coined his "big words:" litigation, just cause, jurisdiction. That was always when Sophie started thinking about her Barbie dolls and what to dress them in after dinner.

Amy, rapidly coming down the stairs when she started sixth grade, wanting to avoid their parents, as she tried to boogie out of the house in the tightest short shorts she could find and low- cut scoop-neck t. Her mom was always a few steps ahead, waiting by the front door and would march her back upstairs to change her outfit and wipe the make-up off her face.

Her grandfather, the previous year, asking her to take over Gold Sounds. "Why not?" he had argued with her on the phone. He assumed she wasn't doing much of anything else out in fluffy California, and he never asked.

"Soph, you okay?" John asked.

Sophie rubbed her eyes. "How are the kids?"

"Big," he smiled. "They look just like Hannah, all of them." His eyes remained on Sophie's.

"I don't know, I think the baby looks like you." Sophie kept her gaze with passers-by. She thought about the last email Hannah sent with a photo attachment of her and the three kids on a bench in Riverside Park. She recognized the path that led to the Tot Lot, near John and Hannah's home on 103rd and West End. She was certain that Hannah had chosen a photo John took, instead of a full family shot, thinking it was salt on an old wound, which it was. Sophie didn't know in what scenario she could ever forgive Hannah. She had a habit of including Sophie in group emails, with captions that read things like, "Zadie's first day at school," "Jack playing soccer with friends." She had the knack for capturing the moment, but the emails always pissed Sophie off. They lacked emotion, never exposing the true feelings that come with something new; trepidation, excitement, nausea, or even terror. And nothing was ever sent to just Sophie, which was no surprise.

Sophie reached for her suitcase, but John took hold of the handle. "I got it," he said. "Did you bring a coat? It's pretty frigid today."

"Yes, in my bag." She noticed how well dressed he was for an early-morning pickup. He wore a beautiful brown cashmere sweater underneath a navy-blue pea coat. Each year she came to visit he seemed to inhabit a more refined look.

They walked to the sliding doors on their way to short-term parking, "How's Amy?"

Sophie registered the small talk. "I saw her yesterday. Pretty good." Sophie placed her hand on the suitcase handle. "I got it," she said, and picked up the pace. She would not confide in him. The cold peace they managed to conjure over the years did not constitute friendship.

"Hannah's been really worried about her."

Good for Hannah. The wind hit them as they reached the curb and waited for the light to cross into the lot. "God, this airport needs a face lift, it's so depressing." Sophie braced herself as they sped to the car and closed their doors against the biting frigid air.

John started the engine. The car felt so intimate as it warmed up. Even the seats were heated. Sophie looked behind her, still amazed that the man she had loved for the first decade of her adult life had three small children, six-year-old Zadie, four-year-old, Jack, and now baby Maddie.

"How's my grandma holding up?" Sophie nestled into the leather seat, thinking of the last phone call they shared. Her grandma had sounded more disoriented, and frail. She repeated the same story to Sophie several times, about Hannah and John's kids, and how they ran into her bedroom every morning and crawled to the foot of the bed, waiting to be told they could come in the covers for a hug and a back scratch. Sophie had loved her grandma's back scratches when she was a kid. She was glad her grandmother moved in with them. They had enough space to provide her with her own bedroom and bath. Amy was right. Hannah had certainly made a killing as head of the ER and mother of three.

"I got you a coffee, black right?" John said, handing her a Starbucks cup from its holder.

"That's perfect."

"I think your grandma is doing great, considering," he started. "She organized an old-fashioned Gold dinner, in your grandfather's honor, for tonight."

'Really? Who's going to be there?" Sophie clutched her bag, considering the small white pills inside. "Where is it?"

"It's at our house. All the kids will be there, and my folks." He backed out of the parking spot.

"Your parents came from Florida?" Sophie said, overjoyed. She hadn't seen Beverly and George for ten years, since she had holed herself up in their house and then fled to California. When she reflected on that period in her life, she felt embarrassed, and so young. What would have happened if she stayed on the tour and married John?

For the first few years after they split, Sophie remained in contact with George and Bev, exchanging birthday cards and holiday notes:

Hers to them: Hope you're enjoying the sunshine. How's the golf swing? Will you be traveling this year?

Theirs to her: How's the beach? Are you enjoying your classes at Pasadena City College? How are the puppies?

Her stomach gurgled. "How are they? I miss them," Sophie said with a smile. She knew that had she stayed with John her life would have been simpler. The car seats in the back would have been for their children. It was such an unimaginable life. Now thirty-eight, she had spent the last years recalibrating; her identity without dance had taken years to decipher, her quest to save Amy from all her vices seemed futile, and the only one left to save was herself. A work in progress.

"They're okay, older you know. Aches and pains of different sorts, but the sun seems to do well by them," John answered. "We took the kids to see them over the holidays. They love it there. The golf course, swimming pool," he trailed off, "You know, I love my life with Hannah and the kids. It's everything I want, but sometimes I wake in the middle of the night and I expect to see you. I don't even understand what happened to us," John put his elbow on the edge of the car door and leaned his head on his hand, looking out the front window.

They had stopped at a light just one turn away from the funeral home, the same one where her mother had been. She would never forget the sterile look of the red brick building. Why would they choose this one? Sophie turned to John, "What's wrong with you? How can you say that to me? You married my sister!"

271

"I'm sorry, Sophie. I shouldn't have. It's just so confusing sometimes when I see you and…" The light turned green and John turned into the parking area and circled. There were plenty of spots, but he drove in a big loop.

She could barely breathe. "There's nothing confusing about it, John. You made a choice." Sophie wiped one tear that torpedoed down her cheek. She hated coming back to New York. Seeing John often shook her off balance, like the tilt of an hour-glass. "Why are you here? Why didn't Jane pick me up?"

"I wanted to see you -"

He finally pulled into a spot. The car idled in the back corner, the furthest distance from the entrance. Sophie wondered if he stopped there to keep a barrier for them from Hannah and Jane. She needed to get out. As her hand went for the door handle the car was pummeled by two little bodies – jumping up and down to see their dad through the glass.

"Climb in guys," John said, as the window glided down.

Zadie pulled open the car door and they jumped in and sat in their car seats, which were on opposite ends, wedged with the baby seat in the middle. "Why did you park all the way over here, Daddy? It took us, like, for-e-ver to get here."

"You remember Aunt Sophie?" John said.

"Of course, Daddy," Zadie answered. "You ask us that every time." Her long blonde hair was in a French braid. It landed on her shoulder, finished off by a pink bow. She had more feminine flare then Sophie and all her sisters combined. Sophie loved knowing that Zadie was prone to pinching her brother when she thought no one was watching.

"Jack, say hi to Aunt Sophie," John added.

"Hi, Aunt Sophie," he said scrambling into the front seat and into his father's arms. He took hold of the steering wheel. "I'm a really good driver," he said in his tiny high-pitched voice.

Sophie was overwhelmed, by both the memory of the day she buried her mom, the desire to punch John, and by her urge to reach over to Jack and take him in her arms. His cheeks were still so full, like perfect little cushions. Almost the same age as Jane had been when their mother died. But Sophie knew that would only make him burrow deeper into John. It always took a couple of days, playing on the carpet with trains, trucks, crayons, before she could steal little kisses on his head, or hold his soft fingers for just a few moments.

"You are quite a driver. Think you can park this baby so I can go in and see your mom?" Sophie knew that Hannah must be standing at the door of the funeral home. She would never let the kids run to the car without her supervision. But Sophie didn't want to look over, not yet. She had a brief longing she needed to shoo like a crazy fly. These were not her kids. This was not her husband, her car, her life.

CHAPTER NINETEEN

Sophie shivered as she hustled to the large white door where Hannah waited. Her hair was in what Sophie liked to call her "mom cut". With each new baby she got a no- nonsense bob.

"Nice to see you," Sophie said robotically.

Hannah wrapped her arms around her own body. "You too. Jane's waiting inside for us."

They walked in and Sophie was overwhelmed by a rush of emotions. Her memory of the funeral home had been spot-on: the ugly light-pink walls with pictures of flower pots in gold frames, the green leather couches and nondescript wooden chairs. Nothing had changed in thirty years. Her heartbeat accelerated faster than when she ran uphill. She wished she were home, taking a hike at Hermit Falls, in the San Gabriel Mountains. Then she would be enveloped in the sound of the waterfall cascading between the gray white misshapen stones, not being reacquainted with the most crushing day of her life.

"The funeral director is waiting for us to make a choice of casket. Jane and I found a lovely one. See what you think."

Sophie turned to her eldest sister, always so practical. Even her outfit screamed sensible: navy wool trousers and a black turtleneck sweater, the perfect pearl earrings, not too ostentatious, but certainly visible. The way her wrinkles and grays came in fit her demeanor, enhancing her forty-four years, making her look mature, but not old. How could this not be painful for her too?

Jane ran over just in time to stop Sophie's ruminating and gave her a gigantic hug. "I'm so happy you came."

She reciprocated, grateful for the tight hold. When they pulled back from each other Sophie paused, noticing the small rounding of Jane's middle. "Are you pregnant?"

Jane just smiled, the mischievous way she had as a child, now radiant and luminous. They hugged again. "Come on. Let's go get this over with." She led the way, her blue jeans snug around her legs and middle.

They headed to the adjacent room. Sophie could smell the bitter aroma of coffee on Jane's breath. "Is it okay to drink coffee when you're pregnant?" she asked, realizing she knew absolutely nothing about this part of feminine life.

"It's okay to have one cup a day. You wouldn't want much more than that," Hannah piped in.

Sophie noted Jane roll her eyes as they linked arms.

The funeral director, a skeletal man in his sixties, waited for them. His body was in constant motion, moving back and forth on his spindly legs, beside a shiny black casket that reminded Sophie of a pair of patent leather Mary Janes. She tried not to stare, but was fascinated by the stretch of his skin around his jawline. You could practically see his skull below, and his teeth were especially prominent, reminding her of a horse's mouth.

"What do you think, Sophie?" Jane asked. Her face looked so fresh, free of make-up, and as white and unblemished as the first snowfall in winter.

"Don't you think Dad should be here too?" She looked forward to seeing her father. "Did you text him a photo?"

"He left us in charge of this so he and Leslie can make the arrangements at the cemetery and for sitting Shiva," Jane said, her green eyes on the edge of tears.

"Who's Leslie?"

"Grandpa's friend."

"The woman who broke up Grandma and Grandpa's marriage? What the hell!" Sophie's face squished up in confusion, "Why is she a part of this?"

"They've been divorced for years, Sophie," Hannah said.

"Yes, but they were married for about fifty," Sophie bit back. "Doesn't that count for something?"

"Maybe I should leave you ladies to discuss amongst yourselves," the director said and bowed out of the room. Sophie had completely forgotten he was there.

"Could we have one visit where you don't snap at me?" Hannah said facing Sophie.

Sophie felt the jetlag creep up on her. "Sure. Let's pick this one." All she wanted was a hot shower and a nap.

"Great. I'll take care of the arrangements." Hannah left the room in a bustle.

"I know she completely annoys you, but maybe this trip you can reach out the olive branch?" Jane said.

Sophie let out a yawn. "I'm not mad any more – I'm just not interested in being close." Was that true, she wondered? "My head is spinning here – Grandpa said, 'He should have married Leslie', the day of mom's funeral." The memory came back to her like a bolt of lightning. "Is this the same Leslie?"

"Let's get back to my place first. You can have a rest and then we can talk… there's something I need to discuss."

"There's more?"

Jane shook her head.

"I booked a hotel room in the city. I needed a little quiet time for this trip." Usually, Sophie loved her stays at Jane's place, a quaint Tudor style house just a few blocks from her dad's. She could jet back and forth between visits with her father, long dance discussions with Sarah while watching videos of her favorite ballerinas, and, best of all, after-hour chats with Jane. They shared and compared single versus family life notes, usually over green tea and Toblerone chocolate bars.

They walked to a nearby sitting room and plopped down on a couch. "Sophie, there's no easy way to say this. I was going to save it for our nightly talk…"

Sophie registered the distraught look on Jane's face. "What? You're scaring me."

"Leslie is a man. He and Grandpa were a couple."

Sophie laughed, partially with disbelief and partially with discomfort, knowing it wasn't Jane's style to lie about anything of importance.

"They were partners since college." her voice cracked.

Sophie furrowed her brow in response. "He had an affair his entire marriage to Grandma? That's – that's despicable."

Jane swallowed hard. "Grandma and Grandpa had an arrangement. Grandma wanted to leave her house and have kids, and Grandpa – well – you know, no one was allowed to be gay then, so they got married."

Sophie sat against the hard back of the sofa. "He duped us all – for all these years? Why didn't Grandma tell us when they split?"

"She's not even fessing up now."

Hannah walked in while stretching her left arm into her camel-colored coat sleeve, "We're all settled up. I'm heading home. See you tonight."

Sophie peered over at Hannah with disdain. Her skin prickled. "Did you know about this?"

"What?"

"This duplicitous situation of Grandpa's. Did you know?"

"This isn't really the time." Hannah's voice remained steady, like the thumping of a metronome. "I can tell you that Leslie is a very nice man."

"You're okay with this – this – double life? What the hell do you call a situation like this?" Sophie wondered why she always fell back into this old dynamic. "Jane – you too?"

"To each his own." Jane shrugged. "We all have our secrets and lies."

Sophie turned in Hannah's direction. "How long have you known this?"

"Not long."

Sophie noted the impatience in her voice, reminiscent of how she spoke with her children when she was frustrated. She could feel the electrical current between them, stirring in her chest.

The room remained still until the funeral director walked in, "Will you be needing anything else?"

"No, thank you. We're just heading out." Hannah stretched her hand out to shake his, always the fucking diplomat.

Sophie observed the creeping of what felt like a long green vine through her torso, webbing its way up and around her ribs and throat, tightening and constricting her body and making it harder to breathe.

"I'm glad that's settled," Hannah said as she pulled her phone from her back pocket and began texting.

"Is there room in your car, Hannah? Sophie is staying in the city." Jane stood, yawned, and reached her arms above her head in a stretch. "I'm so stiff."

"What the fuck is wrong with the two of you?" Sophie blurted. "They lied to us for decades? Doesn't that bother you?"

"Come on, Sophie. You've spent your life around gay friends," Jane said. "You know it wasn't possible to be a gay man or woman for that matter back then. It's still a fight in most of this country. They did what they had to do." Jane tucked the ends of her shirt back into her pants. "I feel bad for them – to have to hide -."

"That's not the point. They raised us for years, pretending to be a couple. Everyone in this family lies." Sophie felt apoplectic. She wanted to rip her hair out or jump up and down screaming. Instead, she clenched her fists and grit her teeth.

"Really, Sophie? That's a gross exaggeration," her oldest sister said.

"Is it? You not only couldn't find your own man for a husband, but you didn't even have the decency to face me. I found out from Jane." Sophie took a long deep breath. "And you," when she turned to Jane she was on the verge of tears. She and Jane had come so far, they were so close. "I know you're not telling me the truth. You and Grandpa have always been so close, you must have known." She wiped her nose and eyes. She was still the outsider.

Jane put her head down and scratched her head. Her voice soft, she said, "I've known for a long time, Sophie, but he asked me not to share it with anyone. He was still so ashamed and worried about what everyone would think."

"What else don't I know?" Sophie said, her voice hardened.

Hannah put on a pair of tan leather gloves, "When you're here for more than a few days at a time, Sophie, then you get the right to judge us."

She left the room.

One beat after, Jane looked over, "I'm sorry. I was stuck in the middle. I really wanted to tell you – so many times."

"You like Leslie?"

"He's great."

They walked to the exit. Jane grabbed her coat off a rack by the door, put it around her shoulders and searched her pockets, then purse for her car keys. "I'm really forgetful now. I can't remember where I put anything."

Sophie opened her suitcase, pulled out her coat, and zipped it to her chin. She looked over at the long staircase looming before her, with the white painted banister. It was thirty years ago when she sat there to escape the many mourners. "Do you remember the way mom used to kiss us?"

Jane looked at Sophie and shook her head no.

Sophie took Jane's pale, angular face in her hands and gave her a kiss on each cheek and the tip of her nose, which was a few inches below Sophie's. "Like that."

***

The taxi ride into Manhattan gave Sophie enough time to meditate on the secrets and lies Jane mentioned. She certainly had accumulated a bunch. She remembered the night that Amy flung her way into Sophie's house at two a.m. wanting to read her poetry and begging that Sophie scratch her legs. Once the cocaine wore off and Amy passed out on the living room floor, Sophie rummaged through her bag to find the drugs she had hidden. She had every intention of depositing them in the toilet, but got sidetracked by the dogs barking at a cat in the yard. Over the course of the next year, she experimented with a few, experiencing the paranoia, hallucinations, and frenetic energy that she had witnessed in Amy. She didn't enjoy any of it, but was desperate to understand the draw and hold it had on her. It proved futile.

And how could she neglect to admit that she had taken plenty of strangers into her bed, men she had just met at a party or sat across on a first date, knowing she would never want a relationship with them, but could certainly enjoy for a few hours? Most shameful were the ones she knew were married, but she needed to prove her worth. If they wanted her and were willing to risk what they had, she must be worth loving. She squandered many nights wanting to be chosen first.

Was her grandfather deceitful or just a man tangled in life circumstances? She remembered hearing him and her grandmother fight. It often ended with him saying, 'When is it our time?' Is that what he meant? He wanted to be with the man he loved? That must have been excruciating. And yet, weren't there opportunities for him to come out to all of them?

By the time they crossed the Tri-Borough Bridge, dark clouds rolled across the city, playing hide and seek with the skyscrapers. The driver kept hitting his brakes as he zig-zagged from lane to lane. Nausea stirred in her belly. She needed fresh air. Heading cross town from east to west proved even worse as he stopped short every other second, along 96th Street from 1st Avenue all the way to Broadway, his foot constantly slamming on the brake.

"You can let me out here, thanks," Sophie yelled through the plexiglass partition. If she stayed in the cab any longer, she was sure to vomit.

The driver stopped short, leaving several feet between the car and the curb. Sophie paid and exited. Her foot sank into a pile of sludge. She cursed under her breath, went to the trunk to retrieve her suitcase, and pushed her way through a mountain of black-stained snow interfering with her path to the sidewalk. She forgot how utterly depressing winter in New York could be. Just as she made it to dry land, her phone buzzed in her pocket.

"Can't wait to see you tonight, Love you – Dad."

A wide smile swept across her frosty cheeks. She loved that her father was contemporary – he had gotten a smart phone and used it to text her often.

"Are you okay?" Sophie wrote back.

"Maybe we can have some time to talk alone tonight."

"That would be nice." Sophie wondered if he wanted to tell her about her grandfather also, not knowing that Jane had already. She would love to hear his version of the story, and thoughts about his father's withholding. Or had he known all these years?

While quickly retrieving her mittens from her coat, she sifted through her family, calculating how each must have taken the news. If her grandmother had made such an arrangement, did she too have another love life unbeknownst to all of them? How was she going to share all this with Amy?

Another buzz.

"Aunt Sophie, where are you? I thought you were coming here to stay with us?"

She hadn't thought of how Sarah would feel about her choice to be in a hotel. "Hi sweetie. Not this time, but I will see you tonight." The wind began to wheel around her, stinging her mouth. She would need to keep this short so she could head down the ten blocks.

"How long are you staying?"

"For the weekend. On my way to the hotel. xo."

Sophie grabbed her suitcase again and began to roll it down Broadway. Perhaps she had exaggerated to Jane and Hannah about how they had all lied to her. It was really just her relationship with Hannah that was stuck in a perpetual purgatory.

With five blocks down and five more to go, Sophie felt an ache in her belly. She needed food and more coffee. Starbucks sat at the corner. She popped in, ordered, and grabbed an empty spot at the windowsill. The place was jam packed and hot. She peeled the layers that had barely kept her insulated enough; coat, mittens, scarf, sweater. She tossed them all on top of her suitcase and crossed her legs, leaning back against the chilled glass.

"Visiting?"

Sophie heard the question to her left, but was not in the mood for small talk. She curtly said, "Yes."

His voice returned, deep and warm, "Tough entrance to the city I guess," he said, but she didn't answer. "It's the coldest day we've had so far."

He seriously could not be a New Yorker, Sophie thought, as she turned just enough to glance at his outstretched legs, crossed at the ankles, and the manicured hands folded in his lap. She appreciated men who weren't afraid to get spa services. "True." She took a long sip from her cup, then pulled open the lid to her oatmeal and added the brown sugar.

"Have you ever been here?"

"Many times," she said, turning to find a fortyish-year-old man beside her. He had the most beautiful complexion she had ever seen, like her black coffee with just a dollop of cream mixed in.

He smiled at her and extended his hand. "Ty."

She placed hers to his and firmly held on. "Sophie."

A moment later she became self-conscious – of her cheesy "I love New York" attire, bestowed upon her from her dear niece, Sarah, and her hair halfway in her ponytail. Had she even brushed her teeth since she left home the previous night?

"What brings you to New York?"

Trying not to stare, Sophie took in the small bump at the bridge of his nose, "My grandfather's funeral." Should she have said something more upbeat?

"I'm so sorry to hear that. I hope I'm not disturbing you."

She stirred her oatmeal, round and round, unable to take a bite. "Not at all."

He pulled on his dark navy wool coat. Sophie noted his physique, sculpted but not bulky. She felt a buzzing inside and tongue tied. He gave her a quick smile – it was broad and alluring.

Go for it, Sophie. Don't let him leave.

He began to gather the remains of his meal.

"Do you want to have a drink with me later?" Sophie asked.

The look he gave her was playful, the edges of his mouth with a slight curve upwards. He took out his wallet and handed her his card. "Where are you from?"

"L.A."

"I'd love to."

It could prove to be a better night than she had anticipated.

A half hour later, Sophie fell into a deep sleep under the hotel's white down comforter. The room already in disarray – all her outerwear hung over the desk and chair in the corner of the room, her clothes on the carpeted floor beside the bed. She allotted three hours for her nap, but it was cut short when her alarm went off. Forgetting East Coast time, she had set it incorrectly. Being pulled out of her slumber, Sophie landed in a crescendo on the ground, flat on her back. She lay stunned and in pain for many minutes, succumbing to the reality that she was wide awake. Before heading into the shower, she stared at the card on the night table. Dr. Tyler Mitchell, Psychiatrist. Her finger caressed the black Times New Roman font.

Regardless of the twenty-degree temperature, Sophie was determined to walk uptown for dinner along Riverside Drive. It was her favorite Manhattan block, especially when all the trees were bare and the branches danced across the flat pale sky. It began tranquil as Sophie marched along with resolving thoughts about Amy; she would make one final attempt at getting her into rehab, and retreat. All the therapists told her, time and again, it was a futile attempt unless the addict wants to clean up. It was just so hard to let go not knowing what might happen. Step after step, she curved along the pavement, letting her white breath lead the way. The early-evening lights from the perfectly measured lamp posts flooded the path. With only a few blocks to go, Sophie caught sight of a homeless woman in her periphery. She was covered in layers of blankets and plastic bags.

As Sophie passed, she called out, "You got a few dollars? I haven't eaten all day." Sophie picked up the pace and so did the woman. "Just one dollar," she belligerently continued.

The pounding in Sophie's chest grew louder as she crossed out of the park and onto Riverside Drive, with the woman still on her heels. She wanted the sun and her car. A few more steps and she could enter John and Hannah's building.

"YOU GREEDY BITCH!" the woman hollered. And to top it off as she about faced, "FUCK YOU!"

By the time she rang the doorbell, Sophie's body, with a bruised ass and shaken spirit, was one long braid to be untwisted.

CHAPTER TWENTY

"Aunt Sophie!" Sarah let out a scream and grabbed her tightly. "Come, I've been waiting for you!" With both hands, Sarah pulled her into the living room, a gigantic space by Manhattan standards, with twin stone-colored leather couches facing one another, a long white coffee table between, and a piano caddy cornered by the windows overlooking Riverside Drive and the Hudson River, covered in ice. The room was in full bloom: Jane and Paul cooing over the baby; Bev and George with drinks in hand; Martha playing "Danny Boy," Sophie's grandmother listening intently, sitting on the piano bench as well, and an old man reclined on the couch.

"You haaave to meet Grandpa Leslie," Sarah said, beaming with enthusiasm.

Was she really hearing this? "Grandpa?"

"I asked him if I could call him that last year when we went away with him and Grandpa. You know they were a couple, right?" Sarah spoke a mile a minute.

The last to know, Sophie thought, "Yes." How could she be surprised? Jane and her grandfather had always been thick as thieves.

"How cool is that?" Sarah continued. "A gay Grandpa. My friend Allison has two moms, but they're not ninety-year-olds."

Sarah continued to babble in her twelve-year-old way, with exaggerated arm gestures and protruding hips to emphasize her points. How long had her niece known this man?

Sophie turned toward Leslie and he returned the gaze with a warm smile and wave. His lap held a napkin full of multiple appetizers, all uneaten. He reminded her of the chicken guy, Frank Perdue: an old white man, bald, and wearing spectacles. He was adorable and forlorn.

George walked over, scotch in hand. "You look very well. How long has it been?"

Sarah continued to yank on Sophie's arm, wanting full attention, which Sophie wished she could give. Instead, she planted a kiss on the top of her head and turned toward her almost father-in-law, who had barely aged. "It's been about ten years."

Sophie thought about all the times she had avoided being at functions where they would have seen each other, Hannah and John's wedding and the three baby showers to start.

"You look just like on TV," Bev chimed in. "It's wonderful to see you. I guess Los Angeles suits you."

They hugged, but Sophie could feel the reservation in her embrace. "It does."

"Agreed, even though you are so far away." Sophie's dad took his turn and they held firmly to each other. He blinked several times rapidly, one of a few remaining ticks.

Sophie whispered in his ear, so she wouldn't upset Sarah. "Why is Leslie here? He's not a part of our family."

He gave her a quick peck on the cheek. "I know it's complicated, but we're all figuring it out." He smiled while his hands tapped his thighs repetitively.

John stood on the coffee table and rang a small chime. "Now that our final guest has arrived – "

Was that a jab?

"Let's eat everyone."

Sophie had barely said hello, let alone taken her coat off.

"Daddy, no shoes on the table," Zadie called out. She took hold of her father's hand and tugged him down. John lifted his daughter onto his shoulders. She wrapped her hands around his forehead. Before strolling into the dining room Sophie caught him glancing at her, like he was skimming the pages of a book.

"Can we sew pointe shoes together later?" Sarah asked, still clinging to Sophie.

Was it that transparent how uncomfortable she felt or was he intentionally toying with her? "You got it. I can't wait."

Sarah darted to her seat at the table. Sophie couldn't help but admire her long neck and beautifully extended spine. She carried herself in full ballerina fashion with her gait slightly turned out.

After hanging up her coat in the front closet and placing her bag on the floor, Sophie closed her eyes and imagined taking a long drag on a cigarette. A chilly sensation travelled along her back and arms like she had just stepped into a cob-web on a dark night. It was such an eerie twist of fate to sit at the table with her family, John, and his, now joined as one. The very situation she had avoided her entire relationship with John now shoved in her face. The irony still stunned her, along with the blasé attitude surrounding it. How did they all find this acceptable? "Here's goes," she mumbled.

Hannah had outdone herself. Her best China, with gold rims, crystal wine glasses, and sterling silverware awaited them. There were three different vases – each with arrangements of exotics in pinks and purples – along the center of the table set for fourteen. If she weren't such a successful doctor, she could have been another Martha Stewart.

Sophie made sure to sit beside her grandma.

"How did you get here, dear?" Her grandmother still took care of her appearance, dressed in cream-colored slacks and matching sweater set.

"I walked, Gram." Sophie leaned in close, knowing her hearing had waned a bit.

She was desperate not to think of the deceit. "Are you doing okay – with Grandpa's death?" Once the words exited her lips, she wondered about her intention.

"You look so pretty. Are you dating anyone?" Her grandmother brushed her hand gently along Sophie's cheek.

Sophie registered a slight tremor from her fingers. Would Ty be a one-night stand or a boyfriend? "Not right now."

"You must have many suitors. A woman as beautiful as you." Sophie flushed with embarrassment.

Jane mouthed from across the table, "How are you?"

Sophie smiled, happy to be beside her grandma, who she imagined must feel more awkward than she did about the dinner invitation extended to Leslie.

"Don't the girls look so happy with their families, Sophie dear?"

Sophie knew "the girls" meant Jane and Hannah. "They do, Gram."

Sophie looked over at Jane again, who turned toward Sarah as she stood. Sophie drank in the beauty of her niece's chiseled arms and confident demeanor. Her powder-white face was freckled like her dad's, but the rest was Jane: the orange ringlets that Sarah happily tamed into a bun and the hint of daring in her green eyes.

"I thought we could go around the table and say something about Great Grandpa Bob," Sarah began.

There was a hum of agreement.

How did she get so mature?

"I loved listening to music with Grandpa. I played him Bach and he played me Ray Charles and Miles

Davis." Sophie watched Sarah look at Jane with a smile. "And he let me eat a lot of cookies when I visited his house."

Sophie reached over and gave her grandmother's hand a squeeze. Her mind told her she should be angry for being complicit in the deception, but her heart felt wider.

"I like how GG Bob let his mustache grow because it always tickles when he kisses me," Zadie said, sitting upright in her seat beside Hannah. There was still not a wrinkle or smudge on her dress from the morning, and her hair remained fully intact.

"GG Bob died, sweetie. That means he's not with us any more," Hannah whispered in her daughter's ear.

"I know," Zadie replied, while elbowing her brother. "Jack, your turn," she added.

Sophie watched, with fascination, the dominance that had already formed. When Jack hadn't instantly replied, Zadie pinched his thigh beneath the table cloth. "Jack, go!"

"Stop it! Stop it!" Jack screamed.

"Okay, you two," John piped in. He had the baby on his lap, who began to wail.

Sophie's father stood up and walked over to his newest granddaughter. Even though he was now in his sixties, he looked more youthful than he had in years, his stature reinvigorated. Sophie knew therapy and Prozac were only one piece of the puzzle. The relationship he shared with Martha ignited his continued healing. Sophie thought her mom would really like that she and her father found each other. If Martha could pull her father back to all of them, then how could there be fault in that?

"My father would be very happy looking at this table. Let's finish this after dinner," her dad said, rocking Maddie in his arms, as her cries became intermittent whimpers.

Sophie watched everyone dig in, serving and passing and chattering. Jane's husband, Paul, talked with John in between bites, Jane helped Hannah serve the kids, Bev and George stood to take a turn doting on baby Maddie, and Martha kept running back to the kitchen to grab another dish.

The pop of a cork interrupted the action.

"I thought we might celebrate life today." With every few words her dad paused to regroup, Martha by his side like a coach telling him to go on and that he was doing great. "Instead of death," he continued. They walked around the table together pouring champagne for the grown-ups. He continued to speak as they went, "I think our family has had enough sorrow and should embrace a life long-lived."

When he got to Sophie, he bent down and gave her a kiss on the cheek.

"How can you be so forgiving?"

"I don't want to waste any more time, Sophie. And neither should you." He touched her shoulder with his free hand and gave her a strong squeeze. How was it that every adult family member was fine with this strange new twist and she was swimming upstream, fighting the current?

A dining room chair screeched against the hardwood floor. Leslie stood, glass in hand. "Sam, thank you for having me here with your family." There were tears in his eyes. "As you can imagine, the road for your father, grandfather, great-grandfather and I was paved in hardship," he said, looking at each of them. "We weren't allowed to be—"

Sophie's grandma rose to her feet. "Thank you, Leslie," she said, her voice unwavering. "That was very nice," she held his gaze. "Robert would be glad to have a dear friend like you here with us. Please, let's continue the meal."

Leslie lowered his eyes and deferred. Jane put her hand on his back as he sat and then wrapped it around his shoulder in an embrace. Was he her surrogate grandfather as well? Jane looked at Sophie a moment later, her eyes wide, and mouthed, "What was that?"

What Sophie wanted to say was − can you blame her? Instead, she shrugged, like, what did you expect? He was the interloper at the table.

After dinner Sophie strolled from room to room, anticipating her late-night drink with Ty, but knowing it would be rude to depart so soon. When she got to Sarah's room, she knocked on the door and poked her head in. "Ready?" Sophie knew threading the needle and sewing each stitch would relax her.

"Can we do it in, like, thirty minutes?" Sarah looked up while her fingers kept texting.

"No problem."

Sophie poured herself a glass of wine and sat on the steps that led upstairs to John and Hannah's bedroom. She leaned her head on the wall and listened to the sound of little feet pounding across the linoleum. "I want you to stay with me forever." It was Jack's voice.

"I will, Jackie. I love you so much."

Sophie took a sip from her glass and peered into the kitchen. Jack nestled into Hannah's lap. They rested on the floor, against the cabinets. Sophie still wasn't much of a drinker, so the few sips she had taken were making her a bit light-headed.

"I love you most of all," Jack replied, as he put his fingers on his mother's cheeks. "Does everyone die when they're really old, like Great Grandpa Bob?"

"Usually, love."

"I want to die with you," Jack said.

Sophie watched them hug so tightly that it looked like their bodies would meld into each other. Hannah enveloped her son with her limbs. The gesture contained an unknown intimacy for Sophie and an appealing side of Hannah.

Her dad sat beside her on the stairs, placing his hands on his temples, "There is nothing like the way you love your children."

"Are you okay?"

"A headache – I get them now and then. I remember your mom telling me when you were about the age of Jack, that she felt connected to each of her girls as if they were still attached to her body."

Sophie leaned her head on her dad's shoulder and listened. It was both comforting and helpful to hear him without watching his eyes pressing open and closed so often.

"She described the connection like the seam of a dress. And each year you grew older a stitch would be released. When Hannah and Amy turned twelve, she remarked the separation felt complete."

"What does that mean for Jane and me then?"

"I wish I could ask her, Sophie." He wrapped his arm around her. "What I do know is that your mom loved you more than anything in the world." He held her tightly.

"Did you know about Grandpa?"

"Your mom tried to tell me – several times, but I wouldn't listen."

"How did she know?"

"I didn't give her the chance to tell me. I wish I had."

"Are you angry at him?" Sophie kept her voice low.

"I was confused at first. I've known Leslie my whole life and never suspected anything. I felt foolish – for some time – but then the puzzle pieces of my childhood began to make more sense." He started to smooth the carpet with his hand over and over, looking pensive. "I'm angry at myself. I should have been a better father to you. I was so wrapped in my own sorrow and guilt that I couldn't raise you. Not the way I wanted, not the way your mom would've wanted."

Sophie could hear the rhythm of his breath truncating into almost a wheeze. If she forged on, would he retreat? And yet this was the most honest moment she had ever had with him. She wanted to know as much as she could. Why did he feel guilty? What would her life look like now if he had stayed present? "What should I do about Amy?"

He placed his hand on her leg and smiled. The change of course restored his equilibrium. "Let her be, Sophie. She has to want to change and get help. That's what I had to do."

"Sam," Martha called from the living room, "Zadie and Jack want to play Chutes and Ladders with us."

Sophie and her father smiled at one another. Sophie released his hand and walked into the kitchen. Hannah hadn't moved from her position against the cabinet, stroking Jack's head as he drifted to sleep. His eyes were three quarters closed. His long spider-leg lashes brushed his lower lids. Sophie crouched on the floor against the kitchen island, across from her sister.

"I'm never quite sure how to answer the death questions," Hannah said, eyes lingering on her son.

"You sounded pretty good to me," Sophie listened to Jack's deep exhales.

"When I got home from the ER a couple of nights ago, I heard the phone ring." She paused. "I thought it was the hospital with an emergency, so I picked up. Grandma had already answered. Leslie was on the other end. He said that Grandpa was lying next to him, but not breathing. He sounded panicked – you know short of breath and speaking very rapidly. Grandma, very calmly said, 'Leslie, call 911,' and after a beat she added, 'You know how much Bob loved you. This is exactly how he would have wanted to die.' Between sobs he answered her, 'Thank you, Eva. I'm okay, now. I'm going to call 911,' and then he hung up."

Sophie's jaw clenched. She didn't know who she felt worse for, Leslie or her grandma.

"I could tell that grandma was still on the line, I could hear her take some long deep breaths, so I took the risk and said, 'Gram, are you okay?' She answered, 'Hannah, is that you?' I said 'Yes'."

Sophie reached up to the counter and placed her wine glass down. She wanted to stay as lucid as possible.

"She hung up the phone. Next morning, she pretended we never spoke."

"I'm sorry." Sophie started to feel that perhaps this information did make sense – maybe it answered some of the questions she had growing up, the fights between her grandparents and his constant disappearances and discontent. Her grandfather had always found a reason to work late. Nothing was what it seemed on the surface.

Perhaps she had judged Hannah too harshly. "I think I've always blamed you."

"For what?"

"Everything. I wanted you to include me. And to love me, even before Mom died."

"It's not my fault that Mom died."

"I know." Why was she always so defensive? "I just – I wanted you to love me the way you did Amy and Jane." Sophie could feel her resistance cracking.

"You were always happy on your own, Sophie. You were independent, and I just didn't think – "

"Think what?"

"That you liked me." Hannah was the first to release a tear. "We all needed saving. Your mom is supposed to make you strong and able to be on your own. Ours was gone, and Dad for that matter. There was no road map for what happened to us." Hannah kissed Jack's head again, leaving her lips nestled in his soft curly hair.

John poked his head through the kitchen doorway. "Hannah, the kids need to go to bed. Maddie fell asleep on my mom and Zadie's spinning out," he said, scanning back and forth between Hannah and Sophie.

"Can you?"

Sophie noticed the quick back and forth facial expressions between John and Hannah. An agreement had been made without words. An interaction they must have repeated day in and out, sharing a life that encompassed not only each other, but three children and thousands of choices. A certain kind of love they never shared.

John ducked out of the room.

"I can't save Amy," Sophie realized she wanted to be forgiven.

"She doesn't want to be rescued."

Sophie gazed out the kitchen window. Snow had begun to fall, just a light dusting so that Sophie could make out the individual shapes of each flake. They were exquisite and fleeting on their own, but when they merged, the momentum of the snowflakes together created power, a flurry of motion and strength.

Hannah readjusted her body, still holding tightly to her son. "So, Dad told you?"

"Told me what?"

"About the accident."

"What about it?"

When Hannah didn't immediately answer, Sophie repeated, "What about the accident?"

"Mom and Dad were arguing in the car." She spoke slowly, eyes down. "Mom knew Grandpa was gay and told Dad that his parents wanted a divorce."

"Did Dad tell you this?"

"No. I read the records at the police department."

"Are you kidding? Why would you do that? Why would they let you?"

"Anyone can access records. You just have to go the precinct and ask." Hannah blazed full speed ahead. "The report said that Dad admitted that he had a lot to drink that night, so begrudgingly let Mom drive." Sophie registered the pain in Hannah's face. "While Mom drove, he yelled at her, that she was wrong, his parents would never divorce and his father wasn't gay. He said his parents had always been deeply in love." Hannah paused to cough a couple of times. "Mom told him the marriage was a facade."

Hannah lowered her head and closed her eyes, as if praying. When she lifted it again, she looked Sophie right in the eye. "They crashed after that. And Dad," she stopped and pressed her lips tightly together, "Dad has never forgiven himself."

Mom died, Dad hospital.

Sophie would never forget the words her grandmother uttered in 1978. They altered everything. Her adrenaline had pumped wildly in her eight-year-old veins. Dogs barked and kids played, but her life screeched to a deafening halt that spring day, with skids marks on the black pavement behind her. And now, thirty years later, she finally heard the full story. One lie – one fucking lie caused her mother's death. Or was it one truth? Or one denial? Any way the prism turned the outcome remained.

"How long have you known this?

"That's not the point."

Sophie repeated, impatient and firm, "How long?"

"A long time."

"Every time I think we can mend our relationship you pull a fast one on me. You are so incapable of being any kind of friend – or sister." Sophie got up and paced the silent room. Moments later, she kneeled in front of Hannah. "You are such a selfish, withholding – bitch."

Hannah's voice was almost inaudible. "I don't know what you want from me."

Sophie put her face as close to Hannah's as she could. They were nose to nose. If her nephew hadn't been there, she would have screamed at the top of her lungs; instead, she kept her tone low, but her voice seethed. "Nothing!" Sophie practically knocked her grandmother down as she fled from the room.

They grabbed each other to steady themselves. "Your mother was a very perceptive woman, but she should have stayed out of it."

"Grandma, how long have you been standing there?"

"The whole time. Go to my room. I'll make us some tea."

Bewildered, Sophie did as she was told, glad for the direction.

It had been years since Sophie stepped foot in her grandmother's room. During visits to New York, they'd met at the local coffee shop. The space was cozy. The peach-colored walls gave warmth to a somewhat sparse décor, with a loveseat by the window, a slim pine wood desk, and twin bed with mauve decorative pillows. Sophie set her focus out the window feeling a mixture of curiosity and dread. Was she going to be scolded by her grandmother for the fight with Hannah?

The aroma of vanilla and cinnamon wafted her way. Grandma handed Sophie a cup and motioned for them to sit on the mini couch. Sternly she said, "I'll never forgive your sister for what she's done – marrying John, rummaging through records that were none of her business. That fight between your parents should have stayed buried with your mom."

Her grandma didn't support John and Hannah's marriage? "You were mad at my mom?"

"My marriage was none of her concern."

"But we all want answers, no matter how painful they are."

"That's naïve, Sophie. All adults have private lives, not necessarily secrets or lies, just what belongs to them."

That was certainly true for her. Sophie never discussed her affairs with her family, so why did she feel so entitled to the information? Sophie placed her tea on the windowsill and took hold of her grandma's hand. "Some of what belongs to you also belongs to us. You raised us."

Her grandma blew on the tea several times before taking a quick sip.

"Did you always know Grandpa was gay?" Her question came out clear, but she continued to spin like she had just stepped off a tilt-a-whirl. There was so much to process.

Her grandma sighed and lifted her head.

"Why did you marry him?"

"You're asking about my private life."

"You invited me to your room, Gram. You want to tell me something. There's always been so much withheld. I don't know how to forgive. I don't know how to love. How do I understand myself if I don't know the truth about my own family? It's all deception."

"NO! It's not. Not everything is as it seems, but that doesn't make it a sham."

"I know this must be terribly difficult – what I am asking from you, but please. It makes me feel crazy to have all these presumptions and no answers."

Her grandmother clasped Sophie's hand, stroked her fingers repeatedly, and began, "We were all best friends, the Three Musketeers. We went on picnics upstate, concerts in the park, dinners at each of our homes."

"Jane told me you all had a pact?"

"I lied. It was less – humiliating – to pretend I agreed to the whole thing for my own gain."

"You didn't know?"

"The first moment I saw your grandfather – he was so handsome, charming, outspoken. I was a kid. He paid attention to me, held my hand, made me feel special. I was convinced he was the one."

Sophie reflected on her relationship with Maurice and Steven. She could have easily misinterpreted the intimacies they shared, especially if falsely directed. "And Leslie?"

"We met him shortly after our wedding. He was our best friend. He had no family of his own because they kicked him out as a teenager. They found him kissing a boy in his bed and disowned him. That made me embrace him in our lives even more. He became a mixture of my best girlfriend and brother."

"They both betrayed you? You must have been devastated. Why is he here tonight?"

"I'm almost ninety years old and divorced. I forgave myself years ago, for allowing myself to be blind, and for feeling desperate to hold on to a marriage that didn't have – marital love."

A steady stream of tears ran down Sophie's face, dripping black smudges of eye-make. She recognized that feeling. She lived a blind desperation with John, holding on to a relationship that didn't fully satisfy either of them beyond deep chemistry, mutual caring, and her deep need to fill the void of her mom's death. She may not have been able to break it off if John hadn't.

Her grandma placed two fingers right below Sophie's eyes and gently wiped the fallen mascara. "The night your dad was born, Robert, your grandfather, disappeared."

Sophie was speechless.

Her grandmother continued the story like a tsunami rolling over a city. "I called Leslie. He sounded distant and cold. There I was, with a new baby, up all night and petrified that something had happened to Robert. I called the police station, every friend. No answers. When Robert returned a week later, he pretended nothing had happened. He refused to discuss where he was."

How had she endured all that? "He was with Leslie?"

"I could see the way they looked at each other after that – and not at me. Your grandfather began leaving for weekends and business trips. He never told me where he was going."

"Why didn't you tell anyone? Divorce him?"

"It was the 1940's, Sophie. Women were homemakers. You didn't question your husband."

"So, you pretended your marriage was real?"

Her grandmother slammed down her tea, spilling it. "It was real – in our own way! You don't get to decide. It's not black and white."

"I don't get it. You forgive him? Leslie?"

"I only have to forgive myself. And I do. I've had plenty of my own intimacies."

Really? Sophie thought, trying to imagine her grandma flirting with different men. *Good!*

Her grandmother went to her bureau and opened the top drawer. When she came back, she held a black and white photo of the three of them. The bottom corner read 1941. They were at Coney Island, sitting on one large towel, laughing and waving at the camera.

"You're my granddaughter. Jane is living back in my era – Hannah, well – I told you how I feel about that, Amy is a mystery, but you Sophie. You're strong and independent. You have your answers now. This," she shook the picture, "this was our lives. It doesn't have to be yours."

CHAPTER TWENTY-ONE

Her grandmother's words swirled in Sophie's head as she chain-smoked. This was her life — standing outside a trendy New York bar at ten p.m. waiting to meet a man she had barely spoken to in Starbucks that morning. Is that what her grandma meant? All Sophie wanted right now was to take this handsome guy into her hotel room and get out all the pent-up residual feelings that built during her rollercoaster of a day.

"You must be freezing out here."

Sophie turned. The wind whipped across her face. He was too early. She had left herself ample time to smoke and then run into the bar's bathroom to Listerine. She dropped the cigarette on the sidewalk and crushed it with the heel of her black leather boot. "I am." When she looked up at him, the first time they were face to face, there was a pull inside she had only felt moments before the curtain lifted, a mixture of anticipation and terror. She became aware of every nuance: the red scarf circled twice around his neck and tucked beneath his jacket, the inches of cold air between their bodies, his immediate smile when she glanced up, her hands hooked on opposite elbows.

"The city is very unforgiving to smokers now." He was soft spoken, each word enunciated perfectly. A sound she wanted to hear more of. He ushered her inside. The feeling of his large hand on the small of her back warmed her.

They ordered two glasses of pinot and sat on crushed velvet purple seats in the corner near the window. "How was your grandfather's funeral?"

His voice was sensitive. Sophie cocked her head to the side and smiled enjoying the way he held his glass on the stem and put his nose just at the rim. "It's tomorrow. Then I head back home." Home – the word echoed in her mind. She'd like to transport them to L.A. in the snap of her fingers. "Today was a family gathering."

"Do you have a big family?"

She reminisced for a quick second on the early days with John when all his questions made her queasy inside. "I have three sisters, nieces, nephews, Dad, Grandma… you?"

"I'm an only child. I always wanted a big family."

"That's what my mom used to say – she was an only child too." Stay on track, Sophie. One-night stand. You live in different states.

He took a sip of his wine and held it in his mouth for a moment before swallowing. "Used to?"

Sophie leaned her elbow on the table and chin in her hand. "She died when I was eight." She liked the attentive way he listened, not taking his light brown eyes away for even a second. "Are your parents alive?" she asked. What would it be like to kiss this man?

"They are. They're retired and living a great life in Santa Monica."

His lips were full and looked soft. "Is that where you're from?"

"I grew up in Brooklyn. They moved to California a few years ago, something they had wanted to do for a long time."

"Do you visit them?"

"A few times a year."

They smiled at each other.

"Would you excuse me for a second?"

He stood and made way for Sophie to walk past. The brush of her side to his front created a tingle in her nose, a feeling that always preceded a rush of tears. She dashed straight to the back of the bar and down the stairs to the bathroom. She sat on the toilet with pants on, head in hands, breathing as deeply as possible. Every man she had any kind of relationship with since John had been cut and dry: a great night of sex, some laughs over dinner and movies. But this brief and beginning interlude petrified her already. It didn't make sense. The toilet beside her flushed three times before she stood again and made her way back up the stairs.

"Are you okay?" Ty asked.

Sophie was hyper-alert of the proximity of their bodies. One slight move and she would be against him. "Just a bit of jet lag I think." Those moments in her life when she felt small and on the outskirts diminished with the way he took her in, like she was the most fascinating creature he had ever seen, a reflection of the way she looked at him.

A group of twenty-year-old girls sat beside them, assorted colorful cocktails in hand, laughing and talking as brightly as their drinks. They were scantily dressed, all wearing a black uniform of spaghetti-strap tops and black pants; leggings, leather, jeans… Clearly, they had been partying for some time, their voices rising while they giggled and leered at the bar a few feet away, their looks reciprocated by older men gawking back.

"What were you like at twenty?"

"The polar opposite of that," Sophie gestured to their left. When she turned back, she noticed him taking in every facet of her face. "You?"

Ty rested both elbows on his knees, his body forward toward Sophie. "Elaborate first."

"Brooding and always filled with discontent, even though I lived in Boston with a boyfriend and danced with a really great modern company."

He moved his seat closer to hers. "That's why you have such incredible posture. Still dance?"

She slid her chair closer to his, equilibrium returning. "Not for the last ten years." Sophie took a deep breath. "Your turn."

"I was a junior in college and partying like crazy. I nearly flunked out."

Their knees made contact. "But you became a psychiatrist?"

"During the summer before that year, my best friend died in a car accident. It took me a couple of years to recover. I had to screw up before I could pull myself out of it."

Sophie rested against the velvet. Could this be for real? A man who experienced a crushing loss like she had – and from a car accident. He might understand her in a way no one else had. How could she get on a plane and go three thousand miles away?

Ty reached for Sophie's hand. "You're pensive."

"I was going to ask you back to my hotel room, but…"

He leaned back in his seat. "And now you aren't?"

Her original desire for a one-night stand waned as they spoke. Not only did she feel intense attraction, but now also interest. She wanted to get to know him, to spend time with him: stroll through MOMA on a dreadfully rainy day lingering over abstract paintings, hit a play at The Roundabout and critique the actors upon exiting, feed each other dim sum in Chinatown and gawk at the fish heads in the markets. "I don't know."

He laced his fingers into hers. The touch stirred a commotion inside like a tornado kicking up debris. They were in the eye of the storm together – perfectly still. The rest of the bar disappeared in the rotation of the wind. All she saw was the slight yellow flecks hidden in his brown eyes that flickered when he spoke, his voice rich in tone. His smile consumed her. She could have told him every secret, every pain, she had never wanted to share with anyone, and had to work so hard to confide in John. Her reaction to him was reminiscent of her first day in ballet. As her feet hit first position, she knew the fit was made. Or maybe she was being ridiculous and juvenile, getting caught in his mesmerizing jawline and perfectly shaped goatee.

"I have an idea," he said. "I'll walk you to your hotel. If you want to invite me in, squeeze my hand."

He had shifted his body to the edge of his seat. One inch closer and her lips could taste his. She squeezed. "This is my hotel," Sophie whispered.

They rode the elevator to the twelfth floor, standing with a foot of empty space between them. Sophie fiddled with her key card the entire ride until she unlocked the door. They stared at one another with coats on. Earlier, before they met for drinks, she had envisioned them tearing each other's clothes off.

How would they get to their first kiss, the one that told if they were compatible? "Do you want anything from the mini bar?" she asked.

"No. Thanks." He slowly removed his leather bomber and placed it neatly on the back of a desk chair.

She slid her own wool coat off her arms and threw it toward the bed, but it landed on the floor. She was fumbling. She heard him swallow as he bent down to retrieve it. Was he as nervous as she?

"I'm sorry. I feel ridiculous. I wanted to have a sexy one-night stand with you," she confessed, "but I find you really interesting and -"

"I have a ticket to visit my folks next week. Santa Monica is less than an hour from Pasadena." Ty bridged the few steps between them and kissed her slowly on the mouth. His hands lightly moved along her face and around to hold the back of her head. She returned each kiss, adding to the intensity until their bodies were pressed against each other, like a rose petal between two pages of a book. Sophie pulled the back of his shirt out of his pants so she could touch the small of his back. She guided him to the bed and they fell on top. He held her face, one hand on each cheek, and whispered in her ear, "You are the sexiest woman I've ever met."

That was exactly how he made her feel. She undid the first two buttons on his crisp white shirt and placed her face on the side of his neck, "Why do you smell so good?"

They lay on their sides facing each other. His hand moved from just under her arm to the bottom of her hip and along the middle of her back. She felt giddy as she pushed her pelvis against his. She thought if she didn't rip all his clothes off in seconds she would explode. Instead, she bolted upright. "I think we have to stop."

He looked at her bewildered, "Really?"

She flopped her back against the head board. "Sorry, it's just – I've always done this. And I like you." *What's the matter with me?*

He pulled her back down toward his body and she rested her head on his chest, "I like you too," he said quietly.

The feel of his skin on her cheek and the sound of his heart beating brought an odd sense of comfort. For thirty years she had waited, thinking in vain, for a feeling of quiet inside, a place she didn't want to flee from. In seconds she fell asleep, having been up almost thirty-six hours.

When she woke the next day at seven a.m. Ty was beside her, on top of the covers, still dressed. She turned sideways to watch his chest slowly moving up and down with a slight sound of a low whistle as he exhaled. Her jeans felt tight against her belly and her brown scoop neck sweater looked crumpled. Quietly she tiptoed into the bathroom, ordered them room service, and cleaned up. She had thirty minutes before she needed to head to the funeral.

"Ty," she whispered, "Do you want some coffee?"

With eyes still closed he shook his head no.

That was all the encouragement she needed. In a beat she removed his shirt and pants, then her own. They were over the covers in their underwear, roaming around each other bodies with hands and tongues.

"I want you."

Once she said the words, she knew it wasn't just physically. As they made-love she already missed him and longed for his visit to California the following week.

**

Approximately one hundred and twenty hours after their first night together, sneakers, shorts, T-shirts, and underwear were all on the floor of Sophie's Pasadena bedroom. The air conditioner's hum competed with John Coltrane playing in the background. After a long afternoon run in the mountains and a hot shower, she and Ty landed in bed for the rest of the night. The plan to cook a meal together and take it to the beach for a California sunset fell by the way side once their towels slid off. They kept dozing in and out of sleep, not wanting to part from each other, their bodies woven together under the cotton blanket. When Sophie opened her eyes, there was just a bit of light coming into the windows, enough to notice a scar along the palm of Ty's hand.

"What's that from?" Sophie whispered while running the tips of her fingers along it.

His eyes were still closed. He pulled Sophie even closer to him. His voice still groggy. "Slicing a bagel while on the phone with a patient."

"Any others?"

"You tell me."

She ran her hands along his chest first. While he insisted he was never a good athlete, his muscles said

318

otherwise. His body was as developed as many of the dancers she had partnered with. "Nothing," she mumbled, and continued down his hips and each leg. Sliding the blanket to the side, she used her body to cover him. "Am I even warm?"

"Perfectly cold."

She turned the other direction, inspecting his arms, shoulders, and neck. He slightly lifted his head to reveal two small scars on his chin. "Ah ha!" she kissed him twice. "How did you get these?"

"First one from playing basketball as a kid. I tripped over the ball and hit the pavement."

"And the second?"

"It's even more embarrassing."

Sophie kissed him on his neck a few times. "Tell!"

"It was last year during a really hot August day. The couple that lives next door to me were having a party. Needless to say, it was loud. I woke up at one point and there was a gigantic water bug on my chest."

"That's disgusting."

"I jumped − and screamed − and fell out of bed. I hit my face on the glass night table beside me."

Sophie wanted to laugh, imaging this six-foot-tall hunk flying out of his bed in fright. "Seriously?"

"Go ahead, let it out, I know it's absurd."

She just smiled − wider than she felt she ever had and placed her fingers on his mouth, outlining each lip.

"Your turn."

"For what?"

"Scars, where are they?"

Sophie lifted her eyebrow and Ty began to scan – every curve with his broad hands and reach. She alternated between laughing and feeling intense heat, like the way blades of grass tickled her skin during the summer.

"You are completely unblemished. I can't find a single scar on you."

Sophie lifted onto her elbow, head in hand. "My mom died in a car accident. My dad was left with severe PTSD…" she shared her family story with him over the course of the next hour.

After listening intently, Ty said, "Those are the scars I call invisible." He sealed the words with a deep kiss on her mouth, "They're the most complicated, Sophie Gold."

She loved the way he said her name. "Come, I want to show you something." Sophie held his hand and led him to the second bedroom in her house. They had to walk through plastic taped up where the door used to be. A new floor had been laid down just that week and the first mirror installed on the wall.

"What's this?"

"I'm making a dance studio. I want to teach ballet to the kids in the neighborhood."

They were still attached by their fingers. "Will you show me something – some move?"

He sat against the bare wall while Sophie walked into the center of the room. It had been years since anyone had watched her dance. A small flutter invaded her chest as she bent her knees slightly and tilted her body to the left. She held herself there and reached her arm out toward Ty with a broad smile. The sun began to light the room through the French doors behind her. A lift of her chest to meet the light and she was off, racing through the room for the first time, like a child rolling down a grassy hill. Small staccato jumps shifted her from one corner to the next, with a playful tilt to her head, her long wavy brown hair spinning with her. Ty found the rhythm of her feet and beat the floor with his hands, drumming for her. Through her periphery she saw his broad brown shoulders digging into the sound. She took a large stance before him and followed his gesture in her shoulders, then waist, then hips. With a grin, she turned – multiple revolutions, with the intention of finishing in a perfectly balanced arabesque. Instead, her left knee revolted sending a shooting pain down her patella. She buckled, "Shit," and lay flat on her back. "I'm so out of shape." Her heart pounded like it would walk away from her chest. "I have to stop smoking."

Ty slid over and placed himself supine beside her. "That was HOT!"

Sophie lay panting beside him, the wind knocked out of her.

He reached for her hand and stroked the inside of her palm. "Teach me something."

Sophie lifted to elbows, "What do you mean?"

"Let me be your first student." A smile unfurled at the corners of his mouth.

"Seriously? I don't have the barre's up." She felt a hint of panic. "It's barely ready for students."

He grabbed her by both hands and pulled her up to stand.

"Okay," reservation in her voice, "I guess we can begin in the center of the room, it's harder to balance though."

"I don't mind lookin' the fool." Ty bumped his hip into hers.

Sophie peered into the mirror, Ty in his navy-blue briefs, his chest and abdominal muscles rippling before he even moved. "Okay, let's do first position. Feet turn out like this." He took the proper stance. As she demonstrated plies, which were always the first exercise done, he followed without a hitch. They took each position, first, second, fourth, and fifth. Sophie spied her own body as they continued — ten years without dance had created a layer of smooth skin, where definition used to be. She shook it off, not wanting to spiral down into a body image drain. "Tendus come next. We start back in first position and you slide your foot against the floor until you can't go any further – pointing your foot at the very end."

Ty followed perfectly. After they did each side, Sophie abruptly stopped. "What's up?" she asked.

"How do you mean?"

322

Hands on hips, a crooked smile formed on Sophie's lips. "You know what you're doing. I thought I was going to have to hold back from laughing, like you would be an awkward muscle man, but you're elegant."

"I confess," he turned to her. "My Mom made me go to ballet as a little guy."

"Get out." Sophie walked over to him and placed her hands on his cheeks and said light heartedly, "You were playing me."

"Just a little," he replied with a grin.

Before she could react, her cellphone and house phone rang simultaneously.

CHAPTER TWENTY-TWO

The kitchen window was wedged open by a piece of plywood left over from the renovation of her soon to be dance studio. The window frames of her bungalow house were only one of many old and decayed spots in need of repair. Sophie jutted her head out and watched her dogs frolic together in the grass. They rolled around each other with their thick, muscular bodies, while releasing playful growls and barks. They mastered the art of complete control even when their jaws were at the jugular. They knew precisely the amount of force to use, and restraint.

Phone in one hand and cigarette in the other, Sophie listened to the curt voice of the nurse on the other end, "She's stable. It took some time to pump her stomach. Let's just say, it was a serious attempt."

Was that judgement Sophie picked up in her tone? "Will she recover?"

"This time."

All the levity from just moments before deteriorated, the way instant darkness befalls a room at night when the light is turned off. After a few more details were given, Sophie pressed end and placed her cell phone on the counter beside a fresh pack of

Marlboro's. Her fingernails dug into the plastic outer layer. She could have plowed through the box, chain smoking the morning away while anxiety seeped through every pore like a forest fire tearing through a quiet wood. Instead, she changed course, crushed the red and white box in her palm and threw it in the trash under the sink. She washed her hands to remove the tobacco smell and splashed cold water on her face and neck, then rinsed her mouth. On route to find Ty, she swiveled on her heels, picked the crumpled box from the garbage and brought the remnants of tobacco and paper to the toilet and flushed it all down, watching the water swirl and suck down the remains.

Ty was in her room, dressed and spreading out her white cotton comforter, "Everything okay?" He meandered her way.

Even in the midst of the news she just heard, she admired Ty before responding, this beautiful anomaly of a man before her. Even in the most casual attire, blue jeans that hugged him perfectly and a basic short-sleeve button down, he looked elegant. Sophie shook her head side to side, "My sister Amy overdosed. She's at the hospital." Sophie leaned against the wall. "One in a succession of failed attempts." She let out a long sigh.

His voice was even and mild. "Do you want to see her?"

The question took her aback, having never considered an option. "Yes."

The first time she received a call like this she had just moved into her house. There were labeled boxes piled in the living room from floor to ceiling. The rest of the room was still bare except for scattered bubble wrap and newspaper. She practically dropped the glass she held when she heard that Amy had overdosed. Foot to the gas she drove to the hospital panicked, alternating between hot and cold flashes. The second attempt occurred as Sophie pulled the key out of her front door and switched on the light at two a.m. drunk from a night out with new friends. She dashed in and out of a scalding hot two-minute shower and called a cab. After that – when the next call came, she finished her hike, fed the dogs, meandered around the house straightening up odds and ends, then departed.

Should she go? This development in thought was like the news story line at the bottom of the T.V. screen when the actual news is being reported, both a distraction and a draw. Her race to the hospital and desire to assist never seemed to help or change Amy. Sophie always felt like she was holding a ladder down a long well that was considerably too short to reach her sister.

"She has a boyfriend and a new job," as the words trickled out it felt more for herself than an explanation for Ty.

Ty held her for several minutes, his long arms wrapped fully around her still underwear clad body,

"Why don't we meet at Zuma Beach later for a swim and dinner?"

There was nothing she wanted more, "Yes!" She felt in awe: could he really like her this much? Be so kind and compassionate?

He stroked her arms, while they stared at one another.

"Why doesn't she just do it already, end it?" Sophie mumbled barely audible. Hands on his beltline, she flirted with the edge where his skin met the denim.

"It's impossible to know, Sophie."

"It's like I condone her desire to die every time I show up. It's so selfish of her."

Ty listened.

"I came out here thinking I could mend Amy, two sisters bonding over their childhood loss, but she just sailed away from the shore before I could jump in the boat. I feel like I'm standing on the dock watching her fade into distant skyline."

Ty held her hands and spoke in a cautious tone. "Maybe it's the reverse."

Sophie looked at him quizzically.

"Maybe you made the distance."

"How do you mean?"

"Self-preservation as not to drown beside her." When Sophie didn't respond, but continued to question with her brow furrowed, Ty continued. "When Eric died in the car crash, I did everything possible to self-destruct: pills, alcohol, cocaine, food, the classic stuffing down avoidance reaction."

Sophie soaked in his words longing to absorb every bit.

"My parents, friends, therapist all had solutions, ideas, love…" "And that wasn't helpful?"

"It was a band aid on an infected wound. I needed time to machete through the depth of emotions I buried."

"Are you suggesting Amy can clean up?"

"I don't know. – She's an addict."

His words felt like a cold blast of air, shocking and refreshing at the same time. She had been told this over and over by Amy's nurses and rehab clinics, but hearing it from Ty, with his frank and non-judgmental tone, it clicked into place.

"I'm saying this for you, the one at the scene of the crime who can't stop watching. You did nothing wrong, but keep feeling guilty or responsible."

"My mom used to tell my how lucky I was to have three sisters and that we had each other. For most of my life it's been a burden."

"Let me make you breakfast."

Sophie reached for him. "Ty," her hand cupped his bicep, then both hands slid up to his shoulders, neck and landed at the back of his head. She kissed him lightly. "I'm so glad we met."

***

Sitting on the hood of her little red sports car, Sophie juggled her keys from hand to hand considering her options: One, turn around and go home, calling Ty on the way to meet her. Two, march into the hospital and force Amy to go to rehab once and for all. Three... she tapped her sandaled feet on the hot pavement multiple times, dashed across the parking lot, moved steadily through the sliding hospital doors, past security, into the large sterile elevator, and onto the 6th floor.

Hands in her pockets, Sophie hovered at the foot of Amy's bed, not daring to touch anything. The dank environment, with an acrid smell, stimulated a headache that had the capacity to last for days.

"What the fuck were you thinking?"

Sophie had never dared to take this hardline approach. It wasn't planned or ever considered, but peering into the skeletal face of her forty two-year old, strung out, sister, who had once been beautiful and vivacious, pissed her off.

Attached to an IV bag, eyes drowsy, Amy mumbled. "You're so pure, so innocent." She tugged on her sheets, squeezing the cotton into her palm. "You're in God's favor, Sophie."

Sophie put a hand gingerly on Amy's ankle. "You always say that. I don't even know what it means."

Amy flinched and crossed her leg over the one Sophie had touched. Her feet began to shake up and down. "It's too hard to be alive. I can't keep," she stopped and pursed her lips together.

"Can't keep what?"

Her voice meek, "No – I can't say it."

"What aren't you telling me?"

The next several minutes felt like a showdown. Amy clamped her eyes shut like a child holding her breath and Sophie crossed her arms staring at her sister, feeling completely inept. What should she do? Should she call her father? Jane? Amy began rocking in her bed mumbling what Sophie suspected was a Bible verse.

Finally, Sophie burst. "Fine – you win." She grabbed the pamphlets she had stashed in her bag and threw them at Amy's belly. "Here's the rehab info for Big Sur. Go – don't go, I don't care." That was such a false statement, Sophie felt crushed as she headed for the door.

"I saw them," Amy's voice was barely audible.

"Saw who?"

The words leaked from her like a dripping faucet. "Grandpa and his – his – friend. I saw them do it."

Gingerly, Sophie turned halfway around and whispered, "Grandpa and Leslie? What did you see?"

Amy began scratching her arms. "You're all so innocent – so pure, but God knows what they did."

Amy began to cry so hard she practically gagged on the combination of tears and saliva that pooled on the corners of her mouth. "In our house, they did it in our house."

Was she ready to hear more? It had only been a week since her grandfather's funeral, Hannah's confession, and her grandmother's coming clean. "When?"

"Before Mom died." Amy squeezed her eyes shut. "I was twelve. Only twelve. I could have prevented the accident. I could have saved Mom." She began rocking back and forth.

Sophie put a hand over her mouth, "Oh, Amy."

"I'm glad he's dead… I need to get out of here." Amy pushed up and began to tug on the tape and IV stuck in her arm. As her forearm turned and twisted, Sophie saw all the track marks she couldn't hide. It was a conglomeration of various shades of black lines, from years of abuse.

"Amy," Sophie held her hand where she tried to tear out the tubes. "Stop."

"Your life is simple – I'm so proud of you – you're the lucky one."

"Lucky?"

"I'm too tired," her eyes batted open and closed, reminding Sophie of her father's multiple ticks.

Sophie slid in bed beside Amy and wrapped her arm around her back, ignoring the smell of old perspiration, "Grandpa is gone. You can move on now."

"It's not that simple, not that simple," Amy repeated like a mantra.

"Why not?"

"I cut out of school, the month before Mom died."

331

Sophie watched her sister.

"It was Hannah's idea. She said she would meet me and we would smoke pot, but she never showed." Amy crossed her legs back and forth over and over. "God had her back." Her legs stilled. She began scratching her arms instead. "They were in our house."

"Grandpa and Leslie?"

Everything rolled out in a fury.

"Mom and Dad were in Houston. Dad had business. Mom went with him. Grandma and – they were watching us."

"I don't remember that."

"You were too young."

"I walked in. No one was supposed to be there. But there he was, with his boyfriend." The words came out in a whisper.

Sophie stroked her straggly hair and held her hand.

Amy clamped on to Sophie's arm. "They were naked." Her eyes looked glazed.

"Did they see you?"

"They didn't even hear me come in." Amy placed her hands over her ears and pressed tightly. "The moaning – I stood at the threshold of the living room, staring. They just kept at it." Her eyes drifted onto ceiling. "I couldn't move. I was stunned, like in a nightmare." She gagged on her saliva. "Finally, I ran out of the house."

Sophie couldn't believe what she heard. How had she kept this in for thirty years?

A fresh group of salty tears spilled from her eyes. "I should have told Mom. They never would have crashed." Her shoulders rounded forwarded, making her chest concave.

"You knew about Mom and Dad's fight in the car?"

"Hannah told me."

"When?"

"After she graduated from med school." Amy wiped her nose with her forearms. "She took a trip to New York. She said she needed to visit Dad, but when she came back home, a few days early, she was all shaken up. She didn't want to tell me, but I forced her. Why did I force her to tell me? It's all my fault."

"Why?"

"If I told Mom, they would have had that fight before they got in the car that night."

Amy wiped her eyes with the back of her hands.

"Look at me." Sophie turned her sister's face. "It's not your fault."

She began to mumble again, another Bible verse. Her body continued to rock, "God wanted me to see it, it was a warning. I failed our mother and all of my sisters."

Sophie wished she could steal the memory out of Amy's brain, carry it into the woods, and bury it, like her dogs with their bones. "You didn't fail anyone."

All these years Sophie felt angry for the tragedy of her childhood, the secrets and lies she knew the adults around her held, but the real trauma lived in Amy. The circumstances were long gone, but the wound so fresh for her. It ruined her.

Amy's body trembled. "God trusted me. I did fail."

Seeing the exhaustion in her face, Sophie held Amy until the shaking subsided.

"Pray for me, Sophie." She repeated over and over softly, eventually drifting to sleep. Sophie tucked the sheets and blanket into the mattress, as if that simple act could shield her sister from further harm.

Wrapped in her own self-pity for years, she hadn't considered what Amy had gone through and why she became an addict. She assumed Amy moved to California to be with Hannah and stayed for her acting career. The decision to never return – ever – had always eluded her.

Continuing to process what she had just learned, Sophie finally headed out the door – Amy deep in sleep.

She had all the pieces now.

EPILOGUE

Spring 2018

It had been months of waiting: for the winter winds to cease, the earth to thaw, and the temperature to slowly rise to above freezing. Sophie had anticipated the first day she could step her winter-booted feet into the garden at her dad's house.

Their planting ritual began in 2014, the year after Sophie returned to New York at forty-three. While the move had been impending, a latenight call from her father nudged the elephant that had been living between her and Ty – having been in a long -distance relationship for six years. They had begun arguing about which coast to move to, knowing that breaking up was not an option, but each had strong emotions tied to their coast. Ty had a thriving practice and lifelong friendships in New York. Sophie loved the year-round warm weather, the ability to go to the beach and hike in the woods at whim, as well as the sweet dance studio in her home. She had to admit she ached for the New York dance scene, having choreographed for years in the late-night hours. She had a handful of pieces ready to start her own company. And she no longer expected her presence to change Amy. Her father's sobering call sealed the deal.

He had been diagnosed with prostate cancer and the prognosis was grim. He had waited too long, not having been to the doctor for years. The warning signs had begun the previous fall, which he ignored. By the time his wife, Martha, brought him to the ER after blacking out in the car, the cancer had already travelled into his bones. The heavy doses of estrogen left him bloated and tired the first year after treatment began, but as he slowly regained his energy, he was determined to make the most of the limited years ahead.

Ty sold his apartment in Brooklyn, Sophie her house in Pasadena, and they landed in Central Harlem. It was in the throes of gentrification which they had mixed feelilngs about, but – it seemed like every month they discovered a new restaurant or building being born – the growth and potential felt like a hot fever. They had walked the streets endlessly with a realtor, passing vacant lots and boarded-up tenements and brownstones in various stages of dilapidation and renovation, and finally fell in love with an apartment on Manhattan Avenue and 115th Street. It was the last three bedroom in the building. For Sophie, the small round green tile work in the master bath took her breath away, as did the rounded kitchen island that looked over into the great room. Ty loved that the master bedroom was on one side of the main space and two smaller bedrooms on the other, and that the living space had floor-to-ceiling windows looking east and north. And Morningside Park was down the block, with a dog run and playground.

Months after the move, at forty-three, Sophie discovered she was pregnant. A little bump had grown around her lower belly that had never been there before. While she knew her body would change in her forties, she had also been exhausted and ravenous. It wasn't planned. It was utterly inconvenient, having so much on her plate: new home, ill father, holding auditions for six dancers to set her first piece, and searching for a venue to house it.

Over the moon didn't do justice to Ty's reaction, he could think of nothing more exciting. For Sophie it took months to go from numb, to lukewarm, to enthusiastic, then petrified. But after twenty hours in labor, she held her daughter, moments after the doctors had cleaned, checked, and swaddled her. All ambivalence dissipated when she looked in her deep brown eyes and stroked her perfectly rounded, bald head. Ty couldn't stop tearing up and giggling simultaneously. He followed their daughter as the nurse wheeled her out of the delivery room to check her thoroughly. Sophie rested her head against the pillows behind her and wept. She had never expected to be a mother, but knew she stood at the threshold, embarking on one of life's most intimate relationships. They decided upon the name Leyla for its meaning: dark beauty.

While, in 2014, Sophie perfected nursing in any situation, quick diaper changes while legs and arms flailed, and waking at any hour, her father sat through rounds of chemo. His nausea abated after a lot of rest and he celebrated by inviting Sophie to revamp his garden. How could she refuse? Leyla had just turned one and could easily come for the ride. It was the opportunity she had longed for, time with her dad.

He had a gardener pull everything out of his backyard, complaining it was all too old and in need of rejuvenation anyway. After new grass seeded, they decided upon a Bartlett pear tree as their first project. Sadly, the tree never fruited and became a longstanding joke in the family.

The following few years the focus was flowers and bushes. This year, 2018, after much deliberating, they decided on vegetables: peas and beans. Her dad had cultivated a patch of dirt at the back of the property, just the perfect dimensions.

Sophie had seeded them weeks before in her home. Ty chuckled often as she watered the soil and talked to it in the mornings while taking her fist sips of coffee, now with a few drops of cream and sugar.

On planting day, she carefully placed them on the floor of her car below the passenger seat. Five-year-old Leyla, with tight curly hair flirting with the edges of her shoulders, Ty's complexion, and Sophie's square jawline and upturned but prominent nose, accompanied her mom to Grandpa's house, as usual. The first year Sophie planted with her dad, Leyla cooed in her Bjorn, year two she ran around bare bottomed pulling the grass and chasing flies, three and four she sat beside them with pail and shovel on one side her of body, and a set of matchbox cars she raced through the dirt on the other side.

Sophie parked the car in her dad's driveway. Before getting out, she pulled down her visor, reapplied her lipstick, smoothed the wisps of hair that drifted away from her ponytail and took a few deep breaths.

"Mama, I want to show Grandpa my scooter. Can we take it out of the trunk?"

Leyla was so proud of her teal blue vehicle, with only three wheels, and a bell she rang incessantly.

"Sure." Sophie popped open the hood, unfastened her daughter's seatbelt and grabbed the planters. "I'll race you to the backyard."

Leyla flew forward with determined face. The path was clear. The rose bushes that used to line the side of the house had been the first to go, but Sophie could smell a hint of lilac in the air from neighboring plants.

As expected, her dad was bundled up on a lounge chair facing a patch of sun, his breath even. He wore a new black cashmere hat and mittens to match. The cold inhabited his body even in summer now. She stood staring for a moment, his impending death like rain clouds ready to burst, then turned and spied Martha in the kitchen window. They waved. Martha blew each of them a kiss, which Leyla returned while jumping up and down.

The air hummed with spring. Sophie heard a lone chirp from a tree above while she placed a hand on her dad's shoulder. "Hi – you certainly look cozy this morning."

He startled awake, pulled the wool blanket tighter around his shoulders. "Sophie, Leyla – my beautiful girls. Are we ready?"

Sophie whispered, "Sure you're up for this today, Dad?"

His eyes fluttered open and shut several times. "Help me up, would you?"

She braced his elbow with her hand as he swung his legs around toward her. It took a couple of pushes and pulls before he made his way upright. "This damn disease, it's making me an invalid." His mouth grew taut with the final word.

"I think you look very well today, Dad. I brought the veggies."

"Grandpa, where's the shovel? I want to dig."

He tugged on Leyla's arm. "First come here and give your grandpa a big hug."

She obliged willingly, resting her head at his hip. "Grandpa, did you see how fast I came around the side of the house?"

"I did. You move like a race car."

"My turn." Sophie gave her dad a bear hug, noting he felt brittle, even with his protruding middle. "Shall we get started?"

"Little one, why don't you dig some holes where I put the stake in the ground. Your Mom and I will be there soon."

"Okay," Leyla hollered as she ran toward the shovel and hoe sitting on the grass.

Sophie took the cue, helped her father back into his chair and brought one over for herself beside him. His voice was scratchy. "There are some things I want to discuss with you."

Sophie tightened her vest around her body and zipped it to the top, covering her chin. She shivered for a few moments, even though it was a balmy sixty degrees.

"I am not proud of the many years I neglected you all."

"Dad -"

He put his hand up. "No, it's important I say this. Your Mom was my best friend since the day we met in college. Losing her the way we did nearly destroyed me – as you know, but I was your father. I was supposed to protect you girls – keep you feeling loved and safe after such a tragedy. I..."

"MAMA – look," Leyla stood on the lawn, grinning widely, while cautiously pointing at the butterfly perched on her shoulder. She knew from a museum trip with school that touching it would be fatal.

Sophie gave her a thumbs up.

"You're a parent now, you know your job is to love and protect before anything else."

Looking at her father made her insides twist. She didn't want to lose him. He was at his most cogent since the accident.

"I missed the most significant years, trapped in my guilt."

He had. What he said was true and yet, now, as a grown woman it didn't seem as devastating. He had been a vacant shell then, but now, he was just a man who had carried a burden for years that nearly eroded him. "You're so much better now, Dad."

"That doesn't change the past. I knew about my father, probably my entire life, but facing it – the admission still challenges me." His head dropped down toward his chest, "Gay – say it Sam, he was gay." He shook his head several times. "It's difficult to say aloud. Your mom, she was astute, and so willing to accept anyone in any circumstance."

Sophie sat back and listened.

"She wasn't even pushing me – it was more a nudge to listen to the truth and I shut her down, lost my temper and that – that took her away from all of us."

His tears fell like a hard rain. Fat, sloppy drops landed on the rim of his upper lip, "We're so foolish in our youth, thinking we're impenetrable."

She peered at him.

"I tried so many times, to stop acting so strange, to make myself engage, but I kept hearing her: a laugh or the cadence in her voice when she told you to march upstairs and get ready for bed. Her voice would sear through me and I would crumble inside. You have so many expressions that remind me of her, Sophie, and the way you've aged is – it's like seeing her again."

It never dawned on her that she resembled her mother. "I like to think I could do it differently if I had been in your shoes Dad, but the truth is I don't know how I would have survived either."

"That's kind, Sophie."

"Look, Grandpa." Leyla started turning cartwheels on the center of the lawn, the sunlight vivid on the new blades of grass below her feet.

His eyes diverted to the lawn.

"It's true. Life is a mystery, Dad. I like to believe there is a reason we went through all this pain."

"Leyla is lucky to have you. Do something for me."

Sophie turned her face to the sun for a moment, trying to hold back the tears pooling. "Anything."

"Sophie, look at me. This is the swan song."

The admission itself was a dagger. She grabbed hold of his hand and held firmly. "I'm not ready."

"There are four boxes on the floor of my closet. The red one is for you." His voice came out strong even though he looked emaciated. "Bring it down. I want to show you something."

Sophie followed his directions, making her way through the back porch door and into the kitchen, pulling a used Kleenex from her jeans pocket and wiped the mucous that threatened to roll into her mouth.

Martha sat at the table with bills surrounding her. "It's important to him to – to get things settled."

"I know." Sophie meandered up the steps admiring all the family photos on the wall. The first stop she always made when going upstairs was to her old bedroom. First peek in revealed a hospital bed in the center of the room and side table with multiple pill bottles and glasses of water. She rushed out and down the hall. It only took a couple of seconds to find what she was looking for and she reversed her steps.

Leyla was sprawled on his lap. "I spent the last few years making one of these for each of you." His fingers ran slowly along the top of the box.

"Mama, open it."

Sophie lifted the lid. Her eyes grew wide like a small child on Christmas morning. Inside there was a pile of photos, a stack of notes held together by a pink ribbon, a jewelry box, and a pair of ballet slippers.

"Those were the first pair you ever wore. I asked your grandmother to save them."

"Can I wear them?" Leyla asked.

Sophie's lips turned down and tears spilled down her cheeks. She picked up the pink canvas shoes and brought them up to her face. With eyes closed, she inhaled – flooded with the memory of running down the ramp to ballet class each week. She passed them to her daughter who quickly threw off her sneakers and pushed her long skinny feet inside.

"The day you were born your mom held you for hours, admiring your thick black hair. Neither Hannah nor Amy had any when they were born." He chuckled, "and the constant movement, you were always in motion." He ran his hand over his daughter's thick brown waves. "On the bottom, grab that," he gestured to the black velvet box.

With a slight tremble in her fingers, she obliged. As she lifted the top, it creaked just moments before a shimmering diamond caught her eye. "It was your mom's."

Sophie swallowed harder than she intended.

"I know you and Ty are unconventional, but should you decide to ever get married, I wanted you to have it. Or save it for Leyla."

"Dad," a turn of her head, "Are you sure?"

"You're a great couple."

Sophie kissed his forehead. "Thank you." She admired the way the light hit the ring and made all the colors within the stone dance. She never doubted the commitment she and Ty made to one another: marriage seemed perfunctory, done for the sake of but not a guarantee of longevity, let alone permanence.

"Come on, Leyla, get those seeds in the ground before the sun goes down," Sophie's dad said.

Sophie hopped up, determined to make sure every seed was planted before departing, "Dad, give us some direction."

"Ley – use your fingers and put the seeds into the dirt, a thumb's length apart."

She walked over and put her pinkie out. "Like this?"

"You got it, pumpkin. Your mom can put the earth on top when you deposit the seeds."

As instructed, Leyla ran off, straight to the planters and nearly tossed all the dirt on the ground, seeds buried beneath. "Careful, sweetie. They're very fragile." She turned to her dad. "I better help her or we will only be feeding the squirrels."

He smiled. "She's got enough enthusiasm for all of us."

Sophie plopped down in the grass ready to get messy. Shifting the soil uprooted a couple of squirming worms causing Leyla to jump up and run about for a moment. She returned, crouched down, "Can I pick one up?"

"Go ahead." Sophie turned to her father, who watched every moment with a proud look in his eyes.

Leyla, nearly crushing it, lifted the worm by one end and dropped it in her other palm. "It feels so weird." She crinkled her nose as the worm scurried off her brown palm and burrowed back to safety. She stood, no longer interested. "I have to pee." She ran toward the back door at top speed.

Martha at the ready stuck her head out, "Can I take her for ice cream?"

"Perfect," Sophie replied.

With much left to do, Sophie finished the job over the next hour. She dug her shovel in and out of the soil, deposited each seed with precision, covered each section, and smoothed down the dirt till it was completely even. Next, she pulled over the hose, held her thumb over the spout half way and let a trickle feed the earth, provoking it to be fertile. Wiping the sweat from her brow, she headed over to her father.

The sun beamed overhead, hot like bright red lipstick, accompanied by a light breeze which crossed her body, seeming to echo her satisfaction. She squatted on his left side. "Dad, let's get something to eat inside."

When there was no response, she tried again, placing her hand on his shoulder, "Dad… Dad," her voice rose. Nothing. She placed her hand around his wrist searching for a pulse.

It took seconds to grab her phone out of her back pocket and call 911.

She followed the ambulance to Long Island Jewish Hospital. It took exactly twenty-three minutes. In that time, she learned from the medics, CPR was performed and paddles were administered. The line remained flat.

Before calling Martha, Ty, or her sisters, Sophie wept while seated on the hood of her car. Her body alternated between rocking without sound and waves of crying noises that erupted without warning. She knew this was coming, but it never would feel like enough time.

Several weeks passed before Sophie opened the box again. She waited for a day when Ty and Leyla had gone. Nestled on the couch with one dog on either side of her like book ends, she read through the multiple cards and letters her dad had saved. The birthday ones from her grandparents were sweet and sentimental, she found a few for Valentine's Day that her parents had written. Her father's handwriting veered to the right with barely any space between the letters, her mother's a loopy script that still had the look of a teenager in love – and a stack of letters her mom used to write, but not give. They were her mom's special notes that marked a moment in time that she wanted to savor and eventually share.

January 3ʳᵈ, 1974
Dear Sophie,

This morning you ran into our room. It was still so dark out. I imagine you must have had a nightmare. I heard the pitter patter of your feet first, then the slam of your small body on the comforter. I am becoming accustomed to your early-morning visits, as they usually come around four-thirty a.m. – are the roosters even cock-a-doodling yet, I wonder?

Anyway, your small arm wrapped around my shoulder and you let out a sigh. These are the moments I savor, Sophie. The times when everything is still, all the problems of the day before and the ones to come are meaningless. It's just you and me. I listen to you breathe – grind your teeth- struggle to find your place in our gigantic bed and I know all is right in the world with you beside me.

I love you, sweet girl, more than I can ever explain.
Mama

Sophie read it over and over before reaching for the next letter. Just as she lifted a piece of pink note paper out of its envelope, she heard the buzz from her pocket.

It was a text which held only one photo.

Sophie readjusted her reading glasses and focused in. A robust yellow pear hung from the center branch of their tree.